drizzle

by Kathleen Van Cleve

Dial Books for Young Readers
an imprint of Penguin Group (USA) Inc.

DIAL BOOKS FOR YOUNG READERS
A division of Penguin Young Readers Group
Published by The Penguin Group
Penguin Group (USA) Inc.,
375 Hudson Street, New York, NY 10014, U.S.A.
Penguin Group (Canada), 90 Eglinton Avenue East, Suite 700,
Toronto, Ontario, Canada M4P 2Y3
(a division of Pearson Penguin Canada Inc.)
Penguin Books Ltd, 80 Strand, London WC2R 0RL, England
Penguin Ireland, 25 St. Stephen's Green, Dublin 2,
Ireland (a division of Penguin Books Ltd)
Penguin Group (Australia), 250 Camberwell Road, Camberwell,
Victoria 3124, Australia (a division of Pearson Australia Group Pty Ltd)
Penguin Books India Pvt Ltd, 11 Community Centre,
Panchsheel Park, New Delhi - 110 017, India
Penguin Group (NZ), 67 Apollo Drive, Rosedale, North Shore 0632,
New Zealand (a division of Pearson New Zealand Ltd)
Penguin Books (South Africa) (Pty) Ltd, 24 Sturdee Avenue,
Rosebank, Johannesburg 2196, South Africa
Penguin Books Ltd, Registered Offices: 80 Strand,
London WC2R 0RL, England

The publisher does not have any control over and does not assume any
responsibility for author or third-party websites or their content.
Book design by Jasmin Rubero
Text set in Bembo
Printed in the U.S.A.

3 5 7 9 10 8 6 4

LIBRARY OF CONGRESS CATALOGING-IN-PUBLICATION DATA
Van Cleve, Kathleen.
Drizzle / by Kathleen Van Cleve. — 1st ed.
p. cm.
Summary: When a drought threatens her family's magical rhubarb
farm, eleven-year-old Polly tries to find a way to make it rain again.
ISBN 978-0-8037-3362-6 (hardcover)
[1. Farms—Fiction. 2. Magic—Fiction. 3. Self-realization—Fiction.
4. Rain and rainfall—Fiction.] I. Title.
PZ7.V2665Dr 2010
[Fic]—dc22
2009023819

In memory of
Anna Lynne Papinchak

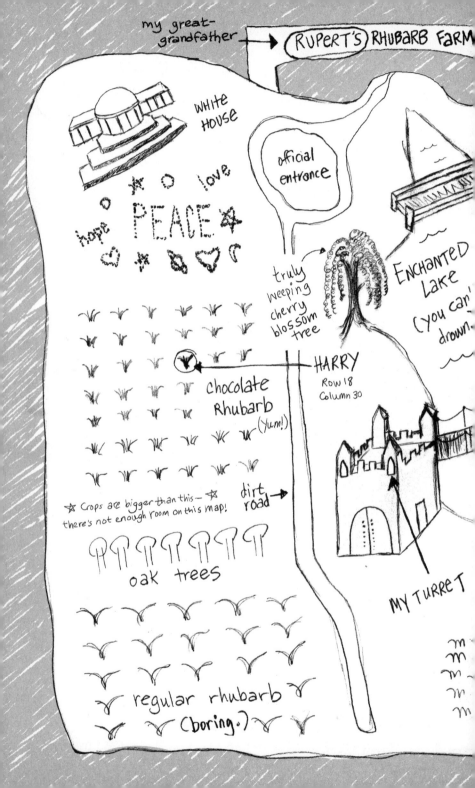

world famous.
LEARNING GARDEN
Umbrella Ride
ruby flowers
ways flowering magnolia tree
more chocolate rhubarb
sugar maples
sycamore trees
MOM & DAD'S CUBE
hammock
ROPE BRIDGE
Giant Rhubarb
40 feet HIGH!
SILO
Dark House (don't go here.)
SHED
Slugsand (really, really gross.)
Dad's Lab
medicinal rhubarb
Grandmom's Bench

MONDAY, AUGUST 18
The Mist Returns

The mist is back.

As soon as I step outside the castle, I see it: a tiny cloud of green mist, swirling above the lake under the weeping cherry blossom tree, dragonflies zipping in and out as if they're sewing it together with some kind of invisible sparkling thread.

It makes my heart almost stop, if you want to know the truth.

Almost four years ago, I saw this same kind of mist stretch across our entire lake. That time, Grandmom had just died and the farm was going crazy.

Today, I'm not sure what's going on. Today, everything seems okay. The rest of the lake is perfectly flat, perfectly blue. I look quickly around the fields, toward the White House and the castle, toward the Giant Rhubarb field and the place where the chocolate rhubarb grows. Everything looks fine, normal.

I peer closer at the mist, which is tucked in the corner of the lake under the truly weeping cherry blossom tree, in *my* special place. It isn't like a normal, all-over-the-place mist. It's small—small enough that it seems like you could pick it up with your arms if you were careful. Grandmom taught me that dragonflies are born in the water, and they have their nymph stage there. Even after they grow up and fly all over the place, they return to the lake, because it's their home. She said dragonflies were made up almost completely of water. "Nature does nothing in vain, Polly, make sure you remember that. These dragonflies know everything there is to know about this lake; they spend their childhoods in the water," she'd tell me. "Any questions, you ask them. They love children." Then she sighed. "Naturally, they think most adults are idiots."

Grandmom was the person who first showed me all the fantastical things about our rhubarb farm—the truly weeping cherry blossom tree, the ruby flowers that cluster in the Learning Garden, the lake that never drowns anyone—so I had no reason to doubt what she said about dragonflies. Plus I was seven, which means that you believe everything everyone says, especially adults, all the time.

Grandmom died soon after that, so I never told her that the dragonflies didn't love me and that I didn't love them. After all, dragonflies are bugs, and as a rule, I don't like bugs, even though I live on a farm where they're literally everywhere.

Now that I'm eleven I know I should have expected Grandmom to die—she was old and she had cancer and besides, like Charlotte in *Charlotte's Web* says, everyone dies. But I didn't get it then. Grandmom kept playing hide-and-seek with me in the Learning Garden and teaching me about rhubarb plantings on Mondays, so I figured that she was sick in the same way that I got sick—that is, she would get better after a lot of sleep and orange juice.

But then, on one rainy Monday afternoon, the twentieth of September, I found her, lying faceup, in between the *P* and *E* of the PEACE maze. The toes of her silly slippers pointed up to the gray sky as rain washed over her cheeks. I turned to see that all around us the rhubarb plants swished their wide green leaves over their heads, pointing to her body. The lake began to roar as if there was a windstorm, even though there wasn't. I turned back to Grandmom and begged.

Please wake up, please wake up.

Then I saw the tips of tiny glittering diamonds popping out of the ground, outlining Grandmom's body. That's when I knew. Grandmom loved the farm so much it was like she breathed it in and it became her lungs and mind and heart. I knew the farm was honoring her by sprouting the tiny diamonds. I knew I should have been in awe of the magic spinning around her. But all I could think of was that she was dead.

My grandmom was dead.

I kept waiting for her to open her eyes and tell me something like "Don't fall into the slugs" or "Rhubarb is almost as pretty as cabbage!" But her eyes stayed shut, and I felt deep in my bones that everything was going to change. I wanted something huge and terrible to happen—I wanted an earthquake to rumble and smash everything: the buildings and the castle and the trucks and the Umbrella. I wanted to fall into the roaring lake and sink to the bottom.

But the ground stayed still. The plants bent over and flapped their leaves good-bye. Flies and bumblebees and spiders and dragonflies fluttered around her, even in the rain. And I stayed there, holding on to her hand, as the tiny tips of the diamonds glittered. She wore her emerald ring, and I wore mine. We had a lot in common, Grandmom and me. We loved the farm. We preferred to be outside. We both had crooked index fingers on our right hands. And we were crazy about the rhubarb on our farm that tasted like chocolate.

I loved Grandmom with every bit of my heart.

For about a week after she died, I did odd, maniac kinds of things: I smacked a rhubarb plant and it smacked me back, I yanked out some of the rubies from the Learning Garden, I threw cinderblocks as hard as I could against the castle walls. Mom tried to help— she put her strong, wiry arms around me as we sat by the weeping cherry blossom tree, thinking, I guess, that if she could hold me in, keep my jittery energy from exploding, I'd start to get over Grandmom's death. Instead, I jumped away from her, away from the tears of the tree, and leaped into the lake, wishing more than anything that things *could* die in our lake, that it *was* possible to drown even when I knew full well that nothing ever died inside of it.

Eventually I pulled myself out, not even noticing until hours later that my emerald ring—the gift from Grandmom herself—had slipped off of my finger. Mom was waiting for me with a big towel and a sad face. I wanted to make her feel better, but I couldn't. I had a riptide swirling inside of me.

I went to my turret that night, and stared out the window. Grandmom had been dead six days, and the lake was still turbulent, the plants at half-mast. I thought that maybe everything was going to die without Grandmom—the plants, the trees, my family, me.

But the next day I awoke to find the green mist spread across the entire lake, with what seemed like millions of dragonflies threading their invisible fabric. Beatrice, our chef—and basically our second mother—brought me breakfast and told me that she thought the mist was like the farm's coat of armor, and that the dragonflies were making it even stronger by sewing their trail of sparks in it. They were making us a shield, in other words, so that our farm would be safe.

It worked. Aunt Edith blew through our house that very night.

"*Remember the great author Willa Cather, Polly,*" Aunt Edith commanded as she breezed in. "*She said, 'I shall not die of a cold. I shall die of having lived.'*" She reached down and hugged me quickly, then straightened up. "*Trust me,*" she said. "*Everything will be okay. Now where can I put my coat?*"

By the next morning, the mist had disappeared. The plants had lifted their leaves and the lake calmed down, and by noon the clouds had gathered and the sky had turned gray. And just like every Monday of my life, it rained at precisely one o'clock.

Aunt Edith gave up her amazing life in New York City to come and live on the farm. She's the kind of person who can hang the sun up in the sky at the same time she pushes a mountain out of the ground. She didn't just come back and save the farm—she saved me too.

So while I was right that a lot of things would change—now it seems as if the whole world wants to eat chocolate rhubarb, and our farm is the country's number six tourist attraction—a lot has stayed the same too. Nothing has died in the lake, the truly weeping cherry blossom tree still weeps, and my older sister, Patricia, is mean to me every chance she gets. It's been mist-free and normal. Not good normal or bad normal, just after-Grandmom normal.

Until today.

SAME DAY, MONDAY, AUGUST 18
Friendship

I'm supposed to be at the White House right this second to meet my family. Mom always hollers when I'm late, but I have to tell my best friend, Harry, about the mist. Usually he has some good ideas. Mom would like him, if she ever met him.

Actually, she has met him—she just doesn't know it. He's always on the farm, west field, row eighteen, column thirty. This is because Harry, my best friend, is a chocolate rhubarb plant.

Obviously Harry can't talk. He's a plant, not a person. Still, he communicates—all plants communicate. And not just on "magic" farms. It happens *everywhere*. If you don't believe it—like some people, *cough*, my sister *Patricia*—it's because you're not really paying attention. I'm not saying they're going to *talk* back. Even I know that would be crazy. But they'll answer you. It's a fact.

When I run up to him, Harry curves one of his bottom stalks into a semi-circle. That's his smile, and he always does this when he first sees me. I think he's the nicest plant in the world.

"Hi." I crouch right by him in the dirt. "I have something serious to tell you." I look him straight in the leaf. As solemnly as I can, I tell him that the mist is back.

Harry doesn't move, which is a little odd.

"The mist, Harry. Remember? Do you know what it means?"

I watch for the smallest of responses: the end of a leaf curling up, the sudden stiffening of a green stalk. But nothing.

"It must mean something, right? It's way smaller than before, and no one's died—" Suddenly my heart thuds. "Is someone dying?"

Harry reaches out his biggest leaf and brushes me on the arm with the underside. He's telling me to relax.

"But—"

He interrupts me by flapping some of his leaves.

"Oh." I sit back down. "You're saying I'll be okay."

He flaps his leaves again. *Yes, definitely,* he tells me. I'll be okay.

"But can you find out what it means? Maybe one of your friends—" I gesture to all the other plants surrounding him.

Harry waves his middle leaf up and down. *Okay.* He'll ask his friends.

"Thanks." I smile and look up. Right now, the sky is perfectly blue and the Midwestern sun shines directly upon us. Our farm is located in one of the driest, hottest sections of the country, in the Midwest. But we're the only place where it rains one day a week—every single Monday at 1:00—and the temperature never goes above one hundred degrees or below thirty-two degrees. It never rains any other time. Dad says it's because of the rolling hills that form a boundary to our property. I don't know how that explains our weekly rain—or the chocolate-tasting rhubarb, or anything else strange on our farm—but it makes him feel better to have a scientific explanation.

Harry reaches over and touches the tip of his smallest leaf to my cheek.

My eyes blink open. This means *pay attention*.

"Pay attention? To what?"

He's about to answer when we're interrupted.

"POLLY!" My sister Patricia has the voice of a whistle. "COME ON! EVERYONE'S WAITING!"

Harry freezes. He doesn't like Patricia, and I don't blame him. Patricia believes all the magical things on our farm are a series of coincidences. Rain the same time every week? It's a weather pattern that no one's bothered to figure out. Real diamonds outlining Grandmom's body? Obviously it's because diamonds are a naturally occurring mineral found in the ground. Plants that communicate? Ridiculous. The wind moves them, or the sun. Not the plants themselves.

Naturally, she's offended Harry so much that he would never ever dream of communicating with her.

"Pay attention to what?" I whisper, trying to get Harry to answer me before Patricia arrives.

But it's too late.

Patricia stands over me, the sun lighting her up like a movie star. She has long, thick blond hair and clear blue eyes, the complete opposite of my own thin brown mess and dark brown eyes. People never believe we're sisters.

"How's Larry the Rhubarb Plant?" she asks.

"His name isn't Larry," I grumble as I stand up. I steal one last look over at Harry, hoping that he'll tell me something. But he doesn't. He just watches us leave, giving me a small twitch of a leaf to say good-bye.

"Do you ever comb your hair?" Patricia sneers. "I mean, ever? In all the years of your life?"

"Just tell me why we're in such a hurry."

"It's a surprise," she tells me. "A *guest.*"

My stomach instantly drops down to my feet. A surprise guest showing up on the same day as the mist on the lake? I sneak another look back to Harry, but I'm too far away and all I see is a blur of red stalks and green leaves, fluttering gently against the light brown soil.

"Who is it?" I ask her.

"A boy—he's eleven too. A *human,*" she says. "Do you think you can handle it?" She snickers, but doesn't wait for me to answer. Instead, she takes off, running to the steps of the White House.

Whoever said that older siblings set a good example should have their head examined. For a second, I consider running back and huddling with Harry. Patricia may be right—every time I've tried to have a human friend, it's been a disaster. Grandmom used to say that friendships were too important to just acquire like things you can buy at the store; that people needed to build roots and history together if they wanted to confide in one another. She was trying to make me feel better, but there was no way Grandmom could understand. As soon as Grandmom smiled, people felt like they could run up next to her and tell her their secrets. Everyone always liked her, instantly. My older brother, Freddy, is exactly the same way—he smiles and the world smiles back. The only Monday it *hasn't* rained on the farm in eighty-six years is the day when Freddy was born, seventeen years ago. Mom is sure it's because Freddy was able to make the sun smile too, so much so that it couldn't allow clouds to ruin his day.

But me? I must radiate something prickly, or ugly, or plain old weird. Mom is convinced my lack of friends is because of the farm; that some people don't understand it, and because they don't understand, they assume it's bad. She wants me to snap at them, tell them that our farm is wonderful and special and that they're out to lunch. That's what she would do. (Actually, it's what she does.)

I don't snap, and I do smile, but none of it matters. When I was at school, I'd feel like the words I wanted to say—the magical words that would make all the difference—got clogged up in my throat. Even people who may have been nice to me soon thought I was strange and uncomfortable. They were right. It didn't have to do with the farm. It had to do with me. I was strange and uncomfortable. I don't know how to do it. To relax, make friends.

I pick up my pace, sighing. I can see the White House up ahead. It would be nice to have a human friend. But there's no reason this boy should be any different.

SAME DAY, MONDAY, AUGUST 18
Aunt Edith

The White House is our farm's headquarters. On the outside, it's so similar to the one in Washington, D.C., that you'd think you were getting ready for a walk in the Rose Garden with the President. Inside, though, it's completely different: there's the rhubarb restaurant and café, the History of Rhubarb Archives, and the office where Aunt Edith works. Patricia's already reached the porch and has latched herself on to her boyfriend, Sam. Sam's big and strong and has curly brown hair and round wire glasses and he's always nice to me, even when Patricia isn't. Honestly, I have no idea what he likes about her, except for the fact that she's beautiful. My mother and father stand to one side, talking to Freddy, their faces lit up, laughing. Beatrice clusters around one of the columns, talking to someone I can't see.

When I reach the very top of the steps, I see a bony hand spread out against one of the white columns. As I get closer, I see the hand belongs to a tall boy with longish white-blond hair that hangs in his face. At first glance, he looks serious. And shy. At least I don't have that sickening feeling I get when I look at someone and know, immediately, that they're mean.

"Polly!" Beatrice strides forward to greet me. She has taken care of me and Patricia and Freddy since we were babies. She's short—even shorter than I am—with smooth dark skin and wild hair that sticks out around her head like a black sunbeam. She was born on a sugarcane farm in Bermuda but came to the U.S. when she was a young girl; she says that finding my family—particularly Grandmom—convinced her she was born under a lucky star.

"I've been waiting for you! This is Basford. My godson. I've been begging for him to come and now, finally, he's here. You'll be in the same class at St. Xavier's." She looks so proud of Basford that you'd think he just won a gold medal in the Olympics. Basford must feel the same way I do: a red streak blazes across his face, reaching the tips of his ears. He's totally blushing.

I shove my hands in my pockets and push my hair back, off my face.

"Hi," I say.

Basford steps out from behind the column. "Hi," he answers. For a long moment, we stay silent. Everyone is looking at us, which makes me nervous.

"Give her a second," Patricia snorts from behind us. "She's kind of a vegetarian communicator, if you know what I mean."

I whirl around, furious, but Freddy gets to her first. "Pipe down," he tells her. Then he turns back to Basford. "Sorry."

It's quiet again.

If I don't talk right now, he'll be sure I'm a complete loser, so I say the first thing that comes to my mind. "Basford. That's a weird name."

Oh no. My face crumples as I press my eyes tightly shut. If Basford was red a minute ago, I'm now the color of the sun. No wonder I don't have any friends.

"Polly!" says Freddy. "Sorry, Basford. She can't help herself."

I squeeze my eyes tighter. It's genetic, it must be. Some ancestor of mine must have been as socially useless as I am. I must be the weak link, the only Peabody who inherited this awful gene. Just my luck.

But Basford just shrugs. "It's okay," he says. His voice is quiet, shy. "It *is* weird."

My eyes dart around, from Freddy to Basford. I'm waiting, I think, for him to scowl or turn away. But he doesn't.

"Polly Peabody isn't much better," I admit, smiling a little. "But at a farm called Rupert's Rhubarb, I guess it's just medium horrible, not horrible horrible."

"Beatrice told me about you," Basford says. He has light green eyes and a small nose, and he seems like someone who doesn't give up smiles easily. I look quickly over to Beatrice, who just nods, and I start to make a list in my head about all the things she could have said. *Reads with a book light every night. Scaredy cat. Loves fried chicken.*

But then, a blue dragonfly appears, zooming in over Basford's shoulder. It swerves around his ear, then flits back behind his head and over to me before looping back in front of his face.

Basford stares, entranced. The dragonfly shimmers in the air, bobbing up and down.

"These are the pretty ones, remember?" Freddy winks at me, as if to remind me that dragonflies are not worthy of my bug anxiety. But it isn't just dragonflies that trigger my bug phobia. Like our rhubarb, our farm breeds both regular bugs (like dragonflies and ants) and crazy, never-before-seen bugs (like Atlas moths that are as big as hawks, or slugs as long as spaghetti). Even Patricia, who likes to think that nothing scares her, runs away from a spaghetti slug.

"Dragonflies are superfast, the cheetahs of bugs," says Sam, Patricia's boyfriend. "People who make airplanes study their flight patterns."

Basford is still tracking the dragonfly. His eyes are bright, but they change as I watch him, growing wider, looking scared.

"Duck!" he yells.

I dive down just as a big black wasp zooms at me,

as full-bore as if it's a rocket. This has happened before. Wasps like me. I hate them. Dad says they target me because they know I'm afraid. Mom says it's because on the inside, I'm as soft and sweet as pudding. Either way, the wasps on our farm treat me like target practice. I run behind a column and down some steps, holding my breath and trying to ignore the panic rising in my chest.

The dragonfly darts in between the wasp and me as if it's my protector, but it's no contest. The dragonfly is fast, but the wasp is mean. Mean wins every time.

"Just don't swing at it," Freddy warns. I hold my arms tightly by my side. Even so, the wasp whooshes by Basford's shoulder and seems to aim at my forehead. I freeze, eyes riveted on its black eyes. Just as my face goes white, a strong, long-fingered hand reaches out from behind Freddy and snatches up the wasp in one quick swoop. It's so fast all I see is the flash of an emerald ring before the hand closes over the bug.

"Got it!"

I'm breathing hard, so I don't look up. Besides, I already know who it is. She has come to save me, as usual. I feel like I always do when she's around—safe, relieved, and awed. She's like my personal goddess, as if Athena stood on Mt. Olympus and said, yes, she's the one; I choose Polly Peabody. I'll watch over her and teach her everything she needs to know.

Aunt Edith.

She's very tall, like Dad—almost six feet—and the power of the sun seems to light her up as she pulls her shoulders back and rises to her full height. It's as if the sun itself—not blood like normal people—makes her move.

She walks over to the edge of the landing and gracefully unfurls her fingers, allowing the wasp to fly away. Naturally it didn't sting her. Not even a wasp would dare sting Aunt Edith. She steps back toward the rest of us. Everyone is watching her, but she looks straight at me, smiling widely.

"See, Polly? Nothing to be afraid of." She waves her empty hand around the porch, her ring gleaming. "Nothing to be afraid of at all."

SAME DAY, MONDAY, AUGUST 18
The Umbrella

Mom and Dad love the farm, but they were the first ones to admit that they didn't know anything about the business side of things the way Grandmom did. That's why Aunt Edith had to come back. Up until then, Aunt Edith was considered probably the best journalist in the world. She wrote for the *New York Times,* and anyone on the globe who was going to do anything important—bad important or good important—called to get her opinion. She was married once, a long time ago, and has twin sons—my cousins Romulus and Remus—but they are grown up and we don't see them much. Dad says that she is one of those people who needed to be alone to achieve her dreams. Grandmom used to say that Aunt Edith wanted to be successful more than anything else in the world, including being a wife and mother. Aunt Edith agrees with Grandmom. She says that she's not ashamed of this, and that no one would tell a man to be ashamed if he said he wanted to be successful.

"You must be fearless, Polly!" she tells me. "People have wasted far too much time on distractions rather than making a real difference, paying attention to the world, *participating*. A life worth living is one that is filled with action, with travel! That will be you, Polly, if I have anything do with it. You will be a *doer.*"

I have no idea why she can't see that I'm about the most opposite thing from fearless in the world. Picture a tiny mouse who runs away, batting her head against corners trying to escape from, well, *everything*, and you have me.

I've tried to tell Aunt Edith this. She says I'm a pearl in an oyster and that I'll thank her someday for forcing me out of my shell. I'm afraid to tell her the truth: that I *like* my shell.

We've walked over to the Learning Garden, which is the place Grandmom and Mom built for children to discover more about "the wonders of nature." Mom's installed water hoses so that kids can soak themselves silly. It's also the home of our most famous tourist attraction: the Umbrella ride. Today's the only day of the year that we close the farm to the public. We call it "Flannery Day," after my grandmom, and we always go up on the Umbrella and look around the farm as a tribute to her.

Chico, my favorite farm worker, stands at the controls as we huddle together on the circular platform under the spike of the Umbrella. Today we're riding on the Umbrella's platform, even though on regular Mondays, people can also choose to ride on the individual umbrellas hanging from the spokes supporting the canopy. (Those are scary swinglike rides that twirl and sway back and forth as the ride rises and falls.) If

I ever come back as another human being, I want to be Chico. He smiles all the time, no matter what, even after a six-inch-long yellow jacket stings him. (Well, he did spend one minute cursing in Spanish, but after that, his smile came right back.) Chico winks at me just as Dad gives him the okay to start the ride.

We lean against the iron railing as the floor of the platform rumbles a bit under our feet. Then we feel it chug, chug, chugging, as it ratchets up in space one click at a time. The Umbrella slowly stretches out above us as we rise—extending its many arms as if it's a giant red pterodactyl clawing the sky. Soon we're floating about twenty stories off of the ground, gazing at the farm and the surrounding lands. The sky has grown dark as the storm clouds gather above us. It's 12:55 p.m.

"Give me a hand," Dad calls out to Freddy. He's carrying two big thermal cases filled with apple-rhubarb juice. Freddy's superstrong—he works out all the time for soccer. He's also supernice, which means he's gentle with the plants even after a harvest, when he carries five stacked bushels at a time. Aunt Edith says he's the most cost-efficient worker we have.

Freddy grips the handles of one of the cases and moves it closer to the center of the platform. Then he opens the lid. At first he pulls out one of the juice bottles, but then he reaches in and grabs a bottle of champagne.

"Celebrating?" He waves the bottle at Dad.

"Not for you, unless you turned twenty-one and I didn't know about it."

Dad hands Freddy the other case. Freddy takes it, but his hand slips and he has to lift his knee so that the juice bottles don't crash.

"Good save," Dad tells him.

Freddy's face flushes red, tired. "Gotta get back to the gym, I guess." He spots me looking at him and quickly looks away.

"Why don't you show Basford the lay of the land, Polly?" Dad says. He looks over to Aunt Edith, who stands, waiting for him, on the other side of the platform. She's put on her bifocals and looks like she's about to go to a business meeting. "I need to check in with the big boss."

"Yeah, Polly," Patricia chimes in. "I'm surprised you haven't started babbling yet. Maybe you can show him your *favorite* place?" An evil smile crosses over Patricia's face when she turns to Basford. "Ask her about the Dark House."

The first thing I always think about when I hear the words "Dark House" is fear. The second is terror. And the third is slugs. Specifically slug*sand*, the stream of mucousy slugs that thrash around in a watery quicksand right near the Dark House entrance.

"What's a Dark House?" Basford asks.

I bite my lip hard. "It's really two buildings: a shed and a silo. They're painted black. We use the shed for the Transplanting. That's when we replant the Giant Rhubarb into barrels and put them inside the shed for about a month, then have a huge party around Halloween," I say.

"What's this 'we' you're talking about?" Patricia laughs. "Polly never goes near there. She thinks it's haunted."

"Haunted?" Basford's eyes light up.

"It isn't," Patricia says.

"It is," I say at the same time. Just last night, I heard terrible churning sounds from my window. As usual, I bolted to Freddy's room and hid under his covers. Everyone tells me I'm crazy, but I'm sure the sounds come from ghosts in the Dark House.

"You can't trust what she says," Patricia tells Basford. "She's never even been inside. She doesn't know what she's talking about."

Beatrice once told me that chanting the same thing over and over again can make it come true, so I close my eyes and chant: *Make Patricia go away, make Patricia go away.*

"Are you okay?" Basford whispers.

"One more second," I tell him, taking a last deep breath, pushing Patricia out of my mind.

"Okay. Now!" I snap open my eyes just as the Umbrella hits its highest point and locks into place, the platform sturdy under our feet. Perfect timing.

Every time I see this sight, I think of how the diamonds popped out of the ground, outlining Grandmom in their final tribute. Even now, with the rain about to start, the farm seems to shine from the inside. From up here, we can see everything—the sparkling stone of our castle, the gleaming green of the cube where my parents live, the mazes and the lake and the trees and the bridges and all the plants in between, on our property and beyond. A familiar pride swells up in my chest; up here, I feel unconquerable. I feel like I can be as fearless as Aunt Edith.

"What's your favorite part?" asks Basford in a low voice.

"I love everything."

Basford raises his almost-white eyebrows; they are even lighter than his hair.

"Okay. Everything *except* for the Dark House." I move

to my left. "Like over there. That's the Giant Rhubarb." I point to the east side of the property. "Our Giant Rhubarb helps fix the hole in the ozone layer."

Basford looks at me skeptically.

"True story. That's why we put it in the Dark House for a month. It grows huge. After the Transplanting's finished, we send it to a place where they take off the acid from the plants and mix it with chalk. Then it gets shot up into the air and forms a shield against all the bad stuff that's tearing a hole in the ozone."

"Acid?" His eyes get big.

"Oh, yeah. Rhubarb leaves are poisonous. But don't worry, you have to eat about eleven pounds to die."

Now he bites his lip. "You could die?"

"It's not that big a deal. Just try not to get the plants mad. Or else they might accidentally-on-purpose swat you with their leaves and you'll get a huge rash."

Basford abruptly turns and looks straight ahead, staring at the lake, and I remember that I'm trying to make a human friend here.

"I'm sorry. But really—it isn't a big deal. Honestly. The only times they've swatted me was when I totally deserved it."

He winces. I remind myself that people don't always understand things like swatting plants.

Basford turns away. Luckily, he's staring at the west side of the lake.

"That's our biggest crop," I tell him. "Regular rhubarb. We sell it to the Juice Company, to mix with all their other fruits to make juice. Don't worry. The regular rhubarb plants never hit anyone." Basford gives me a halfhearted chuckle. I don't think he finds this funny.

"See that house?" Farther down, on the west side past the regular rhubarb, is a small patch of rhubarb that grows next to a tiny cottage. "That's Dad's lab. He's a scientist who cultivates his own rhubarb so he can make medicine."

I turn so that I face directly west. "Over there, next to the oak trees? That's the chocolate rhubarb. Have you tasted it yet?"

Basford shakes his head.

"It tastes like chocolate *and* it's a vegetable, so your parents can't get mad." Just then, the first raindrops begin to fall. I hold up my watch for Basford to see.

"One o'clock." I grin. "It rains at the same time, every single Monday."

I point over toward the White House. "Right there, behind the chocolate rhubarb? That's the PEACE maze. Grandmom transplanted a bunch of Giant Rhubarb plants to make a maze in the shape of the word

PEACE. If you squint, you can see the words HOPE and LOVE too, and a lot of stars and hearts."

He has stopped listening to me. He's turned back, staring directly south, blinking. At first, I think he's going to ask about the Dark House, which he now can see if he looks straight ahead. But he doesn't do that. He's looking slightly to the right.

"Is that—?"

I smile. "Yep."

He sees it. Our castle.

"That's my turret," I say, hating that I can hear the bragging in my voice. But I can't stop myself. I point to the rounded room jutting out from the northwest corner. "I have a window seat there and can look out all night long if I want to."

Basford doesn't seem to notice that I'm bragging. I guess it's pretty hard to think about things like that when you're staring dead on at a real stone castle in the middle of a rhubarb farm.

"And that's—" He gulps.

"The rope bridge." Our rope bridge looks exactly like the kind of bridge that knights race across—usually over a gulch of raging fire—on their way to slay the dragon and rescue the princess. Dad thought it would be cool to have one connecting the kids' house—the castle—to the place where he and Mom sleep—the square cube, made almost entirely of green glass.

"If you ever use that bridge, make sure you don't look down. It's forty feet high. There aren't any rail-ings—just the ropes to hold on to—so if you do slip, you're heading smack into the lake. But don't worry; even if you fall you won't die. Nothing can die in the lake."

He bends down so that both of his elbows rest on the railing. For a long time he doesn't speak, he just looks out at the rain. When he finally does say some-thing, it's barely a whisper.

"This. Is. Awesome." For the first time, he seems to relax.

I totally agree. "I know."

The rain is falling harder now. All the water magni-fies the greens and reds and pinks and browns of the farm; it looks like one of those paintings with thick, bright-colored smeared brushstrokes.

"There's one more part." *Besides* the Dark House, I add silently.

He tilts his head back to where I stand, waiting.

"The Learning Garden. That's the part underneath us right this second. The stuff that grows there is per-fect. The strawberries never get moldy; the roses don't have thorns; the peppers are crisp and delicious every single time. There are other things too. If you lie on the hammock under the sycamore tree, the temperature will always be just right, even if it's way hot outside." I step nearer to him. "It even grows rubies."

His eyes grow bigger. "Truthfully?"

I cross my heart. "Hope to die, stick a needle in my eye."

For a long moment, Basford just stares at the farm. "How does your farm do all these things?"

It's the million-dollar question. If you ask Mom, she would say God. If you ask Dad, he would say it's science, of course. Grandmom, though, was like me. She knew and I know there's only one answer that makes sense, only one answer that's true.

I look Basford straight in the eye. "It's magic."

As soon as I say it, his face lights up and he smiles for the first time, a shy, sweet smile. "Yeah," he says. "That's what I thought."

TUESDAY, AUGUST 19
The Chocolate Rhubarb Harvest

"Now listen up," Beatrice tells Basford and me. "Only take the red stalks, report anything mushy, and make sure you don't hurt any bugs or you'll have to deal with me."

I'm not surprised that Mom put Basford to work just one day after he got here. My mother has this thing about us working. It's pretty simple. If you work hard—as in sweaty, long hours pulling, harvesting, cutting, sorting, packing rhubarb—then you're a good kid who will grow up and become a superstar. If you don't work—if you watch television or play video games—then you're a spoiled, lazy child who will amount to nothing. She and Grandmom thought a lot of the same things.

Beatrice hands me two sets of gloves, and gives Basford the bags.

"Polly will tell you what to do," she says. "Lunch break in an hour. Go!"

I lead Basford into the field, stopping at the first plant in the row. I lean down and break off a stalk from the root. It isn't difficult to harvest rhubarb—you just have to get into a rhythm. *Twist twist snap, twist twist snap.*

"See?" I say. "It's pretty easy. Just *never* hurt the crown," I tell him. "It's the most important part of the whole thing."

Basford stares up at me. "What's a crown?"

"It's the root of the rhubarb plant. It's thick, like this . . ." I make two fists and put them next to each other. "The roots clump together, forming a crown, which stays under the soil." I kneel down and push away a little of the dirt covering the base of the stalks. "See how it's all connected down here?"

Basford crouches down next to me, peering closely at the dirt.

"The only time you ever have to dig up the crown is when you want to *divide* the plant, which is basically like smashing its brain. We don't do that unless we have to.

"Anyway, this is how you harvest. *Watch.*" I lean down, grab one of the red stalks tightly, and twist it hard, once, twice, and then snap off the stalk from the base. "Voila. Chocolate rhubarb."

He takes it and holds it under his nose. "Can I eat it?"

"Sure," I say as I feel a smile slip across my face. "...if you want to get *poisoned.*"

Basford drops the stalk before he notices that I'm laughing.

"I'm kidding. You can eat the stalk," I tell him. "Just not the leaves."

I snap another stalk off of its base and bite into it. "Try it," I say, swallowing.

Slowly, Basford picks up his stalk from the ground and brushes off the sand. I don't think he trusts me.

"Really," I repeat. "You're going to love it."

He takes a big bite out of the stalk, his eyes never leaving mine.

"Yowza." He grins as his face lights up. "This is better than a Snickers bar." He chomps off another piece, and, as he chews, looks around the field. "This is like— this is like the best thing I've ever eaten. It's really like *chocolate!*"

I'm not surprised—chocolate rhubarb has this effect on everyone. Basford gobbles up the first stalk and than snaps off another stalk, eating that one equally fast. Before he finishes his third, he stops, looking around.

"Why don't you just grow this, and none of the other stuff?"

"Well, we make a lot of money with the juice and the Giant Rhubarb." I lean over and keep working, snapping a cluster of stalks in one sharp twist. "But the real reason is that the farm won't let us."

Twist twist snap, twist twist snap.

"What?" He stops eating.

"Yeah," I say matter-of-factly. "I have a theory about it." I lean in close, talking softly. "The farm is like a genie."

"A genie?"

"It's powerful and magical, but it also has to listen to the sun and the rain and the farmers. Us."

Twist twist snap, twist twist snap. "Grandmom always said that the plants would never steer us wrong. So when we plant extra chocolate rhubarb and it doesn't grow, we just listen to the farm and plant something else."

Twist twist snap!

"I won't eat this one," Basford says as he snaps off another stalk. "It's for the harvest." He holds it up for me to see.

I smile. "Beatrice would be proud," I say. "Only two hundred and thirty-one plants to go."

His eyebrows go way up in his forehead. "Two hundred and thirty-one?"

"It's half the field," I tell him. "Don't worry, it'll go fast," I reassure him. "Let me see you do it one more time."

After I'm sure he isn't going to decimate a plant—or else aggravate one so much that it smacks him—I tell him to go to the opposite corner of the field so that we can "meet in the middle." But I'm lying. The real reason is so I can sneak over and talk to Harry.

When I get to his spot, I find Harry with his green leaves stretched out flat to his side, shining under the sun. He's getting a suntan. No joke. All plants want sunlight, but rhubarb is especially crazy about it. He's also happy this is not a harvesting year for him; last year, I pruned him so much, he didn't talk to me for a week.

I check to make sure Basford isn't looking, and then I sit down near Harry and pull out a water bottle from my backpack.

"Here," I say, pouring some of the water around his roots. "Drink up."

It's water from the lake. Obviously, all the plants, including Harry, get enough water from the weekly rainfall, but I know a little bit more will make him extra strong and healthy.

"Don't say I never did anything for you." I smile.

Harry's leaves fold themselves together. *Thank you.*

"That's Basford," I tell Harry. "He's Beatrice's godson."

His middle leaf shakes. This means either *yes* or *I know.*

"He seems nice," I say. "A little quiet. For a boy."

Harry bends his bottom stalk, smiling again. Then he curls up the end of his leaves.

"He's not my friend *yet*," I say. "I just met him yesterday. He might change his mind when we go to school and he sees how unpopular I am." I drink some of the lake water myself.

Harry flaps his leaves up and down. *It'll be okay.*

I tell Harry all about yesterday, beginning with the arrival of Basford to the wasp. Harry listens patiently to my entire story. Once or twice he flaps a leaf to tell me to slow down, or folds up a leaf to tell me to repeat what I just said.

"Okay. So one other question. I paid attention to *everything* yesterday. What were you talking about? Basford? The mist? The wasp?"

This prompts Harry. *No.*

"So what was it?"

Then Harry does something new. He bunches up all of his stalks in one vertical lift so that his leaves look like some kind of strange green bouquet on red stems.

"I don't know what that means."

Harry relaxes his leaves for a second, and then bunches them up again. I shake my head.

"Can you give me another clue?"

Harry stretches his leaves flat and looks like he might respond when I hear a voice behind me.

"Uh, Polly?"

I twist around and see Basford. He's holding out a full bag of rhubarb stalks and is looking at me as if I escaped from a mental hospital. "Were you talking to someone?"

"Me?" I say, my face reddening. "No."

I glance over at Harry.

"I mean I was, to myself, I talk to myself sometimes. But no. No one here." I feel a leaf graze my leg. I ignore it. "I just like to come to the fields and say some words. Out-loud words."

Harry's two biggest leaves scrape my leg. I scooch away from him, but end up touching another plant on the other side.

"Okaaay," Basford says.

"We should get that to Beatrice. She'll be excited you did so much," I say, pointing to his bags. I only have about half as much.

"Let's go!" I say, way too cheerfully.

Harry brushes the underside of a leaf on my ankle. It's pretty obvious. Basford stares at him.

"It's nothing," I say, a fake smile frozen on my lips. "The wind."

"Right." His eyes dart back and forth between Harry and me, confused. There is no wind. I bite my bottom lip and Basford gives up trying to figure it out. As he lifts his bag over his shoulder, I glance back and stick out my tongue at Harry. He has to understand that I can't just go around telling people my best friend is a chocolate rhubarb plant.

"Come on," I tell Basford. "Beatrice will be making my favorite."

"Rhubarb something?"

"No." I grin. "Fried chicken!"

I heave my own bag over my shoulder as Basford steps in front of me, walking down the row of plants toward the road. I glance backward to see what Harry's doing. One of his stalks is sticking straight out, perpendicular to the ground, as if he's watching me. But I don't think he's too mad. If he were, his leaves would be rustling, and they're not. I wink. Harry bends his middle leaf into a smile.

FRIDAY, AUGUST 22
The Turret

Today is Friday, which is always, always, *always* my favorite day of the week. These are the days I get Aunt Edith all to myself. She doesn't do one shred of rhubarb business. Instead, it's all me. Sometimes we see a silly movie. Other times, she teaches me about microfinancing and introduces me to people who have dedicated their lives to helping others. Patricia and Freddy stopped going years ago. I suppose I could ask Basford to join us, but he's watching Freddy's soccer game, and besides, I'm selfish about Aunt Edith. I like when I have her all to myself.

Finally, Aunt Edith's Mercedes rolls very slowly down the circular driveway in front of our castle. Aunt Edith's "driver"—or assistant, or secretary, or butler, whatever you want to call him—likes to make grand entrances. His name is Girard and he's tall with a blocky nose and narrow shoulders that make him look like a long plank of wood, with arms and legs stuck out to the side. He's really smart, supposedly, and works with Aunt Edith so that one day she'll reward him with a high-powered job. That's what she does with all her assistants. If I were her, I'd be looking for someone to hire Girard away right this second. He's unbelievably annoying. He always talks about his time at Cambridge and Wharton, and says things like "Alas, sometimes I think I'd be better on a small pebble in the middle of the ocean, so drawn am I to both sides of the Atlantic." Then he smiles, as if anyone understands what he's saying.

Girard rolls down his window and smiles broadly. He has yellow teeth.

"Polly Peabody. My pleasure. As always." He scurries out of the front seat and walks slowly to the back passenger door. "Your aunt."

He swings open the black door and Aunt Edith steps out, all glorious-looking. "Hello, Polly."

"Where are we going?" I blurt out. Aunt Edith looks at me disapprovingly. "I mean, it's so good to see you. Sorry."

"It's good to see you too, sweetheart," she says. She walks over to me, pulling a tangled piece of hair out from my barrette. "Today I have a surprise for you."

Our last surprise was when Aunt Edith brought me to a science center so I could meet an astronaut who had walked on the moon. Just thinking about it makes me grin.

"Today," Aunt Edith tells me. "Today we're staying here."

Here? I scan the fields, chewing on my bottom lip. "At the farm?"

"The castle," she says. "There's something I've been meaning to show you."

She walks ahead of me to the side door of the castle, the one her father built so that we wouldn't have to use the portcullis. (That's the enormous wooden door in the front of most castles that needs to be lifted up high by chains.) Sometimes I forget that Aunt Edith grew up in this very castle too. I still think of her as a city person. Even when she came back home after Grandmom died, she never became a farm person again. She told me once that she thinks it was a mistake that Grandmom never left, that she didn't explore the world more. But Grandmom always told me that books and poems were all she needed to explore, and that she was quite happy to be on Rupert's Rhubarb Farm for her entire life, "tilling the earth and seeing what magic came forth."

Now Aunt Edith lives about ten minutes away, in a house she bought the very day she returned, four years ago. It's white and rectangular with a flat roof. Inside, the walls are made of concrete that is painted bright white to match the exterior. I've only been there once and I have to admit, I didn't really like it. You couldn't tramp dirt inside, since all the furniture and rugs were white too, and she didn't have any good snacks except for carrot sticks. Honestly, I don't know how she can stand to live there after living here.

"This way," Aunt Edith orders as we walk across the living room to the stairs in the northwest corner. We climb the circular stone steps, on the side of the castle where Patricia and I sleep. There are two rooms down our hall that are never used, so my first thought is that we're going to go inside them.

But Aunt Edith passes those doorways too.

"One more flight, Polly," she says.

The third floor. No one goes to the third floor. Not even Beatrice.

"But I thought—it's locked . . ."

"Of course it is," she says. Aunt Edith fishes inside her black shirt and pulls out a thick golden necklace. Instead of a charm or pendant at the end of it, there's a long bronze skeleton key.

She pushes the entryway door to this floor open. Then she glides into the hall, stopping in front of a wooden door with a keyhole outlined in gold. She inserts the skeleton key into the lock and sweeps inside, as if she always walks into pitch-black rooms. I, on the other hand, freeze.

"Polly?" Aunt Edith calls back for me. I can't believe she wants me to go in there when it's so dark. I take a baby step toward the doorway.

"What about the light?" I ask weakly just as something big and black leaps out at me. "AGH!" I yell, and I leap back into the hall.

A single ray of light glints through the circular window, spotlighting the creature. It's a cricket. A huge cricket. A cricket the size of a squirrel.

"Are you okay?" Aunt Edith uses her calm, stern voice.

"Cuh-cuh-cricket," I stammer.

"They don't bite," she informs me.

"I can't see anything—"

"Oh, Polly, are you afraid of the dark too?" Aunt Edith sighs.

I stop where I am and think about this. "Yes," I admit.

I hear the clopping of her footsteps heading toward the doorway, but before they reach me, they turn in a different direction. She grunts, just barely, and there's a loud clatter as something falls to the ground. The blast of light startles me.

Aunt Edith is standing by a large picture window, a heap of drapes by her feet. She's yanked the entire curtain rod down.

"Well, come in," she says as she pries the frame upward, allowing light and air to spill in.

The first thing I see when I walk over the threshold is the ivy: pretty, green five-pointed-leaf ivy, crawling over all the walls and bookshelves that line this circular wall. It covers the floors in coils and stretches up the window edges and even seems to wrap around the pointed witch's hat of a roof.

I'm about to join Aunt Edith across the room when a strand of ivy literally *lifts up off the ground* and stares at me in the face.

The blood rushes to my head as I stare at it, hovering in the air in front of my eyes.

"Uh, Aunt Edith?"

"The ivy won't hurt you, dear."

I smile at the leaves, thinking that this must be how Eve felt when she was in the Garden of Eden looking at the serpent. The ivy wavers, and then curls back down at my feet.

"Enid's library," Aunt Edith announces.

I don't know much about Enid, except that she was Grandmom's mom, Rupert's wife, and that her father, my great-great-grandfather, was an Italian prince. The story is that when he came to the U.S., he bought our property because it reminded him of his home in Italy. Then he built a castle (also to remind himself of his home) and became a rhubarb farmer. He's the one who started the tradition of giving all the girls in his family an emerald ring. I look sadly down to my finger: I still can't believe I lost my ring in the lake. It's probably gone forever, something Patricia never lets me forget. She flashes her ring in front of my face every chance she gets.

Aunt Edith's face is lit up, her eyes bright. "When I was a little girl, Enid used to bring me up here and show me all her books. Now I can bring you." She steps over to one of the shelves, her long fingers tracing the spines of the books.

"Why is it locked up?"

"I locked it," Aunt Edith tells me. "Only someone who can appreciate the power of words should be allowed in here." She pauses in front of a book, shaking her head in amazement. "Here, look at this."

She gives me an old book with a worn blue cover.

It's called *The Railway Children* by someone named E. Nesbit.

"I spent hours reading her books," Aunt Edith says, looking at the book over my shoulder. "I'm jealous, Polly."

"Jealous?" I turn to face her.

"To be able to read these books for the first time? What better cause for jealousy? You have hours of joy ahead of you." She turns, curling her lips in, thinking. "But at least I have the honor of bringing these treasures to you. That's something."

She goes back to searching through the shelves. There must be thousands of books in here, lining every shelf, hidden behind the ivy and the dust. I could read a new one every day for the next ten years.

I close the Nesbit book and take a step toward Aunt Edith. At the same exact second, *another* cricket jumps out at me. This one's slightly smaller, more like a chipmunk size. I leap out of the way, banging my knee against a shelf.

"Polly," Aunt Edith says in her clipped voice, not turning around. "They're only bugs."

I can't see where the cricket went, but I do see the clutter in the room: small, round, black-edged tables, with tiny colored squares circling around the edge.

Dust specks glint in the sunlight that is now pouring through the rectangular window. Across the room, there are two more windows, hidden by heavy, dark red drapes.

"What are you looking for?" I ask Aunt Edith.

Before she can answer, a blue dragonfly swoops in through the window and flies around my head. It looks like the one that put on the show for Basford. My eyes dart from the dragonfly back to the ivy, which has lifted itself off of the ground and begun to move.

I can't believe what I'm seeing. The ivy stops exactly where the dragonfly flutters, like a bus pulling into a station stop, and the dragonfly *perches* on one of the ivy's leaves. And *then* the squirrel-sized Monster cricket leaps out of nowhere to rest on another leaf. The ivy weaves its way through the air, carrying the bugs across the room, until it reaches one of the dusty tiled tables. It parks at the table, allowing its passengers to jump off. The Monster cricket leaps to an old notebook on top of a stack of books, and the dragonfly zooms over to me, skidding to a stop right in front of my nose. He hovers there, sparkling, wings moving so fast that they create a blue blur. For a second, I just stare at him. Then, without even realizing what I'm doing, I nod.

And I swear the dragonfly nods back.

"I'll find it, I'm sure of it," murmurs Aunt Edith, over in the corner.

I nod again at the dragonfly.

Slowly, the dragonfly nods back at me.

This cannot be happening.

"Can you speak?" I mouth the words, so Aunt Edith doesn't hear.

The dragonfly zooms closer and I think I actually lock eyes—my two, with his seven thousand and three—for a second. He starts to fly through the air, in deliberate movements. Straight up, then down-but-to-the-right, then straight up again. He hovers there, looking at me. Then he starts making a circle. A big circle.

It can't be.

"No?" I mouth. Did this dragonfly actually just spell the word NO in the air?

The dragonfly bobs up and down.

"You can't speak but you *can spell*?" I'm whispering now, but Aunt Edith still doesn't pay me any attention.

When the dragonfly nods again, I reach out and grab on to the back of an old black iron chair. My knees are shaking and I think my heart may permanently stop. I want to tell Aunt Edith that I need to get out of this room, but before I do, the Monster cricket slowly lifts one of his skinny legs up off of the mantel and holds it up to his mouth.

"*Ssshh,*" he seems to say. "*Ssshh.*"

SAME DAY, FRIDAY, AUGUST 22
Self-Reliance

"Finally!" Aunt Edith exclaims from behind me. "I found it! Here," she says. "It's for you."

I turn shakily from the Monster cricket to Aunt Edith. She's so excited that she doesn't notice I'm freaked out. She hands me the book. It's small, attached by a hard leather cover with some kind of stamp on it. "*Self-Reliance,*" Aunt Edith announces. "Ralph Waldo Emerson. Read it a hundred times, and then one time more."

I take the book and glance back to the table. The cricket is still holding his long black leg up against his mouth, telling me to keep them a secret.

"*Trust thyself: every heart vibrates to that iron string,*" Aunt Edith continues. "That's how I want you to approach the world, Polly." She looks sad, kind of wistful. "I'm so glad I found it for you."

I turn the dusty book over in my hand. "Thank you," I say. I can't help glancing back at the window. The dragonfly is hovering over that same pile of books, as if waiting for me. Then Aunt Edith straightens up, stepping directly on the ivy and ignoring the crickets. When I look back, Monster cricket has leaped to the top of the pile of books underneath the dragonfly.

"May we talk for a second?" Aunt Edith asks.

"Sure," I say.

Aunt Edith leans against the bookshelves, her arms crossed over her chest.

"I want you to know something." She gestures around the room. "First of all, all of *this*—the bugs, the crickets, the ivy, the rhubarb—it's *wonderful*. It is magic. Truly."

Relief floods through me. I was never sure what Aunt Edith believed. "I knew it! You thought so too! You think it's magic!"

"Yes but . . ." Aunt Edith steps over to me and lifts my chin. "But it's beside the point."

"What do you mean?" I ask, confused.

"I mean, it isn't *you*. That's why I'm giving you Emerson. Trust yourself. Not the crickets. Not the rhubarb. Not the ring—"

"I lost my ring."

She ignores me. "I watch you, dear. I know how connected you are to this farm. But *you* are bigger, better than the magic. You might not know that now, but you will. I never want you to feel trapped on this farm, or beholden to it."

I don't know what she's talking about—I love our farm. I check out the Monster cricket. He's got one leg up against his face as if he's holding a violin. The other leg is moving back and forth across it like he's playing a song. I almost giggle, but then I see the intense look Aunt Edith is giving me.

"Things are going to change, Polly," she says. Her voice is strong and hard, scaring me. "I want you to be prepared."

As she speaks, I feel something inside me rip, like a piece of fabric torn from my bones.

"What do you mean, *change*?" I grip the book tightly across my chest as the image of the green mist flashes through my mind. I must look terrified, because her voice shifts, and her eyes become reassuring.

"I just meant . . . don't worry, sweetheart. All of life is change. That's all I'm talking about. Life."

I want her to explain, but she doesn't. She's just waiting for me to answer. I don't think I have any choice but to say what she wants to hear.

"Okay," I say. My eyes dart over to the bugs. They're behind Aunt Edith, just watching.

Aunt Edith doesn't notice. She's still apologizing. "Sometimes, I forget you're still a child. We can come back," Aunt Edith says. "Would you like that?"

Before I have a chance to nod, the ivy springs up behind Aunt Edith and two of Monster cricket's friends leap on top of the leaves. They jump from leaf to leaf, as if they're on platforms of different heights. The Monster cricket springs up to the very top of the vine.

Aunt Edith smiles tenderly at me, patting down my messy hair. "Would you like to come back here?" she repeats.

I try to pretend I'm paying attention. But it's hard. Behind her back, above her head, the dragonfly is spelling out another word.

Y . . . E . . . S.

"Yes," I tell Aunt Edith. "Yes."

"Wonderful," she says, and she strides past me to the doorway. Before I walk through the doorway, I glance back into the turret one more time.

The dragonfly bobs up and down in the doorway, while the Monster cricket stares at me from the ground. Slowly, he lifts up his leg and waves. *Good-bye.*

"I'll be back," I whisper.

SAME DAY, FRIDAY, AUGUST 22
Beatrice

After Aunt Edith leaves, I go into our playroom, sitting on the soft couch opposite an oil portrait of Enid, set above our fireplace. I glance up at her quickly, then lean back into the soft chair and open *Self-Reliance.* It begins with a poem.

Ne te quaesiveris extra
Man is his own star; and the soul that can
Render an honest and a perfect man.
"An honest and a perfect man."

I frown and shut the book. You would think that Mr. Ralph Waldo Emerson never knew any honest and perfect women. Only men. I rest my head on the back of the couch just as Freddy slams the door and walks inside, with Basford right behind him.

"We won," he says. "Four zip."

"Freddy scored two of the goals," Basford says, gazing up at my brother with what can only be described as worship.

Freddy grins. My brother's red cheeks are blotchy, and his shirt is soaked from sweat. "You need a shower," I tell him. "You reek."

"Yeah," he says. "I'm totally beat." He heads toward the stairs and stops. "Where's Aunt Edith?"

"She left."

"Where'd you go today?" He grins. "The Museum for Smart People?"

At that second, Beatrice walks into the room, an orange and white and red skirt cinched in at her wide waist.

"Laundry time," she tells Basford. "And don't forget to wash the clothes you're wearing." Beatrice makes all of us do our own laundry, which she insists will be helpful when we're grown up.

Freddy takes off his sweaty shirt and tosses it to Basford. "Do a friend a favor?"

"Sure." Basford says as he catches it.

"Excuse me?" Beatrice interrupts.

"It's just one shirt," Freddy groans. "I'm tired."

"It's no problem," Basford says softly. Then he turns

and leaves the room, before Beatrice can order Freddy to take his shirt back.

"Tired?" Beatrice stomps over to Freddy and tries to look him in the eye, which is pretty funny to see, since Freddy towers over her. She motions for him to lean down and presses her lips against his forehead.

"You have a fever," Beatrice pronounces.

"No, I don't," he says.

"You do. To bed."

"I'm fine. I'm just hot from the game." Freddy pinches his shirt so that it's away from his skin.

"Go upstairs and take a nap."

It's impossible to win an argument with Beatrice, and Freddy knows it. "Fine," he says. "But not because I'm sick. Because I'm tired." He walks out of the room, and Beatrice turns her attention back to me.

"What book is that?" Beatrice steps over to my chair and picks up *Self-Reliance.*

"Aunt Edith gave it to me," I tell her.

"Where did you get it?"

"Upstairs."

"Enid's locked library, you mean."

"You know it?" I'm shocked.

"I've worked here for thirty years, of course I know it." Beatrice hands the book back to me.

"It's a really weird place," I say. "Beatrice, there's ivy growing on the *inside* and there are these bugs that were so big you'd have to kill them with a baseball bat—"

"Polly!" Beatrice turns her head sharply. "What kind of a grown-up are you going to be if you just go around blabbing secrets all over the place?"

"Secrets?"

"If Edith wanted to show you and *only* you the library, I'm sure she had her reasons."

"She did. She said things were going to change and she wants me to be prepared."

Beatrice looks me up and down. "Now why'd you go and tell me that?" She holds up her hand, waving the dust rag in my face.

"Do you know what she means?"

"No," Beatrice says quickly. "I'm not a mind-reader, Polly." She seems to scrub the top of the fireplace mantel with her dust rag. "And neither are you." She stops dusting. "Everything changes. Every single second on a farm brings something new."

"Is that what she meant?"

Her face scrunches up.

"I don't ask a lot of questions. I just hope that when I need to do something, I do it. You never know what kind of person you'll be until that moment of crisis: the kind who sits and watches, or the one who moves. I want to be the one who moves."

She puts her hands on her hip, thinking.

"Okay, but—"

"Go read your book, Polly."

"Beatrice—"

She turns one last time to face me. "And for God's sake, don't talk about killing any bugs with baseball bats!"

I stare at her, but it's clear she's finished with the conversation. A long time ago, Beatrice made us all sign a contract swearing that we wouldn't kill any bugs on the farm on purpose, even if it had stung us or hurt us or anything. "Your dinner or your signature," she insisted. Anyway, if she'd just let me speak, I could tell her that I *wasn't* planning on killing any bugs. I was just trying to tell her how big and strange these bugs were.

But Beatrice is long gone. I clutch my book and trudge up the stairs to my room. At moments like this, I think I really do have the weirdest family—and live on the weirdest farm—in the whole wide world.

SAME DAY,
FRIDAY, AUGUST 22
Jennifer Jong

I flop onto my bed, arms behind my head, and then glance absently at the bright blue folder sitting on my desk. Mom has left me a bunch of orientation materials about St. Xavier's, the new school I'm starting in precisely eleven days.

I suddenly understand. I know *exactly* what Aunt Edith was talking about. She was telling me to be prepared for my new school. Seventh grade.

Of course!

I pick up the folder and stare at the bright picture of the beautiful stone building in the center of St. Xavier's campus. Pictures of kids with big smiles and straight hair stare back at me. They look happy. Maybe *I'll* be happy.

I close my eyes and let myself imagine all the *good* things that can happen at St. Xavier's.

58

I have friends. I talk in class. No one thinks I'm weird. I'm one of those normal kids, the ones with their picture on the cover. I'll even comb my hair.

At my old school, nobody paid me much attention until this one terrible, awful day when a big, smiling kid from my class named Max Keyser noticed my finger.

My right index finger is crooked. Not just kind of crooked, *really* crooked. It literally makes a right angle at the top knuckle, like a road sign announcing a turn. It's genetic. Aunt Edith has one and so did Grandmom; perfect Patricia—of course—doesn't. Usually I hide it, but on that day, I was looking through my backpack for a book to read so I didn't look too stupid alone on the playground. I dropped the whole bag and some papers flew out. Max picked some up for me, but when he brought them over he glanced at my hand.

"Hey, what's that?" His eyes locked on my finger. I tried to curl it up, but I was too slow. "Eww!" he yelled, jumping back, dropping my papers.

He made so much noise that a girl from my class— the most popular girl in my class—sauntered over. Her name was Jennifer Jong, but everyone called her Jongy. We were the two best spellers in our school.

"Let me see," Jongy said.

I crouched down on the ground, pressing my fingertips against the palm of my hand. We had been in the same class since first grade. Up until fifth grade, she ignored me. Then I beat her in our school's spelling bee. She told everyone I had taken some kind of secret rhubarb potion, and that I was a cheater. The teacher had told her to stop, but Jongy just kept saying "You can't make me, you can't make me."

I didn't take any potion. I just knew how to spell "broccoli."

Anyway, this was the first time she had spoken to me in a year.

"It's just my finger," I told her. "It's a little crooked."

"I'm sure it isn't that bad," she said sweetly. "Let me see." I straightened up and extended my hand, palm up. She leaned forward and inspected it, like she was a scientist. She smiled, and I smiled back, relieved.

Jongy turned my hand around so that my palm faced down. She still smiled, but now she closed her lips. She traced the curve with her own straight, manicured finger. Then, in a flash, she let go of my hand and turned to Max and the other thousand classmates I suddenly seemed to have.

"I knew it," Jongy said. She glanced over at me and then twirled back around to the crowd. "She's a witch."

She said it as matter-of-factly as if she was saying the sky was blue.

"What?" I said.

Jongy's mouth opened wide in a big, glaringly bright white smile. "There's something weird on that farm. It rains every week! At the same time! Come on! We live in one of the driest states *in the country.* Daddy always says he doesn't know why it isn't being investigated." She said "investigated" as if it had about twenty syllables. "I think the police are scared that they'll end up burned at the stake or whatever it is witches do."

I stood there, wishing I really *was* a witch so that I could disappear. My whole body felt hot, embarrassment pouring into my blood, and I'm sure I turned as red as our most thriving rhubarb.

"No!" I said. "No, I'm not—" But I looked around at all my classmates—they seemed to have tripled, quadrupled—and I stopped. "I'm—"

Tears flooded my eyes. I tucked my head down and picked up my bag. I could feel myself start to cry and I *really* didn't want Jongy to see that. Aunt Edith *hates* girls who cry. So I pushed by her and walked as fast as I could into the school, into the locker room, and hid in the bottom of the sports equipment closet. I didn't leave for the rest of the day.

After that, every time I walked by Jennifer Jong, she and her friends hissed *"Witch!"* Sometimes they wore garlic around their necks as if I were a vampire. I couldn't wait to get out of that school and away from Jongy and her friends. But now I *have* gotten away, and I get to start at a whole new school.

I study the material from St. Xavier's, and before I know it, I'm falling asleep. I dream of crickets and drag-onflies, leaping and flying over Basford and a group of smiling girls and boys—all of them surrounding me, Polly Peabody, who no one thinks is weird at all.

It is a very good dream.

SUNDAY, AUGUST 24
The Organic Psychic

I love Sunday mornings—the last day of peace and quiet before the tourists swarm on Monday—and this one is especially warm and sunny and perfect. Basford and I are about to go swimming in the lake when Ophelia Baird's red, white, and blue minivan screeches into the driveway, jerking to a stop.

"Polly!" Ophelia jumps out.

"Oh boy," I mutter.

"Who's that?" asks Basford.

I don't even know how to answer him. Not because I don't know Ophelia. Because she's hard to explain.

Ophelia's an Organic Psychic.

Yep. An Organic Psychic.

An Organic Psychic is someone who can talk to the spirits of the natural world that have not been messed up by people, chemicals, or gossip. (That's what Ophelia says, anyway.) Mom doesn't really believe her, but she enjoys Ophelia's company.

She's supertall, like over six feet. When she gets out of the car, she lifts her head, looking like a giant, and gazes around the farm. For a couple of seconds, she closes her eyes and touches the middle of her forehead with her right hand, almost like beginning the sign of the cross. When she opens her eyes, she snaps a smile firmly into place.

"This is Basford," I tell her.

"Of course it is!" she says, as if she's met him twenty times before. "You sweet boy. You did the right thing, coming here, you know. Just like your father said."

Basford raises his eyebrows but I just shrug. Ophelia's always like this. She's the looniest person I know. "Is your mother inside?" she asks me.

"I think so."

"Good. I've brought some new pesticides." I watch her as she grabs a big paper bag out of her van. She holds the bag to her chest, about to walk, but then she stops, closing her eyes. She sniffs. "Now that's a new one." She frowns. "Distress." She sniffs again.

"What are you doing?"

"Hmm. Perhaps it's the larvae. I'll talk to your mother."

"Larvae?"

"Or the curlicues. I'm not sure. I'm feeling gray. And red. And perhaps some brown. Definitely brown. The auras, you know. Yours is wonderful, by the way. Yellow and green and blue. Just superb. Yours is lovely too, young man."

She smiles briskly before she walks into the castle through the side door.

"How did she know what my dad said?" Basford asks.

"She's a good guesser," I tell him truthfully. "She once told me she could predict the future by looking at the shape of a zucchini."

Basford's eyes widen. "Can she?"

"What do you think?" I ask. We've reached the edge of the lake. "She's really nice, so it's okay she's kind of a kook."

I swing my foot in the lake, gauging the temperature. "Ready?"

Basford grins, and I jump in the water. He cannonballs in after me. Yesterday I showed him all around our property—that is, when he wasn't playing soccer with Freddy or listening to my father explain his rhubarb research. He's so patient he even listened to Patricia talk about her latest shopping trip. Still, I have to admit—it's pretty fun having someone my age on the farm.

"Race ya!" Basford says as he takes off for the other shore.

"Cheater!" I yell, swimming after him. I go as fast as I can, but it's a little weird because with every stroke, I feel a strange tingle in my finger. When I finally reach him, I hold my hands up out of the water, examining them. It must be what my health teacher calls growing pains, or "the passage into adolescence." I'll be twelve in December. It doesn't really matter; they don't hurt that much.

"Watch this!" Basford calls as he plunges his head below the water line. As the minutes pass, I figure out that he's testing out our non-drownable enchanted lake.

Just when I'm starting to get bored, Basford swims up, breaking the water's surface. "I can't believe it! Four minutes and I'm not even dizzy!"

"One of Freddy's friends made it for an hour once," I tell him. "Mom said he was an overachiever."

Basford smiles widely, looking like a little kid. He dives back under and I see him examining all the sparkling rocks and colored fish. There's something about our water that magnifies everything, almost like you're scuba diving with high definition goggles. The seaweed on the bottom, the random fish, and the stones in the sand—everything is as clear as if you saw it through a sparkling clean window.

He pops up and splashes me. "Marco!" he yells.

"Polo!" I yell back.

We swim and play games for the next two hours. Even Patricia joins us for a while, though she just swims boring laps, touching one side of the lake and then the other, over and over again.

When Beatrice comes outside to tell us that lunch is ready, Basford and I paddle over to the edge next to Patricia. But before we climb out, my sister scrunches up her face. "Did you pee?"

"What?"

"Did you pee in the water?"

"No!" I'm insulted.

"Then why is the water so warm near you?"

"I'm hot-blooded," I say. The water right around me suddenly *does* feel really warm. But it's positively *not* because I peed.

"Yeah, right," says Patricia. I check to make sure Basford isn't listening; it's so typical for Patricia to want to embarrass me.

"Could you just quit it?" I hiss.

She holds her nose. "Sure. I won't tell anyone THAT I'M GOING TO SCRUB MYSELF BEFORE DINNER."

On cue, Basford turns. Patricia smiles sweetly.

"Never can be too clean," she burbles as she pulls herself out of the lake.

I'm positive that Basford is going to ignore me after that, so I'm surprised when we get out of the water and he tells me that Ophelia was right.

"I didn't think anything would change, but I was wrong."

"What did you want to change?"

A sad expression shoots over his face for just a second. Then his face brightens up. "It's a long story. Besides," he says as he looks around the farm, "this is the kind of place where nothing bad happens. Right?"

I decide not to bring up Patricia. Or the mist. "Right," I tell him, just as Mom opens up the castle door. "It's the best place in the world."

After lunch—and after Ophelia told us that there really are such things as giant beanstalks—I leave Basford with Freddy so I can go talk to Harry. It's the first time I've seen him since I've been in Enid's turret.

He's happy to see me, waving his leaves all around when I stroll up the row and sit down next to him. As I tell him about Ophelia and everything that happened in the turret with the Monster cricket, and the ivy, and Aunt Edith, Harry flicks his leaves a little, but not enough for me to understand what he's saying.

"No, really. What do you think?"

I expect a real answer from him, so I'm annoyed when I see he's doing the bouquet maneuver, pulling his stalks together like he is a bunch of celery.

I roll my eyes. "I don't know what that means."

But he does it again.

"You don't have anything to say about a cricket so big it could almost drive a car?"

Harry hesitates, but then repeats the gesture. I stand up. "If you're not going to talk to me, I'm leaving," I tell him.

I wait for him to say good-bye or at least say *something*, and when he doesn't I spin around and start to stomp off. But as soon as I take a step, I feel guilty. I'm not very good at being mad. I'd much rather be friends with Harry than fight with him. Plus, I want to talk to him about Basford. I want to tell Harry that I may actually have a human friend.

So I turn back around, ready to apologize. But what I see stops me in my tracks.

Every single plant is spread out flat, stretching out its leaves to touch the edges of their neighboring plants.

"Hey! What's going on?"

As soon as my words hit the air, the leaves spring

back to position and the field goes back to normal.

I step closer to Harry, suddenly panicked. "What were you doing?"

Harry reaches out and touches the tip of his leaf to my cheek. *Pay attention.*

"I *am* paying attention. You're not telling me anything."

Harry waits a second, and then tosses one of his leaves around, twirling the end of it. This means *tomorrow.*

"Tomorrow?" I glance around at the other plants. I know they're listening. "What's tomorrow?"

Harry pulls his leaves up in that bouquet position. I glare at him.

"You're driving me insane, you know that?"

He doesn't even crack a smile (by bending his leaf) when he answers. *Yes. Sorry.*

For a second, I wonder if Harry's jealous I may have a human friend. He's never acted this strangely before.

"Is everything okay?" I ask him.

It takes him a long time to answer. And when he does, I'm surprised.

No.

MONDAY, AUGUST 25
Spark

Last night, I heard the haunted noises from the Dark House again. I'm not crazy. The sounds are as real as Patricia's annoying voice, but much scarier. Usually when I hear them, I run to Freddy's room. I know he can hear the noises too—noises sounding like the mangled screams of a ghost going through a shredder. But he always says they're nothing but the normal farm sounds that bugs and animals make. (There's nothing normal about those sounds. And we don't even have animals on our farm.)

For once I didn't run to Freddy's room last night, though. Instead, I just jumped to my window seat and stared at the farm, scared out of my mind. All I could think about was how Harry said something was wrong. I thought I'd stay awake all night, but I fell asleep, right there on the window seat, sometime after 3:00 in the morning.

Now I have a crick in my neck. From my window, I can see the orange blockade of tour buses near the White House, with people spilling out of the White House porch. I check my watch. It's almost time for the rain; I can't believe I've slept this long. I get dressed as fast as I can and pull my hair back into a loose ponytail. I speed outside, sprinting by the truly weeping cherry blossom tree. I glance quickly over to see if the mist is still there. I almost stop running: The mist is not only there, it's bigger—what was the size of a tiny cloud now looks like a wet, green down comforter, filling up most of the space under the tree limbs. As I run, I have a sudden vision of the mist leaking through the cherry blossoms, oozing out like some kind of gas attack over our farm.

The thought makes me feel sick, like I've eaten something rotten. But I can't think about it now. I promised Mom I'd meet her in the Learning Garden to help with the tourists and I'm superlate. I'm running as fast as I can when the blue dragonfly suddenly appears, flying by my ear and spinning circles around my head.

I slow down just a little, panting. "Can't talk now. I'm in a rush."

But the dragonfly goes nuts, zipping this way and that in the air in front of me. I stop running, placing the palms of my hands on my thighs, breathing fast.

"What is it?"

The clouds are thicker now, changing from gray to black. I can feel the moisture in the air. The dragonfly soars up in a straight line, against the black sky. Then he doubles back, flying perpendicular to the first line.

"T?" I ask.

He pauses to agree with me, bobbing up and down. Then he continues to spell.

"R . . ." I say, still breathing hard, as the first raindrop splatters against my arm. "Y."

The dragonfly pivots around and dives in front of my face, nodding maniacally.

"Try?"

The dragonfly nods again.

I glance over to the Learning Garden. The Umbrella ride is way up in the air, canopy fully extended. Even from here, I know it's packed. I can make out the tourists, crammed together along the platform railing, and I can see legs dangling from the Umbrella swings. I can even hear the squeals of glee as the rain falls harder, sprinkling my head, my shirt, the ground.

"Try what?" I ask the dragonfly.

He flies away from me then, toward the Learning Garden.

"Hey!" I call out. The dragonfly doesn't turn around. "Hey! Blue Dragonfly!"

The dragonfly slides to a stop.

"You want me to follow you?"

He nods and starts to zoom away again. I jog after him.

"Listen," I say, panting. "Do you have a name? I can't keep calling you 'Blue Dragonfly'!"

The dragonfly zips in front of me really fast, and then dives back. He starts to spell.

S . . . P . . . A . . . R . . . K.

As I read it, I start to smile. "Spark? That's perfect."

A cheer goes up from the crowd on the Umbrella as a full rain shower pours from the gray, clouded sky. I should be used to it by now, but I'm still always surprised that people deliberately come here to stay out in the rain. Any other place, they'd be running indoors as fast as they can.

The row of sugar maples encircling the Learning

Garden comes into view. I pick up the pace so that I can huddle under the always-flowering magnolia tree while it downpours. The dragonfly—er, Spark—flies in front of me, darting through the first line of trees. I'm right behind him, getting soaked.

Just as I duck under a branch, a terrible noise spreads through the air. It's a creak and a scream and a crack, all at once.

Spark skids to a stop. I hear a snapping sound, this noise even louder than the first.

We both turn to the Umbrella at the same time.

People are screaming. *Screaming.*

I don't understand at first. But I look closer and see the people on the individual swings spinning around, out of control—I hear the *clickclickclick* of the rising Umbrella shaft, relentless, unstopping.

I'm close enough that I can see Chico waving his hands like a banshee behind the controls.

I look up to the Umbrella again, just as the platform seems to slip just a little and the screams become even more awful.

The Umbrella.

It's stuck.

SAME DAY, MONDAY, AUGUST 25

The Umbrella

I jump out from under the tree and rush to Chico. Above me the Umbrella sways. The tourists' screams sound like the roar of a tidal wave.

"What's happening?" I ask Chico.

"No sé, no sé!"

He throws me his phone and tells me to call 911. I try to keep my voice calm.

"There's an emergency. Rupert's Farm. Off the pike. Take the entrance from the front."

"What type of emergency, ma'am?"

"The Umbrella's broken," I tell her.

She gasps. "The Umbrella?" Then she goes back to her original, professional voice. "The Umbrella, really?"

"Yes," I say. "The Umbrella."

"Oh my," she says. She recovers more quickly this

time. "We'll be right there." She pauses. "In a second. Oh my."

I snap the phone shut and look back at Chico. He's putting all of his weight against a lever, but it's not moving.

The Umbrella pitches to the left. The swings are dangling above me now—people's legs and feet flapping like bats against the rainy sky. "Do you think they'll jump?" I stare up at the platform.

"They can't jump!" Dad runs up behind us, his face red with worry. "They're twenty stories high."

"But what if—"

Dad yanks out a wrench from the pocket of his pants and places it around the big rusted bolts attaching the iron plate to the Umbrella's motor. He turns the nut in one big swinging movement, then swings it again and again until the first bolt falls off.

"*Dios mío!*" Chico exclaims a minute later. Inside the motor case, wrapped around the cogs and gears of the engine, are the white, stringy thick roots of the nearby chocolate rhubarb plants. The gears stop and start as they try to spit out the roots.

But the roots are winning.

I think back to one of the last conversations I had with Grandmom.

You're gonna figure this out yourself in your own good time, Polly, but I can give you a head start. Just a little nudge. If it's from the earth, it's the winner, and it's a gracious one, so don't try to fight it. The ocean, the water, the earth—they're on our side. Remember that.

Chico grabs an axe and hacks at the roots.

"NO!" I yell.

But Chico hacks and hacks and hacks, his clothes plastered to his body from the rain. He seems to have cut away all the roots that were attached to the motor pieces, but when he turns around, he's clearly frustrated.

"Can't get it," he mutters, wiping his forehead with the back of his hand. He looks to Dad, who bends down and examines the motor. Then Chico extends his arm into the motor casing to try to pull out the root strings still caught inside, but his hand is too big for the inner plate. It won't fit.

Dad tries next, but his hand is even bigger than Chico's.

I think I hear a small child scream from high above me. Everything inside of me—my breath, my heart—has stopped; someone has to fix this. Now.

Dad slams his hand against the metal guard over the motor. My eyes widen. Then Beatrice runs out, grabbing Dad's wrist.

"Basford! He's up there!" She looks wild, as if she's transformed into some kind of crazy animal. "Get him down! GET HIM DOWN!"

I hear Beatrice say Basford's name, but it's as if it runs through my ear canal slowly, tangled, and it takes me seconds to understand that Basford, my new friend, is up on the ride. When I look up, the platform sways and another thundering creak slashes through the air.

"It's the roots," Dad tells Beatrice. "I can't pull it out."

Beatrice leans down, helpless. She looks over at Chico, her face broken. "Help," she begs.

And then it just comes out of my mouth, like a breath. "I think I can try." An image of Spark spelling the word against the sky flashes through my mind.

Dad snaps, "No. Absolutely not."

Chico looks quickly over at Dad, but Beatrice just stares at me. She doesn't say not to go. I push through them, wiping the raindrops from my face, and look inside the casing. There is one big string of root that is clogging the gear.

"Polly, don't you dare—" Dad shouts, but it is too late. I stick my right hand inside the gearshift.

"Dios mío," Chico mutters. "Policita—"

I stare straight ahead, not blinking, ignoring Chico

and Dad. Instead, I move my hand closer to the motor and try to think clearly. I need to pull out that one string, that one piece of root, and the motor should churn easily again. Right now the motor seems to be coughing, working one second and then stopping the next.

"POLLY!" Mom shouts from behind me. I don't turn around. "Get your hand out of there right this second!"

I can feel the heat of the motor close to my hand. My heart is beating so fast, it feels like a jackhammer.

"Stop that motor right now!" Mom screams.

"He can't," Dad says anxiously. "If we shut it off, we may not be able to get it down."

A shoe falls off someone's foot, landing near us.

Chico kneels down next to me. More screams, more cries from up above.

"*Tú puedes,*" he whispers. "Polly, *tú puedes.*"
You can do this.

Slowly I open my eyes and look at the single root, white and thick like a braid of hair. My right hand wavers—I'm trembling—and I see how close the cutting rotor of the motor is to the root. I don't feel the rain at all.

My shoulders tense, and my hand trembles harder. I

want to make a fist, but I can't unless I want my hand chopped in half.

This is a mistake. This is a very big mistake.

"Polly." Aunt Edith is here now too. "Remember Emerson. *Trust thyself.*" She speaks slowly, calmly. "You don't have to do this. But it would be a good thing if you can." I can feel her put her hand gently on my shoulder. "Try."

Try.

I turn back to the motor, ignoring the screams from the ride and the sound of sirens drawing closer. I forget about everyone and concentrate.

Try.

I reach in and touch the end of the root, which is still about six inches away from the motor. I tug, gently, and then, gripping the root more strongly, I pull harder. I do my best to ignore the running motor, but it's like looking at the bottom of a vacuum cleaner that keeps rolling and rolling, just waiting for its chance to suck up a finger. I grasp the root then, as hard as I can, and *yank!* It comes out. I snatch out my hand and fall backward, about one inch away from amputation.

I'm still holding the wayward root when I hear the people on the platform cheer. About one hundred sets of eyes are looking down at me in a circle, including those of some firemen. Beatrice and Patricia and Freddy have all run up to the controls.

Mom jumps in and pulls me up by my armpits. "My baby, my baby," she whispers, and I can feel her body shake underneath her thin shirt. She hugs me so hard that my head is pressed deeply into her shoulder. When she releases me, I realize the rain has stopped. The Umbrella is still high up in the air.

"It needs to go through its cycle again before it can close," says Dad. He wipes his eyes with the back of his hand. "Oh, pumpkin." He leans down and hugs me too.

"I'm okay, Dad," I lie, still trembling.

Beatrice stands about three feet away from me. Tears stream down her dark cheeks. "Come here, little girl. Come here." I move to her, allowing her strong arms to circle me. She used to call me "little girl" all the time. "Thank you, Polly. Thank you." I can feel Beatrice shake as she hugs me; her words are whispered and her breath feels warm.

"What happened?"

Beatrice releases me a little, looking me straight in the eye. "Foolishness," she says as she deliberately steps on the leaf of a plant. "Foolishness!" she repeats angrily.

"Irresponsible. People could die!" She kicks a plant. "My Basford could have died!"

It's like the whole world blurs as I realize what she's saying.

The plants.

They were clogging up the ride. On purpose.

"Seriously," Patricia interrupts my thoughts. "I would have never thought you had that in you."

Freddy puts his arm around my shoulder. "My little sister. Braveheart."

Aunt Edith and Mom and Dad and Freddy and Beatrice and Chico and Patricia and everyone are looking at me like I've sprouted wings and am going to fly. I cross my arms and look toward the Umbrella, which has finally come back to the ground. People are jumping off, wet mothers hugging their wet children, young boys shaking their hands in a wild kind of drying dance, teenagers wrapping their arms around their wet shirts, firemen walking around, smelling the flowers. It's like the whole farm has breathed a heavy sigh of relief.

Actually, the farm isn't relieved. The people are relieved. The farm—*my* farm—*wanted this* to happen.

"BASFORD!" Beatrice yells. He's walking over to us, taking small steps, his hands shoved deep in his pockets. Beatrice darts over to him as fast as her little legs can carry her, almost knocking him over. "I'm so glad, I'm so glad," she says as she smothers him with another one of her hugs.

"He must have been so frightened," Mom murmurs. She puts her arm around my shoulder. "I can't believe you did that."

"I can't either," I murmur.

"That was crazy!" says Freddy, his eyes bright and proud. "You just stuck your hand in a motor! Are you sure you're my scaredy cat sister?"

Beatrice and Basford join us. Beatrice clings to Basford's arm, as if letting him go would make him lift up like a helium balloon.

"Dude, she saved your life," Freddy tells him.

"She did," Patricia echoes, as if she can barely believe it.

Basford flips his hair off of his face and then takes a step away from Beatrice. He's not smiling. He doesn't even look happy.

Then he thrusts out his hand. I take it, and he shakes it up and down, awkwardly. "Thank you," he says quietly. "Thank you very much."

"You're welcome," I say, equally quietly. We look at

each other without smiling, like we're the only two who understand how terrible it was.

"What was it like up there?" Freddy asks. "I would have been freaking out."

Basford glances back at the Umbrella. He blinks, as if he's looking at the sun even though he isn't, and then swallows. "Everyone was afraid."

Beatrice jumps over and gives me another hug. "That was so darn brave of you, honey. So darn brave."

"She's right." Aunt Edith stares at me, her eyes shining. "You were fearless, Polly. Absolutely fearless."

I have to look away. I don't feel like I was fearless. I was afraid too. Scratch that. I am afraid.

The plants on the ground are bright and healthy-looking, as if they're the most innocent things in the world. A picture of the green dragonfly mist flashes through my mind, making my stomach turn upside down. I realize suddenly that Spark must have known too. It's like our farm is in revolt, starting some kind of war with all of us.

"Let's go inside," Mom says.

I catch eyes with Beatrice.

"In a second," I tell Mom. "I have to do something first."

SAME DAY, MONDAY, AUGUST 25

An Explanation

Harry won't tell me anything.

"Come on, Harry. I saw the roots," I say accusingly. "That was bad, really bad. Your friends could have killed a lot of people."

Harry stares back at me defiantly, then he bunches up all of his stalks in that unreadable, familiar bouquet.

"Stop it!" I yell. But it doesn't help. I look around the field and *all* of the chocolate rhubarb plants are bunching themselves up.

"You could have *killed* people, Harry. You could have killed Basford! Do you understand?"

I hear a footstep behind me. "I'd like to hear the answer to that too."

Aunt Edith. Great.

"Hi." I turn around.

"Quite a day for you, Polly." Aunt Edith beams.

I don't say anything. I don't feel happy. I feel like a person betrayed by her best friend.

"So." She looks around the field. "You were talking to a plant." This is a statement, not a question. "Does it talk back?"

I shrug.

Aunt Edith nods. "I had a plant once. I called him Teddy."

This doesn't sound like Aunt Edith at all.

"Teddy? Teddy who?"

"Roosevelt, of course," she snaps. "American history, Polly. You must learn it."

This sounds exactly like Aunt Edith. The one who *doesn't* talk to plants.

"He's still alive actually. He's the Giant Rhubarb plant by the bench outside the Dark House."

When Grandmom was alive, she liked to sit outside the Dark House and look at the lake. She said it was the original site for the farm and made her feel connected to her past ancestors. *If you ever have a question for me, Polly, and I'm not around, just come and sit down right on this bench.* Which I'd love to do, but I can't. As much as she tried, and as much as I loved her, Grandmom could never convince me that the Dark House wasn't the scariest place in the world.

"Do you still talk to him?" I ask.

"No. When you get older, the plants stop talking." She scans the field. "Which one is yours?"

I point to Harry. "This one. I call him Harry."

"Hello, Harry," she says.

Harry doesn't move. I'm not surprised. But I know he's listening to every word.

"I heard you accuse him of murder," Aunt Edith says. "You're giving these plants a lot of credit."

"It was their roots clogging the ride up!"

Aunt Edith looks at me sympathetically—like I'm a person who still believes that the dinosaurs are roaming around the earth. "I'm worried about you, Polly. You're doing the exact opposite of what I asked you to do in Enid's library."

"What was that?" I wish she would go. I just want to talk to Harry.

"You're not treating this farm for what it is. A distraction. You showed your mettle today. You put your hand in a motor, Polly, and you saved hundreds of lives!"

She doesn't understand. I thought she did, but she doesn't. "The plants know more than you think," I insist.

"Not true. Simply not true," Aunt Edith insists. "They're plants. They're not creatures of free will, like humans."

I don't say anything because at that instant, I feel really fragile, like I could break into a bunch of little pieces.

"Oh, Polly," she says. "You look terrified." Aunt Edith walks over to me and puts her hand under my chin. She brings my eyes up to hers.

"I just want you to know how smart you are, how quick-thinking. I want you to see yourself doing big things, great things. World-changing things."

I can't help it. I start crying. Aunt Edith keeps trying to make me someone I'm not. "I won't do world-changing things. I can't believe you don't know this already. See? I'm crying. You hate criers. I'm the biggest crybaby chicken you've ever seen."

"You just put your hand in a moving motor to save the lives of hundreds of people. Not exactly chicken material." She pauses, an amused smile playing over her face. "And I don't hate criers."

"Yes, you do."

"Okay." She grins. "I do. A little. But only because I used to be one myself."

She could have dropped a million-pound weight

on my foot and I wouldn't have been more surprised. "You?"

"Yes, even me. Until the day I realized that an entire ocean of my tears had been wasted and I had nothing to show for it. You'll figure that out too, I'm sure of it. But in the meantime, Polly, *please* stop worrying. Everything will be fine."

"Did you really cry?"

"I did." She shrugs. "Not so much in public, naturally. Bad for my image." Aunt Edith leans over as she gently wipes my eyes with the back of her hand. "Listen very clearly, dear. Are you listening?"

I nod, blinking back my tears. I'm sure Harry is listening too.

"Then trust me, Polly. I have everything under control."

WEDNESDAY, AUGUST 27
Headlines

This morning, when I come down for breakfast, Beatrice showed me the front page of the local newspaper.

RUPERT'S RHUBARB FARM IN DISARRAY: UMBRELLA RIDE BREAKS AND RIDERS IN MORTAL DANGER!

By Debbie Jong

EXCLUSIVE

Rupert's Rhubarb Farm—the only rhubarb farm in the world that can guarantee rainfall once a week—suffered the setback of its life on Monday. Its notorious Umbrella ride got stuck while thousands of feet in the air, tossing hundreds of passengers around in what-seemed-like-certain-death.

Naturally, this could have been a catastrophe of catastrophic proportions. Reports allege that an offending weed was finally wrenched from the motor of the ride by an underage girl, although this has not been confirmed. An eyewitness confirmed that the girl looked shaken and a bit vapid, utterly incapable of such a feat. It is this writer's opinion that relevant authorities need to come and review the business practices of this company. Just because this particular farm happens to be managed by Edith Peabody Stillwater should not mean special treatment . . .

I read it over and over again until Dad walks into the kitchen, slamming the door behind him.

"Hey, pumpkin!" Dad says, giving me a kiss on the head. Only Dad can be so flaky that he can he act cheery after such a disaster.

I hand him the paper. "Did you read this?"

Dad laughs. "I did. Ah well. Don't fight city hall."

"What does that mean?"

"You can't take it too seriously, Polly. People will

say what they want to say." He reaches into his pocket. "Plus, Debbie Jong's a moron."

"That's Jennifer Jong's mom, right?"

"Yes. She was in Edith's class in school. Edith used to tell people that Debbie was proud of being dumb. I think the words she used were 'aggressively stupid.'" Dad pulls out a bunch of receipts and coins from his pocket, not what he's looking for. He reaches into his other pocket. "I'm not surprised she targets us in a news article. She always wanted to be Edith's friend. Horrible position to be in, especially with my sister." Dad smiles as he pulls out what looks like a tiny glob of yellow Jell-O. It's a vitamin. "Here," he says, handing it to me. "Vitamin E. Take it so—"

"I live to be a hundred and four. I know." Dad always pushes Vitamin E. He says it's the closest thing to a wonder drug that exists.

I look back to the paper. "But what if someone believes it?"

He glances at the article and shrugs. "The Umbrella did break. We do need to figure out what happened."

"We know what happened."

"We do?" Dad looks up at me, genuinely curious.

"Yes." Why are the adults pretending they don't know? "The plants did it."

"The plants?"

"Dad! Didn't you see them tangled up inside?"

He looks at me blankly for a second. Then, like it's a gust of wind he can't stop, his mouth opens and he roars with laughter. "I'm sorry. But even you have to know that the plants didn't—couldn't—do any such thing. They're *plants*. I know them, I study them, you might even say I was intimately involved with them."

There's nothing worse than when parents think they're being funny. "Yuck."

Dad takes an apple out of the refrigerator. "No. Just science."

"I think it's magic."

"I know you do. And that's fine. But if you ask me, all of the questions we have now will be answered someday scientifically. Not today, not tomorrow, maybe not in a hundred years. But in a thousand years? I think so. When I was younger I thought I'd try to figure out the rainfall. Eventually, I gave up. Not because it wasn't interesting. Because it became more interesting to study the properties of the plant itself, and that's how I developed my area of expertise. Hopefully I'll find some—*some*, not all—answers as I continue to work. Your area of expertise could be something different. You could figure out why the diamonds sprout—"

"Or why the rhubarb tastes like chocolate—"

"—or why no one drowns in our lake. There are a million things you could study, if you choose. Or you could do something else altogether. You can write plays or sing songs or play sports." He bites into his apple. "I just hope that you find something to do that you love. Otherwise, it's just treading water till you're gone.

"Anyway," Dad says as he tilts my head back, smiling brightly. "Chin up, sweet pumpkin," he says. "Good things are coming." He points to the stack of papers he holds under one of his arms.

"Like what?" I try not to sound too excited.

"You'll see. For once my dear sister might be impressed with her little brother," he says, putting his cap back on his head. "Wait till the Sunday dinner. It'll be a doozy." Dad leans down and kisses me on the cheek. "Take your vitamin!" he repeats, and strolls out of the castle.

My eyes brighten. I feel like Dad just threw me a life preserver.

Good things are coming? Really?

I jump up and push open the door. At first, I just peek to make sure that reporters like Mrs. Jong aren't on the other side, waiting to pounce. But no one's there. The farm seems normal: I see pickup trucks and workers carrying shovels and plants waving their leaves at the sun.

I hesitate for only one more second. Then I spring out of the castle and race to the cherry blossom tree. If Dad's right and good things are coming, then the mist will be gone.

It only makes sense. In a minute, I'm on my way.

SAME DAY, WEDNESDAY, AUGUST 27

Heartbreak

"Dad said good things were going to happen," I murmur to Beatrice, who stands next to me under the weeping cherry blossom tree.

The mist is above us, crowding the limbs of the weeping tree. It's gotten a lot bigger. I can see the dragonflies zipping through it. I automatically lift my arm up, scraping my fingers at the bottom of it. It doesn't feel at all like I think it will. I assume it would feel like fog—that touching it would be like touching steam. But it doesn't. It feels like a cotton ball that's been drenched in water and squeezed so tightly that it's heavy and thick.

And wet. When I look at my fingertips, they're dotted with drops of green water.

"Weird," I mutter.

Beatrice flinches, as if I've just woken her up.

"The dragonflies know what they're doing," she announces. "Stop trying to figure them out." She puts her hand on my shoulder and twists me around. "Aren't you supposed to be at the Learning Garden?"

I cross my hands around my chest. "I'm scared," I admit, glancing back up at the mist.

Beatrice's eyes scan the mist too. "Yeah," she murmurs. "I get that." She turns so we're side by side, her arm still around my shoulder. "People always get scared when they don't understand something. But really, what's the use? Does it change anything?" She pulls me alongside her as we walk out from under the tree. "Anyway, I trust the dragonflies. You should too."

"But—"

"Polly," Beatrice says calmly. "There's nothing you can do here."

She taps me on my shoulder, and I start to walk away from her. She's probably right. But I still can't help turning around and peeking at the mist as I leave. The good news is that by the time I reach the Learning Garden, I can't see it at all.

"You two are going to put out the new pesticide in the Giant Rhubarb field," Mom tells Basford and me after I arrive. "Ophelia brought over a new one. Says it won't harm the plants or the bugs." Mom walks over to a yellow star lily and plucks it. Another one instantly grows back. She sticks the flower in my hair and smiles. I take it off as soon as she turns around.

Ophelia's new pesticide turns out to be beer. Plain old ordinary beer.

"Ophelia says all we have to do is pour it into little saucers and leave them in between every third plant. In a week, she promises they'll be teeming in bugs! Happy, happy bugs!" Mom smiles as I hold out my saucer for her to fill. "Start in the Giant Rhubarb field," she directs us.

"Mom—" I protest. She knows that I don't especially like working in the Giant Rhubarb field, since it's so close to the Dark House. Mom shakes her head. "You do the north side. Basford can do the south side. You'll be fine."

We finish pretty quickly. When we're done, I stop by the lake to fill up my water bottle. I want to go back and talk to Harry. I don't invite Basford to come along with me, but I don't tell him *not* to come along with me either, so we end up walking across the entire farm together. At first, we don't talk that much. But then we walk over the iron bridge to the west side of the farm, and I see him gazing at the water. I think that maybe he's missing his home.

"Are you sad you left Bermuda?" I ask.

He shrugs. "Sometimes."

"I've never lived anywhere but here," I tell him.

Basford keeps looking at the lake. "Who would want to leave here?"

The answer pops into my mind so fast it surprises me. "Aunt Edith."

He turns, interested.

"She lived in New York until she had to move back here after Grandmom died. She was so busy she couldn't even come to the funeral. She was in Russia and had to take cars and planes and even a donkey to get back. She was interviewing someone really important. Like a king. Or a sheikh." I pause, thinking. "It may have even been a terrorist."

This makes me think of those six days before Aunt Edith showed up, when I was going totally out of my mind because of Grandmom's death.

"Grandmom was totally different from any old person you've ever known. She had cancer but wouldn't get treatment because she said that if she couldn't walk around the fields, there wasn't any use to her being alive in the first place. Then she'd say that if the plants couldn't help her, she didn't want to be helped."

Basford squints in the sunlight. We're off the bridge now, heading over to the chocolate rhubarb.

"Remember I told you that Dad is a rhubarb scientist? That's because of Grandmom. She thought rhubarb could cure anything if someone could only figure out how to get its magic from the plant into the person. That's why my father is always working in his lab, trying for some big cure. He was so sad when Grandmom died. I mean, we all were, but he was really sick about it. I think he thought that if he were a better scientist, he could have found a cure and made her better."

Basford doesn't say anything, and my head is now so filled with images of Grandmom and me that I'm quiet too. We've almost reached Harry's field when Basford speaks.

"My mom," he says softly. "She had cancer too."

I'm so surprised, I forget to breathe, and I end up having a coughing fit. Basford hands me a water bottle. I drink some and try to sort out my thoughts.

"Did she die?"

Basford nods. Suddenly I feel like all my worries

have dissolved and in its place is an image of Basford, alone in Bermuda without his mother.

"Is that why you're here?"

"Yeah. My dad was really worried. I stopped talking."

"For how long?"

"About a year. Maybe more."

I look down and watch a two-headed spider scramble in front of me toward a plant. "Why didn't you talk?"

"Nothing to say." His cheeks seem to tremble, and I think he's going to cry. But then he looks at me and his eyes are just sad and empty of everything, including tears.

We just stand there for a long time.

"Hey," I say. "Do you want to meet my best friend?"

SAME DAY, WEDNESDAY, AUGUST 27
Welts

In five minutes, we're standing in front of Harry.

"I talk to plants," I confess. "This plant especially." I lift my head and look Basford squarely in the eye. "Go ahead. Laugh."

His eyes flicker over me for a second before he leans down and studies Harry, like a scientist. "What's his name?"

"Harry," I say. "Harry, meet Basford. Basford, meet Harry."

Harry's bottom stalk bends in half.

"He's smiling," I tell Basford. For the first time during our long walk, Basford cracks a smile too.

"Nice to meet you, Harry." He looks back at me. "Do I shake something?"

"No. He's a plant. Not a person. Plus there's that poison, remember?"

Just as he says that, Harry stretches out one of his leaves and brushes Basford's knee. Basford recoils.

"Poison?" he mouths.

"No," I laugh. "He's telling you to relax. There's no poison on that side of the leaf."

"How long have you been friends?"

"Since I was six," I tell Basford, although in my head, I say, *Until Monday, when he didn't warn me that his friends were going to try to kill people.* I look sternly over at Harry. "I'm kind of mad at him right now."

"Why?"

"You know when you know someone's going to do something bad but you don't do anything to stop them?" I kneel down in front of Harry. "That's what he did."

Harry starts flapping his leaves up and down, upset.

"Maybe he had a good reason not to stop them." Basford looks at Harry. "Is that it?"

Harry shakes his middle leaf.

"That means yes," I explain. "And I already know that's what he thinks. He's just not telling me what the reason is. Right, Harry?"

At first Harry doesn't move. Then, as if he deliberately wants to make me mad, he pulls his leaves up and makes the bouquet sign.

"ARGH!"

"What does that mean?" Basford asks.

"I have no idea. And he knows I have no idea. But he keeps doing it."

"Maybe we can figure it out," Basford suggests. "Are you mad?" he asks Harry.

He shakes his middle leaf again. *Yes.*

"At Polly?"

He lifts up his leaf and turns it back and forth.

"He's saying no," I tell Basford. "Listen," I say, frustrated. "Harry, didn't you hear what Aunt Edith said? You don't have to worry. She has everything under control."

Harry doesn't answer.

"Whatever it is that's bothering you—whatever it is that made your friends try to hurt the people on the Umbrella—"

He lifts his leaf, vehemently turning it back and forth. Basford shoots me a confused look.

"Well, if you weren't trying, you messed up, because you really did almost hurt people. How would that make you feel?"

I know what's going to happen before it does. The bouquet.

"Just stop it!" I yell. "You have nothing to worry about. Aunt Edith told us! You were right here, listening!" I realize I'm trying to convince myself as well as Harry.

Harry's stalks stiffen and rise up, so that my face is directly in front of his largest, healthiest leaves. *I'm mad at you.*

"You're acting just like a crybaby. You can't be mad at me. You're the one who tried to kill people for no good reason!"

Harry picks up his biggest leaf and slaps me.

I hear Basford gasp. Tears crowd my eyes and my cheek stings.

"I don't care," I say stubbornly, tears falling. "You

can hit me as much as you want. You're wrong."

He doesn't slap me again. He just starts rumbling his leaves, drumming them on the ground. The other plants join him. Basford's face has gone white, but I can't think about that now. I scramble to my feet and rush out of the field as fast as I can. Welts form on my face as I run, I can feel them. He *hit* me.

I hear Basford running behind me, but I don't stop running. I can't believe it. I just can't believe it.

Harry hit me.

SUNDAY, AUGUST 31
Ask What You Want To Ask

I've refused to see Harry for the last three days, and I don't even feel guilty about it. Nope, not a bit. Basford thinks I just need to go out to the field and get Harry to explain. But I won't. It's Harry's fault. For hitting me, and then for ruining my life at St. Xavier's—because that's what's going to happen as soon as everyone sees the huge welts on my face, courtesy of my once-best-friend.

Besides, even if I wanted to see Harry—which I don't—Mom's kept me working every second. I wasn't even allowed to have a Friday tutorial with Aunt Edith. Tomorrow, the Monday before Labor Day, is the farm's biggest tourist day, so we've all been sweeping and folding and packaging during every spare minute. Well, all of us except for Dad. He's been holed up in his lab, working furiously on something top-secret. He's going to finally tell us about it at dinner tonight.

"Polly, take this." Mom hands me an hors d'oeuvres tray, olives and cheese and roasted almonds, just as Aunt Edith walks through the door.

"How lovely!" she exclaims, taking an olive. "Special occasion?"

Mom sets down a white ceramic basket filled with bread. "Always, Edith."

Girard steps inside. "Good evening," he says, then looks over at me. "Good Lord, Polly. What did you do to your face?"

I take a deep breath. "I tripped," I say as I hear Patricia snicker. Aunt Edith raises her eyebrows but Girard nods, like it's an acceptable answer. He doesn't know anything about rhubarb. Or farming, for that matter. One time he literally yelled at the dirt because a speck got on his fancy English shoes. (Then he stepped in a puddle of mud, which hadn't been there one second earlier. It made me giggle because I knew the farm was getting back at him.)

We eat the olives and almonds and drink apple-rhubarb juice. Freddy's not with us because he's been feeling sick and running a fever again, and Dad's not here yet either. Finally, when we're all just listening to Girard drone on about something none of us cares about, Dad rushes up the stairs, beaming.

He's holding a crate-sized box.

"Just had it copied," he pants. "One for all of you. I'll explain after dinner." Dad says, breathing hard. Mom smiles nervously, but Dad's so clearly happy that it's not long before everyone's joking and laughing.

Everyone, that is, except for Aunt Edith. All through our meal, she's distracted, constantly glancing at Dad's box. Finally, when Patricia, Basford, and I finish clearing the table, Dad picks up his mysterious box and takes off the lid.

"Pass them around, please," he asks, handing out what looks to be a bound notebook. On the cover is the name DUNBAR INDUSTRIES.

"What's Dunbar Industries?" Patricia asks.

"It's the name of the pharmaceutical company I've been working with for the past three years," Dad says. He takes a deep breath and looks up at us, grinning. "I found out this week that they've just granted me a bigger, better underwriting for funding. That's how promising the initial results of the rhubarb medicine study were!"

Honestly. He may explode. That's how excited he looks.

"Which study is this?" Girard asks.

"I'm developing a strain of medicines for the nervous

systems, medicines that specifically attack certain genes."

"Marvelous," Aunt Edith says slowly. "Just marvelous. But how is this different from what we've been discussing?"

Dad beams. "It's a continuation of our discussion." He pauses, as if he's saying the most obvious thing in the world. "Edith! This will solve your problem!"

"My problem?" Aunt Edith says, echoing our thoughts. She says this softly, but Mom, Patricia, and I all notice the change in her voice.

"What you've been talking to us about. This solves it." Dad smiles again, but his teeth are clenched and I notice that he's gripping his notebook so hard that I can see the plastic cover denting in the middle.

Aunt Edith takes her notebook and opens it to one of the last pages, where there are numbers charted in graphs. She studies it for a long moment. The rest of us have become silent, watching her. Then she closes the notebook and looks up at my father.

"When will you get the money, George?"

The money?

Dad blinks. Mom tries to light a candle on the table that went out. It takes her three tries to light one match. It feels as if all Dad's excitement has been sucked out of the room, leaving everyone tense.

"Edith—"

"No, I don't want to discourage you. It's all good news, and good work, but I thought I had made myself clear," Aunt Edith says quietly.

I look toward Dad. His lips tremble, as if the upper one can't follow orders from the lower one.

"What's the matter, Dad?" I ask. My head feels wobbly. Something is definitely wrong.

Dad turns and looks straight at me. When he speaks, he sounds grim. "Your aunt needs money."

"Ha!" I snort. I can't help it. "Right. And I'm going to go to Mars. On my wings." I instantly feel better. This is the craziest thing I've ever heard. I'm sure Dad's joking.

But he doesn't look like he's joking. He's glaring at Aunt Edith, his gaze sharp and pointed. My smile fades away.

"Aunt Edith's the richest of any of us!" I look over at her, my mind filling with confusion. "I mean, you're famous!"

"Don't be slow-witted, Polly!" Aunt Edith snaps. "As if fame has anything to do with anything."

It feels like Harry slapping me all over again.

"It's too late," Aunt Edith declares. She puts the notebook on the table.

"Dammit, Edith!"

We all jerk our heads toward Dad. He never curses. Never.

"What is going to be good enough for you?"

"Honey, not now," my mother begins.

"She wants to sell the farm, do you all know that?" My dad whirls around as he speaks.

I must not be hearing correctly. Aunt Edith wants to *sell the farm?*

My mom's hand catches on a platter on a side table, and it makes a *clink*. "Worst idea I've ever heard," Mom mutters.

Aunt Edith raises her head sharply. "Frankly, Christina, this doesn't concern you."

"Mom?" I try to stop this craziness. If I can just interrupt this argument, things will go back to normal.

Mom ignores me. "You want to sell the farm and you think it doesn't concern me? Is that what you're saying?"

"Yes," Aunt Edith says. She pushes her chair out from the table. "We'll talk about this at another time. Without the children."

"Wait—Aunt Edith—" I try again, but it's a wimpy sound, and Mom's voice overpowers mine.

"My children can hear all of this," snaps Mom.

"No," Aunt Edith says. "They may not, because I don't want them to. May I remind you that there are two people who own the farm. My brother and me. No one else." She's breathing hard. "And let me tell you one more thing. It is *my* decision. The farm *will* be sold."

I hear the last word like a tumbling brick, like the concrete block I threw at the castle long ago when Grandmom died.

"Aunt Edith," I say, confused. "Are you really—I mean—what are you—?"

Aunt Edith looks at me straight in the eye. When she talks she sounds kind, not mean. "Remember Emerson. *Truth is handsomer than the affectation of love.*" She pauses, taking a deep breath. "Ask me what you really want to ask me, dear. I won't get mad."

Okay then. "Do you really want to sell the farm?"

"Yes." She pauses. "Actually, it's already done. The farm is sold for a very generous price. I'm just waiting for your father to sign the papers."

I'm rocked. Truly, completely rocked. I'm a baseball that's been hit out of the park, out of the county, out of the universe.

"Edith." Dad speaks gravely, more serious than I've ever seen him. "I told you, I am not going to sign."

She lets out a short, harsh laugh. "Of course you are."

Dad shakes his head and pushes his chair back from the table. "No. I own half of this farm, the same as you. And I say *no*."

Aunt Edith swallows and her face hardens.

"I'll ask you again tomorrow, George." She puts both of her hands on the table and stands.

"I'm not going to change my mind," Dad insists.

"We'll see about that." She gives Girard a small nod. "We're leaving."

"Do not—" Mom starts, but Aunt Edith cuts her off. She gives Mom a small smile, and then turns to us. "Good night, everyone."

"But—" Tears form and spill from my eyes. I can't stop them.

"Oh Polly," clucks Aunt Edith. "Please don't."

She is staring at me with such sadness and such pity that I can't stand it. But the fact that Aunt Edith wants to sell the farm makes me not like Aunt Edith.

And I cannot *not like* Aunt Edith. I just can't.

Then, in an instant, she walks out.

Even after we hear the door shut, none of us move for a while.

"Aunt Edith is rich," I say. "She has a Mercedes. She knows the President."

Mom laughs, crazily. "A Mercedes and a president, yes," Mom says.

I get mad that she's laughing. "You must have done something," I tell Dad.

"Polly—" Mom begins.

"What did you do to her?"

"Polly—" This time it's Dad.

"Just give her the money," I say.

"You don't know the first thing—" Mom says.

"You're being cheap!" Aunt Edith is the one person in this family who actually knows anything—who actually *is* anything, and Dad's making her want to sell the farm. That has to be it. I jump up from my chair.

"Sit down!" Dad orders.

But I run out of the house, with everyone staring after me. I don't care. I'm mad, more mad than I've ever been. At my parents. At Aunt Edith. At Freddy. At Patricia. At Harry. It feels like all my anger is pooling into one hot, ugly stream. My cheeks burn; my heart pounds. I think my brain has blown up; nothing makes any sense.

I run over the rope bridge and through the castle and I run and run as fast I can over to the chocolate rhubarb field, row eighteen, column thirty.

"Harry, please talk to me!" I stare down at him, panting. "Tell me what's happening!"

Slowly Harry moves all his leaves up to the *same bouquet position.*

I wipe my eyes to get rid of tears I didn't even know were falling. "Why do you keep doing that?"

The other plants start to make bouquets too, one by one, until the entire field is covered in chocolate rhubarb bouquets.

"HELP ME!" I plead.

Suddenly, Harry slowly releases his leaves, stretching them out, flat, like he's finally going to answer me, tell me what I need to know. I take a deep breath, relieved.

He stays there, outstretched, for a long, long moment.

"Yes, Harry?" I whisper.

Then, Harry's leaves snap up into the bouquet position, that same terrible, unknowable, frustrating position.

And I snap too.

I don't know what that means I don't knowwhatthatmeans Idon'tknowI . . .

I don't think, I just reach over and start ripping, leaf by leaf, yanking out the stalks, throwing down Harry's stems, digging at his crown deep in the soil.

The other plants thunder around me, raising and

lowering their stalks, rustling their leaves, but I ignore them, I ignore my parents' disappointed faces, and most of all, I ignore Aunt Edith's voice saying *the farm is sold, the farm is sold*.

I don't stop until Harry is shredded. I'm gasping, but calmer. The other plants are now still. They're watching me, probably certain that I'll turn on them next.

My crooked finger throbs. Burning, terrible shame washes over me, and I'm sure I'm going to start sobbing, but I don't. I can't. I'm suddenly empty inside— as if by shredding Harry, I've destroyed myself too. I flop to the ground like an old ragdoll, falling on top of the tattered remnants of Harry. I just lie there, rubbing my finger and looking up at the dark and empty sky.

MONDAY, SEPTEMBER 1
Trust the Plants

I wake up late, looking up at the window in my turret. I have no idea how I got back to my bed.

The farm looks just like it did yesterday. Thriving and green, a swath of yellow where the tour buses park. There are people everywhere.

Then I remember.

HARRY.

I pull on clothes and rush out my door, sprinting down the stairway, out the door, through the fields, until I reach him. As I run, I tell myself that it's all a mistake. That Harry will have magically reappeared, just like all the plants in the Learning Garden.

But when I get there, Harry's leaves—what's left of them—are flattened, shredded, in small and big and in-between green pieces. The stalks are torn in the middle,

flung everywhere. I kneel down in the mound of black dirt. Some white roots are sticking out, green leaves and broken stalks scattered. I have no way to absorb the return of the river, *the ocean* of shame that floods through me. This is the worst thing I've ever done.

"Trust the plants," I hear my grandmom say. *"The plants will never steer you wrong, sweet thing."*

I look at the other plants, who are reaching out as they did a couple of weeks ago, touching their neighboring plants. Like they're getting ready for some kind of battle.

Carefully I pick up Harry's pieces, all the remnants of leaves and stalks and roots. I put them into my pocket. It looks like maybe, just maybe, there's still something there in the crown—like deep in the soil, there's a part of Harry that may have escaped my craziness. It's very thin, very frail. I'm not usually that religious, but I make the sign of the cross, and then lean down and kiss that part of the plant.

The other plants have flattened out, touching each other like giant fans. I step around them, walking in tiny zigzagged paths throughout the field. Their stalks flutter slightly, but they stay where they are, stretching to connect with their neighbors.

"It affects everyone. It affects the whole farm." I pause,

realizing. "That's why you clogged up the Umbrella."

And then I understand. Harry was trying to signify that *the entire farm* was in danger, so he was using every bit of his plant body. That's what the bouquet meant.

"You all knew Aunt Edith had sold the farm."

The plants shake their middle leaves, in one unanimous yes. I look over to Harry's place. He was trying to tell me. I glance over to my cherry tree. The mist hangs heavily under the branches, dense and mysterious. I want to collapse. But before I can do anything, I hear someone calling my name.

More like yelling my name.

"POLLY!"

I turn. Running down the entry road is Freddy, and Patricia, and Basford.

"POLLY!" they repeat.

Freddy reaches me first, panting. He can't speak because he's coughing so much; he must still be sick.

"What is it?" I ask.

He wheezes. "You don't know?"

I shake my head.

"What?" I ask again.

Patricia lunges through the plants. "Look up," she gasps.

I tilt my head back, looking up at the sky. It's blue.

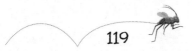

Brilliantly blue. A perfect, cloudless, bluer-than-blue sky.

Freddy flashes his watch at me.

It's 1:07 p.m. On a Monday.

There is no rain.

TUESDAY, SEPTEMBER 2
Scientific Inquiry

"Polly Peabody! Do you have any comment?"

The reporters are worse than slugs. Slugs can't move any real distance; reporters travel, like the mosquitoes in Africa that cause malaria. It's my first day at my new school *and they're here.*

We should have expected this. They've been swarming our farm, scrambling over the fields and popping up near the lake, one of them even taking samples of the water from the lake. Mom and Beatrice have been slamming the door in their face all night long, giving lots of great news footage for people who want to know the burning question of their day: *Why didn't it rain on the Peabody farm?*

This morning, when Freddy got in the driver's seat of Dad's old station wagon, Mom had kissed us each on the cheek, even Basford.

"Freddy was born on a Monday when it didn't rain," she said earnestly. "This could be a *good* sign." Her voice sounded clipped and her eyes had a desperate look, which she was trying to hide by packing us in the car and sending us to school as if everything was normal. "And Polly's welts are down, so that's good too." I slammed the door when she said that, because while Mom's right, the welts have calmed down, it now looks like someone smashed a piece of pizza across my face. Perfect for the first day at school.

Not that it matters. The photographers would take pictures of me if I had a bag over my head. Meanwhile, the reporters are throwing so many questions at us that it's making me dizzy.

"Patricia! Did you know this was going to happen?"

"Have you checked with any meteorologists?"

"You there, blond guy? How are you connected to the Peabodys?"

Basford freezes. "Come on!" I hiss as I grab his arm and pull him through the line of screaming reporters and flashing photographers' lights.

"Are you prepared for this emergency? What's your Plan B?" shouts another reporter as we pass. Luckily, the headmaster, Mr. Horvat, storms over and extends his long arm in front of the reporter's face, like a barricade.

"This is private property," he snaps. "And you should have better sense than to assault children at their school." Soon, he's ushered us into the school through large Gothic doors and brings us to his office. After telling us that he would guarantee that we would have a "normal" school life, he wished us luck and told us that we should come to him with any questions or problems.

"Maybe we should ask him how to make it rain," Patricia jokes.

I don't say anything because I'm now staring at something other than reporters and big black cameras. I didn't think anything could take my mind off of the farm, but here I stand, gawking, at St. Xavier's School.

It isn't that I haven't been here before. I have, with Patricia and Freddy. But I guess I never really paid attention. I'm now realizing it's one of the most beautiful places I've ever seen.

I used to go to school in a place built of orange brick, in the shape of a rectangle. I think there may have been some straggly trees and some green lawns, but there was nothing noticeable about it, and certainly nothing even a little bit beautiful.

But here? This is a *school?*

There's a huge gray stone building with a clock

tower and arched walkways and polished stone floors that shine. Thick, cropped green grass spreads from the edges of the walkways down to a small pond on one side and to a gully on the other. Flowers are pruned and bright, trees are as tall as giants, with outstretched branches, as if they too were welcoming the new students as much as the smiling teachers. There are tennis courts and soccer fields and an indoor swimming pool, and there's the Common Room, which is essentially like a big living room in someone's mansion.

Even the classrooms are perfect. When I get to my science classroom, it's—well, I've never seen anything like it. It's on the top floor for one, but while half of the classroom has a regular wooden floor, the other half has *grass*. That's because the "ceiling" of our science classroom is really a retractable roof, so that on the sunny days, the teacher can roll it back and we can learn science while sitting on green grass under a bright blue sky.

When I sit down, in the second-to-last chair in the very last row of desks, I feel myself relax. No reporters. Basford sitting next to me. And call me a geek, but I feel kind of proud that I get to go to a school that looks like this: It seems like you'd have to be special to be allowed to even cross the doorstep of this magnificent-looking place.

But then *she* walks in and everything changes in a second. The girl walking onto the grass is my height, but bigger everywhere: her head, her body, her legs, probably even her toenails. She has thick dark hair and big blue eyes and big teeth and big lips and a big, big mouth that is always smiling, even if she says cruel things.

Yep. Jennifer Jong. St. Xavier's plummets down my expectation ladder: If they let her in, they'd let in anyone. Luckily, she sits down in the front row. I'm not even sure she knows I'm here. I tuck my chin into my chest and stare at my desk. I'll stare at it all day long if it means she leaves me alone.

Then a man rushes in and I automatically lift my head. He has crazy wild blond hair that's really long, a crooked nose, and a slanted smile. He's wearing a short-sleeved, bright orange Hawaiian shirt, like he just came from the beach.

"Hey!" he says. "Owen Dail, at your service."

Basford and I look at each other. He's grinning; I'm not. Maybe this is common in Bermuda, but I've never had a teacher like this.

"Some quick rules." The teacher moves briskly around the classroom, picking up beakers and plastic bottles and strange, silver implements. "Call me Owen. You get a demerit if you call me Mr. Dail."

"What's a demerit?" asks a girl in the back row.

Owen wheels around, looking down at her. She's wearing all pink. "A demerit is my catch-all phrase that means 'bad thing.'" He starts to lope toward his desk.

"But would it affect our grade? If we get a demerit, I mean?" Owen stops again, mid-row. He turns to face the girl.

"Your name?"

She looks around nervously. "Dawn. Dawn Dobransky."

"Well, Dawn Dobransky, for you, yes. Demerits will affect your grade."

"Just me?"

Owen shrugs. "I don't know." He looks around. "Perhaps everyone? What do you think?"

Dawn Dobransky stares at him uncomprehendingly. "I don't know."

"Well then, I don't know either. Let's keep going, shall we?"

He runs to his desk, puts the palms of both of his hands on the top and propels himself up, so that he can

sit on top of it and look back at all of us. He's remind-ing me of Chico's dog, back when he was a puppy.

"Roll call. My favorite part of the day. I'll know all of your names by December. Scout's promise." He holds up his fingers in a peace sign. "I mean, Scout's honor."

I can't help it, I smile. He's so weird.

He starts reading off names, making funny comments along the way. For someone named Charles Lafayette, he salutes. For a kid named Joseph Josephs, he simply says "My condolences." And then he gets to me.

"Polly Peabody!"

I raise my hand.

"Peas! Do you know what that makes me think of?"

Now everyone has turned to me, including Jongy. I keep my eyes trained on Owen and shake my head, scared of what he's about to say.

"Gregor Mendel!" Owen says gleefully. "Do you know who he is?"

I shake my head again.

"Anyone?" Owen asks. "This is a science class, think science. Gregor Mendel. Not a scientist. A priest. An Augustinian priest—whatever that is—who is the founder of . . ."

129

He waits. A pretty girl with thick blond hair and blue eyes raises her hand.

"Yes, Marsha?"

"It's Margaret."

"Absolutely. Margaret. Continue. What does Miss Peabody have in common with Gregor Mendel?"

"He studied pea plants?"

"It isn't a question." Owen yells, "That's the answer! Be confident! Yes! Gregor Mendel is the father of modern genetics!"

Margaret smiles nervously.

"Let me see." Owen peers at his list. "Basford? Someone named Basford Von Trammel?"

Basford looks uncomfortable.

"Is he here? Mr. Basford Von Trammel? Or is he off running the State Department? Perhaps he's an ambassador? Maybe a spy? Perhaps that's why he's so quiet?" Owen scans the room.

Jongy stands up, pointing. "That's him. I saw him on the news last night. He lives with the Peabodys."

Basford immediately casts his eyes down to the floor.

"Hello, Mr. Von Trammel," Owen says. "May I ask where you got your first name?"

"It was the name of my father's favorite teacher," he says quietly.

Owen's face splits into an incredibly big, lopsided smile. "I love this story! If any of you want to name your child Owen or Dail, talk to me after class. We may be able to figure out an arrangement."

Owen turns back to Jongy. "And you, our public service student. Who are you?"

Jongy's eyes narrow. "You called on me already."

"I did?"

"Yes. Ten seconds ago."

"Oh, yes. You're Eve."

"Nope."

"Pia?"

"No."

"Sylvie?"

"Jennifer. Jennifer Jong."

"Right," he says. "Do you know everyone in the class?"

She looks around. "I'm new here. But I know *some* people."

"Like our ambassador, Mr. Von Trammel?"

"Like Polly Peabody."

I close my eyes.

"Wonderful," Owen says.

"I was actually hoping I could make an announcement to the class," Jongy continues.

"Go right ahead."

Jongy clears her throat. "I know I'm speaking for everyone when I tell Polly that we're all so sorry for the Peabody family. It must be so hard to start a new school the day after you find out your farm is going to be ruined."

Everyone's quiet. I stare at my hands. This is not how I wanted to be introduced.

"You need to sit down," I hear Owen say from across the room. "That was unkind."

I sneak a glance over to them. Jongy sits down slowly. As she does, she removes her lip gloss and starts to apply it, looking Owen straight in the eye as she does.

"Excellent," Owen says. "You are providing me with an excellent basis to begin our discussion, Miss Jong."

"What?"

"Scientific inquiry. I'm sure you've heard of it. You seem like an uncannily aware young woman."

He starts to walk around the front of the classroom. "Let's say you're puzzled by something. Something happens and you want to be able to explain it." He steps toward Charles Lafayette. "Like, let's say Billy—"

"Charlie."

"Charlie," Owen continues. "Let's say Charlie won-

ders why his hair is brown. Do you ever wonder why your hair is brown?"

Charlie shakes his head. "Nope. My mother's hair is brown. So is my dad's. I'd wonder if my hair *wasn't* brown."

"Excellent!" Owen grins. "You not only set up the 'inquiry'—why does Charlie have brown hair—but you've come up with a 'hypothesis'—that is, I have brown hair because my parents have brown hair. Then you test it—not literally, but instinctively—because you correctly assume that hair color is genetic, and you consider the color of your parents' hair." He snaps his fingers. "You have a fine mind, my friend!"

He's clearly someone Grandmom would call "excitable." But it works; I think I'll like him.

"Don't look at me like I'm crazy," he says to the class. "Although someone did tell me once that the crazies were the only people worth knowing." He pauses, biting his lip. "Except that he was crazy himself. Well, anyway. You get my point." He takes a couple steps, then stops, looking confused. "The point?"

He looks straight at a guy named Christopher. Christopher's eyes widen.

"The point?" Christopher echoes.

"Exactly! The point is the process! You have a prob-

133

lem. In trying to solve it, you come up with a hypothesis, a theory. And then you test it out, to see if you are right. That's all it is, scientific inquiry in a nutshell. Understand?

"Now, Miss Jong." Owen spins around, catching Jongy and Joe whispering to each other. "Hello, Joe Josephs of the unfortunate name." He moves over to Jongy. "Miss Jong. I have a hypothesis for you. May I have that stick of makeup you thought was appropriate to apply as you spoke to your esteemed science teacher?"

Jongy looks around, unsure what she should do. Owen just stands there with a big smile on his face. She gives him the lip gloss. He takes it back to his desk, puts on a pair of reading glasses, and studies the small print.

"Hmmm." He takes off his glasses and returns the lip gloss to Jongy.

"What?" Jongy's worried.

"My hypothesis,"—Owen gives Jongy a reassuring smile—"is that your lip gloss may be dangerous to your health. Why do I say that? Because I suspect it flattens the natural protective layer of your lips, allowing rays of sunlight to penetrate directly through the skin, causing skin cancer and other non-cancerous disfigurations."

"Disfigurations?" Jongy mutters.

Owen seems not to have heard her. "How do I test for this?" He continues, "I read the label. And sadly . . ." He looks over to Jongy. "I'm right."

"English, please," Jongy says, annoyed.

"Lip glosses without sun protection act like a magnifying glass to the sun."

"What does that mean?"

"I think you should invest in some new lip gloss. With sun protection. You'll thank me for it later, trust me."

Jongy smirks, but then quickly uses the back of her hand to wipe off her lip gloss.

"So again," says Owen. "Someone tell me. Scientific inquiry is . . . ?"

"Problem, hypothesis, testing, analysis," says the blond kid in the back.

"Excellent, Charlie," Owen says.

"My name's Christopher."

"Right. Of course it is." He walks over to his desk. "Scientific inquiry is just a fancy way of describing what you already do instinctively, and putting names to all the steps. Now listen. We have a lot to get through this year. Some of it may actually be helpful to you.

"And some of it may not. Throw some spaghetti against the wall"—he lifts his right arm and pretends to

pitch something against the back wall—"and see what sticks. Now. Let's talk about our first assignment!"

As he continues, Margaret, the pretty girl who answered the first question, turns to me.

"Don't worry about Jongy," she says. "We went to camp together. I know how she is."

"Thanks."

I'm so nervous, I can't really look at her. But I think she's still staring at me.

"I'm sorry about your farm," she says. "It sounds scary. Was it?"

I grip the edge of the desk. Nothing's changed. "Uh, yeah." I turn away from her and look out the window.

"Are you okay?" she says.

Exhibit A. Polly Peabody. Hypothesis: She's a freak. Testing: Express concern at her farm's condition. Conclusion: Freak.

It's never going to go away.

I don't speak the rest of class, staring so hard at my desk that I think I'll burn a hole in it. When it's over, I run away as fast as I can—so fast that I don't even notice that I'm colliding into some classmates: Will, Joe, and Jongy.

"Hey!" Will says. "You're Freddy Peabody's sister."

"Yes." I try not to look at any of them. But Joe sud-

denly leaps toward me. Before I can move, he grabs my head and locks it in the middle of his elbow.

"Ow!"

"What's that about?" Will asks Joe. "Leave her alone."

But I know what Joe's thinking, what he's doing. I know what everybody's been thinking since they've seen me on campus.

"I DON'T KNOW WHY IT ISN'T RAINING!" I yell, flailing my arms. "LEAVE ME ALONE!"

Joe releases me and they all take baby steps away from me, like there's a lion loose in the hallway.

"Uh," mumbles Joe. "I was just getting back at Freddy for hazing me last year. I didn't mean to . . . uh, hurt you."

Jongy smiles like the fake person she is.

"She's stressed," she says to the guys. "Leave her alone. Her farm's going kaput." She puts her arm around me like we're best friends.

I try to duck out from under her, but her hand grips my shoulder tightly. A crowd has gathered around us, including all the people I don't know yet.

"You know, I can't wait for our class trip." Jongy grins.

I groan. Every year, Mom insists that our classes take a trip to our farm so that they can learn about "responsible farming."

Jongy keeps going. "Maybe we can take that great Umbrella ride. You know, the one that tosses its passengers all around?" She's *pinching* my shoulder. I wrench myself free of her just as she's snarling through her smile. "If it ever rains again, that is."

"It will rain again," I say weakly.

"What does your aunt say? Mom says she saw her leave on a private plane today. Pretended she didn't know her, like she always does." Jongy smacks her lips, smearing her lip gloss. She must not be too afraid of disfigurations after all, since she's obliviously reapplied it. "I guess she's getting out before it gets any worse?"

I'm confused and she can tell.

"Okay, show's over." Owen steps out of the stairwell and crosses over to where I'm standing. "Give her a break."

"But she's the Rhubarb Princess!" yells Joe. "Let me just ask one—"

Owen flicks his eyes over both of them. His face is harder: He's no longer the goofy guy from the classroom. Now he's a grown-up—with long hair and a Hawaiian shirt—who seems pretty mad.

"I expect more from you guys," he says quietly. "Don't behave like this again."

"I didn't do anything," Joe says. "She's crazy."

Owen glares at him. "Go!"

"Okay, okay," says Joseph. Before she goes, Jongy winks at me, which causes me to feel even more sick.

"Polly?" Owen asks. "Everything all right?"

I nod.

"Because the ambassador and I can lay down the law, right, Ambassador?"

He winks at Basford. Basford smiles faintly.

"Now listen, Gregor Mendel," he says to me.

"Who?"

"Don't you listen? Father Mendel, the pea plant guy. You want to be literal? Okay. I can do literal. Now listen, Polly Peabody." Owen leans against the wall, his head turned so he can look me in the eye. "From what I know, your farm is a really cool place that gets a lot of attention and does good things. So maybe people just bring it up because they're genuinely interested in it." He cracks a crooked smile. "And maybe, maybe possibly, they're genuinely interested in you too. Right, Ambassador?"

Basford nods. But he has to be interested in me. He's living at our farm.

Anyway, I know what Owen's trying to say. But adults must get some mist of their own in their brain, making them forget what middle school is like. I come from

the weird farm with the weird rain. Plus I'm weird, I'll always be weird. If I could kill this part of me, if I could strangle it, I would. Genuine interest in me from people my age means only digging into my weirdness. I wish it weren't true, but it is.

"Thanks," I tell Owen, and then I run away from him and Basford as fast as I can. St. Xavier's is a big place. There's got to be some places to hide.

SAME DAY, TUESDAY, SEPTEMBER 2
Scraped Knees

After school, I tell Mom that she has to cancel the class trip.

"Nonsense," she says.

"Mom, they're just coming to gawk at everything."

"No. They're coming to learn. I have a whole plan. We're actually going to use your class for help with the Transplanting!"

"What if doesn't rain? Will it be fun then?"

"Yes," Mom says stubbornly. "Honestly, Polly. We're not doing it to torture you. We're doing it because,

140

hard as it may be for you to believe, some of your classmates may actually care about responsible farming practices."

I'm sure Jennifer Jong really cares that our rhubarb is organic. It's probably tops on her list after "Find out what they sacrifice at the midnight rituals" and "Look for the cauldron where they burn their newts."

I give Mom the meanest look I can muster.

"School will get better," she says.

"Can I go to my room?" I answer.

Mom reaches out, as if she's going to touch my shoulder, but her hand stops in midair and she simply nods. I run up the stairs as fast as I can and shut the door behind me. Even though it's a sunny day, I feel like everything's turning rotten. A school like St. Xavier's can give refuge to someone like Jennifer Jong. Aunt Edith has gone somewhere on a private plane. I may have killed Harry.

And it didn't rain.

I stare at the Tupperware container where Harry's leaves and stalks float in water. Did I think they were going to miraculously reattach themselves? Well, they haven't. They're just scattered pieces of Harry, floating apart from each other. This is how they'll be tonight, tomorrow, and next year unless I figure out a better plan.

In seconds, I'm clutching the Tupperware container under one arm, and holding my water bottle in the other. I run to the lake, dunking the water bottle inside, letting it fill up to the top. Then I jog over to the chocolate rhubarb field, eighteenth row, thirtieth column. Harry's home.

It's empty, of course, although I dive to the ground and start pawing at the dirt with my hands, the soil warm under my touch. I calm down just a little when I see it—Harry's lone root, the skinny little white string, barely long enough to poke out above the ground. Carefully I pour the water over his root. Then, very solemnly, I kneel and again make the sign of the cross.

I'm not going to give up on you. I promise. And, if you're listening, please don't give up on me either.

I walk back to the castle slowly, kicking the dirt as I walk. I can't figure out how to feel about school or Harry or the fact that it didn't rain yesterday. My brain is stuck, and I guess the truth is, I just want the answers *now.*

"What is going on?" I find myself blurting out to my cherry blossom tree. Instantly teardrops form on its petals.

"Sorry," I say quickly. "I'm sorry." The tree often

cries by itself, but there are times—like now—when I'm the reason it starts to weep, which makes me feel awful.

I reach out and grab one of the drooping limbs. The petals are stunning: pink and lacy, cascading from the top of the tree down to my toes. I'm pretty sure the tree is attached to me in some way, which is why I always feel so comfortable coming here when I want to read a book or just be alone. But I wonder for the first time whether this attachment is a burden to the tree. It would probably be much easier for a tree to have an attachment with someone always happy, like Freddy. He's never prickly. And he'd never, ever make anything or anyone cry.

I raise the branch quickly and duck underneath it. The mist has risen as high as the tree itself and it's filled every spare space. Now that I'm really focusing on it, I can see it isn't ugly at all. It's actually pretty— individual strands of water, green and sparkling, spun together in some kind of magic net. I reach up and try to pinch some of it off, but it's woven too tightly and again, I just get green drops of water on my hand. There must be a million dragonflies working furiously on this mist—they are at least as disciplined as ants.

"What are you doing?" I yell, hoping that Spark or one of his friends may answer me. "Why are you making this?"

I wait for a second, and then sit on the ground, under the mist, leaning against a big rock on the edge of the lake. I want to take a nap, right here. Maybe I could be in a fairy tale, and when I wake up, the mist will be gone and Aunt Edith—*my* aunt Edith, not the stranger who wants to sell the farm—will be in front of me, ready to teach me about, say, the Aztecs.

"Spark?" I try again.

I'm focused on the mist, so I've forgotten the basic annoying fact that mosquitoes think our lake is their playground. I'm an easy target, so when I get bit on my lower neck, I slam my hand against my collarbone, nailing it. *Sorry, Beatrice.* I jump up, angry, just as something whizzes by me, a fast, flying, colorful bug. Spark. I watch as he dives under the lake's surface, zooming back up again.

Spark doesn't know yet about Harry. The only person who does know for sure is Basford, even though he hasn't said anything to me about it. But I know he saw the empty space in the field yesterday, when they had all come running to tell me it wasn't raining. Even as I was absorbing what was happening, I was able to

watch Basford glance from the ground back to me, his face solemn, a surprised look in his eyes. I had to turn away.

"I need to tell you something, Spark." I stand up and follow him over to the water's edge. "I didn't mean to do it, I just—"

Spark flies by me, heading for another pile of rocks about thirty feet from where I stand. I get up and run after him, barely able to see his pin-width-size blue body around the edge of the mist. I dodge a branch, duck under the mist, and finally see what he's doing: He's stalking a group of mosquitoes, each one larger than the one I just smacked. Dinnertime. Just as he dives in for his feast, I smash my right foot against a pointy gray rock, kicking something that shatters. I tumble, hands outstretched, and end up pressing the heel of my right hand on something sharp. I yank my hand up, but my knee's cut too—I seem to have kicked a bottle that broke. My fingers rake around the thick grass, picking up shards of the bottle as Spark returns, flitting around me.

"Ouch," I say quietly. Spark zooms in front of my face, bobs up and down, then heads back to a rock and slurps up another mosquito. My hand is bleeding. Figures. "How to Make a Rotten Day Even Worse," by Polly

Peabody. I suck on my bloody wrist, blinking back tears as I brace my back with my left arm. Only my left hand touches something else in the grass, something that is smooth, not sharp. I lift it up in front of me, wiping the tears away with the back of my bleeding hand.

It's a key. A long, bronze skeleton key, with a cut-out on the top. On the base there are words etched on the side:

WATER. NATURA NIHIL FIT IN FRUSTRA. +/−

I forget all about my hand as I realize that I'm holding a key that looks *exactly the same* as Aunt Edith's key that opened Enid's turret.

My mind is whirling—Aunt Edith's key? Here under the cherry blossom tree? Spark darts in between me and the key.

"Did you know about this?"

I wait for Spark to spell, but he just bobs up and down, until he swoops over my shoulder and literally eats a mosquito in midair.

I stare back at the key. Water, I understand. But plus minus? And the words in Latin?

"Hey. Your mom told me to find you." Basford pushes through the boughs of the tree. His eyes are drawn immediately to the mist. "Yowza." Then he eyes me strangely, looking at my knees, my face.

"You're bleeding."

"It's nothing," I say as I press my hand into my shirt, blotting the cut.

"Not that. Your leg."

I look down and see blood gushing out of my knee.

"Aw, cheese and crackers," I groan. "Here, hold this." I hand him the key and stretch out my shirt, pressing the cloth into my knee. "I broke a bottle."

Basford examines the key in front of his face as I soak up the blood on my leg. "I just found it," I explain. "I'm going to Google the words as soon as I get inside."

Basford's eyes flicker toward me, a slight smile playing across his lips.

"You don't have to Google it," he says. "It's Latin. I know Latin." His cheeks flush red. "I mean, I know some Latin."

"Well, what is it?" I ask him. "Tell me."

"It means," he speaks carefully. "'Nature does nothing in vain.'"

The words hit me square in the chest. "What?"

"'Nature does nothing in vain,'" he repeats as I feel my face turn white. Basford's smile slips away.

"Are you sure?" I ask.

"Yes," he says. "Polly?"

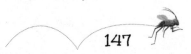

I hear him, but I can't answer because I'm thinking about all my afternoon picnics with Grandmom, all my strolls around the White House, all our talks under this cherry tree.

Nature does nothing in vain, Polly. Make sure you remember that.

Grandmom's words. On the key.

Someone's trying to tell me something. I glance up, searching for Spark. There's a million dragonflies in the mist, none of them paying any attention to me.

"I could be wrong," Basford says. "I could have screwed up the translation."

"No," I tell him, hearing Grandmom say the words again in my head. "You're absolutely right."

SAME DAY, TUESDAY, SEPTEMBER 2
Enid's Necklace

I feel bad about ditching Basford, but I'm not ready to show him Enid's turret. It isn't because I don't trust him, because the truth is, he's the only kid my age who's been nice to me in my entire life. It's not even

148

because he might freak out at the crazy things that go on in the turret, because I don't think he would. It's just that I have a feeling the turret is mine, only mine.

And Aunt Edith's. Of course.

I'm trembling as I climb the stairs. Going up here makes me think of Aunt Edith. It also, unfortunately, makes me think of the crickets.

I force myself to focus on only one step after the other: Take out the key, put it in the lock, turn it slowly, hear the bolt slide out of place. I breathe fast, shallow breaths as I push open the heavy door, then jump back in the hallway quickly, in case any cricket decides to terrorize me. Nothing seems to move. I cautiously take a step, crossing over the threshold into the turret.

And *then* the Monster cricket rushes me, leaping up on my shoulder.

"Hey!"

Monster cricket jumps off, landing on a stack of dusty books. He waves his legs around like he's swaying his arms to a funny song.

"Are you laughing at me?"

The cricket picks up his front leg to answer, but I'm suddenly distracted by the strand of ivy that comes off the walls. It weaves its way from the wall over to where I stand, and then forms an archway over my head. Then

another strand detaches itself from the wall, doing the very same thing.

They're creating my own pathway, my own personal, magical maze.

The light is soft, shining in wide arcs throughout the room. I cast my eyes around quickly as theories pass through my mind.

Did Spark bring me to the key? Did he want me to come here? Is this part of a plan? Am *I* part of their plan?

The maze pushes me through the room, passing by stacks of books and drawing me right around the curved wall where a big drawing of the farm hangs. The ivy moves just ahead of me, winding me slowly over toward the window. Finally, it stops at a round, dusty, tiled table.

The Monster cricket leaps onto it, startling me again.

"Aaaah!" I yell. "Please stop doing that!"

He extends his leg, pointing to a small black box lying dead center on the same table. I pick it up and glance back at the Monster cricket. He nods his big black head.

There's a small card inside. In old-fashioned hand-writing, it reads *For Enid*. I pull apart the white tissue paper, finding a long, gold roped necklace.

"It's just like the one Aunt Edith wears. The one that holds her key." The Monster cricket nods. "Is it for me?"

When I ask, about fifteen new crickets start to jump all over the place, joining with Monster, who hops to the highest book on the stack. Honestly: The crickets perform some kind of quasi-cheerleading routine, each of them perched on a different book at a different height. Then the ivy twirls around me, and more bugs—big, ugly stinkbugs—show up too, extending their front legs so that they form a circle. It's like they're playing ring-around-the-rosy. Kind of cute, and at the same time, incredibly gross.

The ivy spells out a word in its archway. Y E S. 4 U.

I take the key out of my pocket and thread the necklace through the keyhole at the top. When I look up, I have another visitor: Spark. He's just flown in through the window.

"Hey!"

I dangle the necklace in front of him, but he's not interested. He flits around the room, rushing over to the cricket. It seems like they have a full-blown conversation; Spark's bobbing and weaving, Monster cricket is leaping and extending his long black leg.

Things are quite dire if my only option is to ask a stinkbug.

"What's going on?" I ask the biggest one.

He doesn't answer for a long time. And when he does, I'm pretty sure he gives me a stinkbug fart. Yuck.

Luckily, Spark flies back to me when he's finished with Monster. He flits around the room quickly, in small little darting moves, always turning around to make sure I'm looking. I think he's nervous.

"Do you want to tell me something?"

He bobs in the air.

"Wait," I say. "I have to say something first." I take a deep breath. "I didn't mean to hurt Harry. I swear, *I swear*, I'm going to make him come back, I'll do anything—"

I . . . K . . . N . . . O . . . W.

But he's making it too easy. This is the first time I'm saying aloud what I've done, and I want to make sure it's really clear how sorry I am.

"There's one root left and it's small, but I'll water him every single day if I have to," I continue.

Spark bobs up and down impatiently. He's annoyed. So am I.

"What is it that's so important?" I ask him.

W . . . A . . . T . . . C . . . H.

"I'm watching," I tell him. He backflips away and begins to spell.

152

"Is than an S?"

He bobs up and down before he flies in a straight line up to the ceiling.

"I?"

Again, he bobs his answer. His next letter also seems to be a straight line. Up. To the right. He does it again. Up, to the—

"L?"

SIL? Uh-oh. My smile stiffens.

"Spark? I hope it isn't what I think I it is . . ."

He finishes, flying round and round in one perfect circle.

Silo.

I see our enormous black Silo in front of my eyes, like some kind of living, breathing monster. No way.

Spark hovers in front of my face, almost defiantly. The ivy stops moving, the stinkbugs drop their legs, and the cricket leaps to the table. They are all watching me.

I squeeze my eyes shut. "Is this your way of getting back at me about Harry? Making me go to a place that's *haunted*?" I stop, opening my eyes and sweeping around the room. "A place that's full of *mutant slugs*?"

Spark zips around my head, ending by my right ear. He won't give up. The other bugs stay silent, frozen, even the Monster cricket.

"I told you I was sorry about Harry. And I am. I've never done anything so awful to anyone. I'll do anything I can to bring him back to life. But there's no way. There's just no way I'm going to the Silo. I'm sorry. I just can't."

The ivy drops to the floor when it hears me refuse. I look over to the Monster cricket, who's waving his long black leg.

Tsk, tsk, tsk, he seems to say.

"No," I say louder. "I'm sorry, but no." I swallow hard, then trudge over to the door. "Thanks for the necklace."

I slam the door shut and bolt it quickly, as if this would stop the bugs from following me—as if I have any real control over them.

When I get to my room, I put the necklace and key in my top drawer and sit by my window. I force myself to stare in the one direction I always avoid.

The Silo.

From my window, the Dark House looks like a capital letter *L*. The flat part is the shed where the Giant Rhubarb grows in barrels without any sunlight, and the tall part is the Silo. The Silo has been here forever, back when that Italian prince founded the farm. But the shed was built when Grandmom called up some scientists at Yale after she read about their work taking oxalic acid from rhubarb leaves and shooting it into the atmosphere. Dad said it was one of those classic Grandmom moments: She had an idea about something, called the right person, and bam! We were growing Giant Rhubarb for a lot of money and for the good of our worldwide community. Dad called it a "win-win" situation.

The Giant Rhubarb gets giant because of something called "forcing." We dig the plants up from the field and plant each one of them in tin barrels, moving them into the shed for about six weeks. We water them while they're in the shed, but we keep it completely dark: That's why the shed and the Silo are painted black. Like all plants, rhubarb will literally grow themselves to death searching for the sun. All their energy is forced into the leaves, which is why they grow so big, and we're able to extract so much of the acid that helps with the ozone. Then, after the six weeks, we take them out of the shed before they die and replant them in the ground. The whole thing is called the Transplanting— even though most people only know about the big party that happens on Halloween, the same day that we replant the plants into the field.

Dad insists that the shed isn't a terrifying place, and

155

that I'd realize this if I just let him show me around. But I can't. My fear is rooted so far deep that I think it's probably part of my bones. Some people are scared of black cats; others are scared of roller coasters. I'm scared of the Dark House.

And I'm especially scared of the Silo. At least the shed has a purpose. The Silo does nothing. It just stands there, looming over our farm, casting its deep black shadow over everything that's good.

I look away from my window.

Sorry, Spark. I can't do it. I never claimed to be anything but a coward.

FRIDAY, SEPTEMBER 5
The Water Cycle

So far this week, I've ignored Jongy when she whispered to me that she thinks Aunt Edith went to Antarctica. I've ignored Charlie and Billy and Christopher when they asked me if they could buy up our remaining chocolate rhubarb, before it all dies. I've ignored the nice person who left an article on my desk about droughts in Africa.

But I can't ignore today's science class. When I first see the topic on the SmartBoard, I think it's a joke.

THE WATER CYCLE.

The availability of fresh water is the single most important element in sustaining our global community.

Jongy hoots from the corner. "Maybe we can move this whole class over to the Peabody farm. I think they need some water now that the rain dances aren't working."

My classmates giggle. I get that St. Xavier's is a

prettier, richer school. But it turns out to be exactly the same as any school on the inside. I suppose that shouldn't be surprising. I shut my eyes and try to think of something good. Charles Dickens. Chocolate rhubarb. Silly movies.

"Miss Jong, would you come up here?" Owen barely looks away from the papers he's skimming at his desk.

Jongy rolls her eyes. "Why?"

"I'd like to ask you a question."

Jongy strolls to the front of the classroom.

Own puts down his papers and leans back into his chair.

"Would you please explain the history of rain dances for the class?"

"What?"

"I just heard you referencing rain dances. I'd like to hear what you know about them. It's a tradition that has been a major element of many ancient and contemporary societies, particularly those that rely on the weather for their food. So, please, elaborate. What do you know?"

"You're just mad I picked on your pet."

"My pet? My dog is here? Winston!" He looks to us. "I can't imagine you wouldn't see him. He's an eighty-pound chocolate Lab." His head whips around to Jongy.

"Did you pick on him? Pick a flea? Pick something else? What are you talking about?"

"You're not funny," Jongy says.

Owen pushes his chair back hard, so it makes a squeaky sound. When he stands, his expression changes.

"Neither, Miss Jong, are you."

I close my eyes, breathing deeply. I know that Owen was technically doing this for me, but there's something about their interaction that makes me think he's doing this for him too. He seems determined not to let someone like Jongy act the way she usually does. And it's working.

When I open my eyes, Owen is saying, ". . . lab partners. We're going to measure the temperature of the shifting phases of water molecules, which, I promise, is *exactly* as boring as it sounds. So try to pick an interesting partner so you don't go a little nutso."

I immediately look at Basford. He nods and I feel a sense of relief.

"Basford!" Jongy breaks into my thoughts. "You'll be my partner, okay? That's all right with you, right, Polly?"

She could have a zillion lab partners. I have exactly one friend here and she's trying to ruin that too.

I look at Basford. He's clueless.

"Polly." Owen smiles. "You can be with Dawn."

Owen points over to Dawn Dobransky. The one who wears pink. Pink headbands, pink shirts, pink socks. I gather my things.

"Sorry," Basford whispers. Jongy smiles at him with her big dimples and he actually smiles back. Ugh. Boys. I shake my head and walk to where Dawn stands.

"I've already begun," Dawn informs me. She's very fair-skinned and has thin, pink lip-glossed lips. "I downloaded copies of all the labs during the summer. Did you do that too?"

"No," I say.

"Okay, well, you're going to be so happy you're doing this with me!" She grins. "We get to watch water heat up and become vapor, and then watch as it condenses—condensation, naturally—and then be able to see it precipitate!" She beams. "Just like rain! I love science! Don't you?"

"Sure." I sigh.

Owen walks around the classroom as Dawn assembles plastic soda bottles and shoelaces. I pretend to help.

"Doing okay?"

Dawn smiles. "Yes, Mr. Dail! I mean, Owen."

I focus on threading the shoelace through the hole

in the cap of the soda bottle so I don't have to look at him. Dawn keeps talking to me, telling me exactly what to do. We fill the bottom of one of the bottles with about three inches of water.

"Now take it over there," she orders, pointing to the grass section of the classroom. "I'll fix up this bottle while you're doing that." She starts to pour dirt into the bottom of the other bottle.

I pick up the bottle with the water and carry it toward the grass. I purposely avoid Jongy, but again, she steps in my path.

"Rhubarb witch," she whispers.

I turn and run into Margaret. The bottle hits her on the waist.

"Ow!"

"I'm sorry," I say immediately.

"It's burning hot," Margaret says, pointing at the bottle.

I look down, surprised. The water in my bottle isn't boiling, exactly, but condensation has started and the water's swirling. I lift it higher so I can see it against the light.

Owen turns around. "What's going on?"

I look at him guiltily, even though I haven't really done anything. "Here," I say, handing him the bottle.

He takes it, curious. Then he looks up to the sky. The whole class is watching.

"Guess the sun heated it up," he says. He looks at me as if I'm the one who has water steaming out of my ears.

"That's what's supposed to happen, right?"

He nods slowly. "Yes." He stares at the bottle. "Kind of." He places the bottle down on the floor, against the brick partition. "Exactly. Kind of."

I sense all my classmates gawking, as if weird things like this could only happen to freaky Polly Peabody. I walk back to Dawn's table as fast as I can. When I turn around, I see that Owen is still watching me from his desk.

Dawn is impatient. "Here's the other one." She hands me another plastic bottle, this one filled on the bottom with dirt. "I already put in the grass seeds." This time I rush to the other side as fast as I can and place it down. I don't know if anyone is watching me, but I examine it after I put it down, to make sure nothing's boiling. The bottle just sits there and soon I feel foolish, watching dirt.

After class, I head toward Basford, but Owen stops me.

"Got a second?"

He's still thinking about the soda bottle. "That was pretty cool. Any idea what happened?"

"Nope," I say. I shift my backpack to the other side. "Is it that weird?'

He stares at me for a long second. "Nah. The pyramids, they're weird. Walking on the moon? Weird-o-rama. Wax museums? Have you ever been to one? Totally weird. Nope. On a scale of one to ten, this is just a . . ." He smiles as he searches for the word. "Not even a number. A mystery."

"I thought you said it was the sun."

"Maybe, but I kind of doubt it. The bottle got awfully hot, awfully fast." He shrugs. "But no harm, no foul."

I bite my lip. "So it's okay?"

"Yes." He grins. "Are you always this worried?"

I look him straight in the eye and answer truthfully. "Yes."

SATURDAY, SEPTEMBER 6
Spiders

It was stupid of me to expect that Aunt Edith would be waiting for me yesterday afternoon. But on the way home from school, I suddenly believed that Aunt Edith would be there and we'd go on a tutorial where I'd learn something amazing, something so special and important that I'd be the envy of everyone.

I know my face showed how disappointed I was when we pulled up and there was no Mercedes waiting in our driveway. It's my fault anyway, for even hoping. I'm pretty sure Aunt Edith is traveling now—she would travel to a different country every second if she could. She says there's no way to learn about the human condition without seeing it from a front-row seat. I've been reading *Self-Reliance* every night, though, and Mr. Emerson doesn't agree with her. *The wise man stays at home,* he says, sounding more like Grandmom than Aunt Edith. But the real truth is, I have no idea what Aunt Edith is doing or thinking. She could be anywhere, doing anything. I don't know her as well as I thought.

Yet she was right. Things are changing around here. This morning, I walked outside and saw that the thick mass of green mist under the cherry tree had begun to leak out from under the branches. I ran over to the tree and gasped. Now a part of the mist floated a few feet past the branches, hovering over the water. Cautiously, I leaned over to touch it. Again, it had that wet, cottony feel. But this time, it wasn't quite as tight—as if the net had loosened just a bit, allowing the strands to pull apart and cover this new section of the lake.

When Grandmom died, I never thought to touch the mist itself. I wonder if it was the same thing. Maybe this is how it starts? Under the tree, to gather strength, and then pushing itself over the water? Perhaps it will continue to stretch out just like last time, wrapping itself around our lake, waiting for our next savior to come and fix us, just like Aunt Edith did four years ago.

And then I think, if that's true, I wish he or she would hurry up, because there's a general feeling that we're all walking along the edge of the world, ready to fall off if it doesn't rain on Monday. The truth is we

have no Plan B. It's always rained. That's all we know.

Gently, I pour some water on Harry's spot. I come here every morning before school, making the sign of the cross, hoping to see some sign of progress. But so far, nothing's happened. Today, Saturday, I stare at his one white strand of root so hard it hurts. It hasn't changed at all, but there's a part of me that's clinging to that skinny little string. As long as it exists, I have a chance.

"Is there anything else I can do?" I ask the spindly root as nicely as I can. Then I turn to the other sagging, unhappy plants. "I'll do whatever you say."

But it's like all the plants are asleep. Or they're ignoring me, their friend's shredder. I don't blame them. Coming here every day, knowing how all the plants must be mad at me, is part of my punishment. I want them to know that I'm genuinely sorry and that I'm not going to give up.

Suddenly I feel something faintly scrape my ankle. I look down, full of hope, expecting to see a leaf rustling or a stalk reaching out to me.

It's neither. It's a spider.

A big, black, long-legged spider with two heads and three stripes on its body.

"Eww!" I recoil.

"Seeek!" I hear in response. It's so faint that I think it may be a mouse lost in the fields.

"Seeek!" I hear again, louder. I look to the plants, feeling suddenly panicked. Now the bugs are *really* talking? Am I hearing correctly?

The spider scrambles up the leaf of the plant directly in front of me.

"Seeek. Seeek." The spider speaks from his left head.

I didn't even know spiders had mouths.

"Seek." The spider quickly scuttles to another plant, dropping from one leaf to another as if on stairwells. Then he speaks with his right head. "Seeek!"

"Seek?" I ask.

The spider shakes his right head no.

"Seeek!"

"Sick?"

Both heads move up and down. Then the spider moves, crawling from the leaf in front of me, down the stalk and onto the ground.

"Who's sick?" I hear my voice catch in terror.

I watch as the spider scampers away. "Wait!" I hurry after him.

The spider pauses, turns his right head so that it's facing me.

167

"Seek!" Then, without a second glance, the spider darts into the field. I follow him into it. Then I stop. I stop because in front of me are hundreds of black two-headed spiders. A virtual army of them, thousands and thousands of skinny black legs and striped bodies, all standing still in the middle of this chocolate rhubarb field, all of them looking straight at me.

"Seeek! Seeek!" I gawk at the bugs, mouth open, eyes wide. In one sweeping moment, the spiders fall silent. And then they're gone. Every single one of them.

Gone.

MONDAY, SEPTEMBER 8
For Real

Yesterday I read one Mark Twain story for English and did two chapters of math homework, but I wouldn't be able to say one word about of any of them today.

All I'm thinking about—all any of us are thinking about—is whether it's going to rain at one o'clock. I'm meeting Freddy, Patricia, and Basford in the Common Room as soon as this class is over.

Meanwhile, Owen is attempting to teach us about the atmosphere.

". . . this is the troposphere, the layer of the atmosphere that is closest to earth. All together now, say *troposphere* . . ."

I check my watch. It's 12:48 p.m. Owen says something about argon.

12:49 p.m. He uses the term *electromagnetic radiation.*

12:50 p.m. Class is over.

I jump out of my seat and am the first person at the door. As I try to spring through it, Owen taps me on the shoulder.

"You know that you and your family are stronger than a few raindrops, right?"

"Sure," I lie as I look for Basford. He's scrambling around the desks. "Come on!"

Patricia's in the room, sitting on the couch near Sam, Freddy's by the window, his cell to his ear. I check my watch. It's 12:59 p.m.

"Talking to Beatrice," Patricia whispers.

I try to sit, but I can't, not now. Finally I run over to Freddy, pulling on his shoulder. "Tell us!"

Slowly, Freddy turns around. He isn't smiling.

"Okay then," he says. "Thanks." He snaps the phone shut, holding it in midair.

It's 1:01 p.m.

"Nothing." The words sound like gravel crunching. "Not a cloud in the sky."

I move away from Freddy and fall into a chair. Sam and Patricia sit up against the cushion, and Basford looks at me, then back to Freddy.

I follow his gaze. It's like Freddy's whole face has lost its color.

"Wow," mutters Freddy. He's drawling almost.

"Maybe it is really over. If there's no rain, there's no rhubarb . . ."

I cover my eyes.

"Um . . ." Basford whispers.

"What is it?"

"Company," he says, and he points to the entryway. There, in the hallway, are about fifty of our friends. And non-friends. And perfect strangers.

In front of the crowd stands Jongy. She holds her pink cell phone, reading off of it.

"Says here it's the third time in eighty-six years . . ." she announces. We catch eyes and she smirks at me.

"Get out." Sam looms over Jongy, all two hundred and twenty pounds of him. "Now."

Power is relative; Jongy's a big deal for seventh grade, but she's nothing next to the captain of the high school football team. She spins around, but not before she sneers at me one last time.

It's only then that Patricia and I turn back to Freddy, who has slumped onto the couch. "Are you okay?" I ask him.

"I—uh . . . I feel like the wind's knocked out of me." He tries to smile, but he's out of breath. I suddenly have a terrible, terrifying thought. Could the spiders have been talking about Freddy? Is he the one who's sick?

171

No.

At that second, Mr. Horvat, our headmaster, runs into the room. Freddy tries to stand up. "I'm okay," he says. And then his knees buckle. "Maybe if I could just lie down a little."

Mr. Horvat acts quickly. "You all have two minutes to get to your next class or to study hall. Any of you who are still here, except for the Peabody siblings and you"—he points to Basford—"will be suspended." He looks at his watch. "Go!"

Our classmates push and shove each other as they scramble to turn around. Sam kisses Patricia on the cheek.

"I'll see you all later," he says softly.

Mr. Horvat looks back at us. "Freddy, why don't you go and see Nurse Skalley?" Freddy nods and slowly gets to his feet. He has his arms folded, across his chest, and he looks at the floor as he takes his steps.

It can't be. Can it?

"Maybe when Freddy's all checked out, you should go home." Mr. Horvat says it as an order, not a suggestion.

"Yes," Patricia agrees for all of us. "Okay."

Simple facts are making my mind spin. The spiders told me that someone was sick. Today Freddy basically collapses after the news. And on the day he was born

there was no rain, just like today. Just like last week.

What does it mean now, for Freddy, if the rain has stopped? The worst possible thought flashes through my mind, worse than anything conjured up by Jennifer Jong, or slugs, or even the Silo. I wish I could stuff it back where it came from, but it's gushing, over and over in my head, repeating the same sickening thought over and over again.

If it stops raining for good, does that mean that Freddy's going to die?

SAME DAY, MONDAY, SEPTEMBER 8
Dad's Plan

I don't say what I'm thinking to anyone.

And anyway, Freddy is now acting anything but sick. Nurse Skalley gave him apple juice and a banana, and now he's bouncing around the infirmary. Mom is on her way.

"I freaked out," Freddy argues. "Wouldn't anyone?"

Nurse Skalley nods impassively and hands him a piece of candy. "Your blood pressure's normal, so that's good."

"Please, I'm begging. I've got practice."

"Not today you don't," she says.

The rest of us slouch in chairs or against the iron cots. It is almost silent up here, except for the sounds of Nurse Skalley walking around. I stare out the window, looking at the green leaves of some maple trees.

No rain.

Patricia taps her fingernails together, murmuring. "I wonder what we're going to do."

"We'll irrigate," Freddy says. "Just like Dad said."

"It won't be enough," she says matter-of-factly. "It's over."

"Why do you always have to do that?" I ask. "Why can't you even pretend that there might be a way out?"

"Polly." She looks at me like I'm a toddler. "Think about it. If there are pipes, and we don't even know if there are, they'll be rusted. Nothing's set up. Nothing on our farm is figured out. Our whole family has just relied on . . ." She looks so exasperated that she sputters. "They just relied on clouds to show up on Monday morning and then built this entire empire around it."

"We have a lot figured out," I tell her angrily. "What about the rhubarb? What about the café, the Umbrella, the Transplanting?"

"If there's no rain, it all dies."

"Shut up, Patricia," Freddy snaps. "Mom and Dad won't let that happen."

"Freddy?" Mom pushes open the infirmary door. Mr. Horvat follows her inside. She runs over to Freddy and hugs him so tightly I think he's going to suffocate.

"Mom, Mom, I'm okay!" He wriggles free of her. "Really, don't worry. I think I was just expecting different news."

"Me too." Mom smiles halfheartedly. "Onward and upward!"

Patricia rolls her eyes.

"So now can I go?" Freddy asks.

"Go?"

Freddy puts on a hopeful smile. "Soccer?"

"Absolutely not," says Mom. As Freddy opens his mouth to protest, she cuts him off. "Don't waste your breath."

Mom and Freddy go back and forth about potential irrigation schemes while we drive home, but I spend the ride staring through the windows, feeling sick. Grandmom dying was the worst possible thing for me. But she was old and had a disease—not that it made losing her any better, it just made it more *understandable.*

I don't understand what you're supposed to do—how you're supposed to *think*—when your favorite aunt wants to sell your home and your brother may be getting really sick because it's stopped raining. I don't understand this at all.

When we get to the White House, Dad pulls Freddy out of the car to hug him. Then he abruptly releases him and switches to doctor mode, looking Freddy over as if he were some kind of specimen.

"I've arranged for a full blood workup," he tells him.

"Dad," Freddy says. "I'm fine. Really."

"There's a nurse waiting for you." He points to the archway of the White House.

"Uh, Dad?" Freddy gives him a half smile. "Maybe we should try the medicine you're working on? If you're so worried?"

"Not funny," Dad mutters. "It's not nearly ready for testing on people, especially not on my own son."

Mom steps toward Dad. "Nurse Skalley thought he just had a scare."

"Healthy seventeen-year-olds don't just collapse."

"I didn't collapse," Freddy says.

"Enough." Dad puts his hand on Freddy's shoulder, ushering him to the steps. "Come into the library when you're done."

As I walk up the steps, I turn around and look around the farm. I squint, trying to see the tips of the leaves from the PEACE maze. They're stretching out, extending their leaves up to the sky, begging, I imagine, for the sun to go away for just a second. Maybe I'm imagining it, but it seems like the edges of the plants look a little saggy. I try to see beyond the maze. But from this distance, it seems green and pretty, exactly like it usually looks in September.

We go into the sitting room of the Rhubarb Archives, the place where we have a library of sorts about all things rhubarb. I sit down next to Basford on the sofa. Dad stands in the middle of the room, next to a large, square-shaped easel with a PowerPoint chart on it. Beatrice, Patricia, and Mom sit all around him in various soft chairs.

"We're going to take turns," Dad says. "I've rush ordered five lake-side pumps and hoses for Wednesday. Chico is responsible for getting them to work. Here's the work schedule . . ."

Dad's spent a lot of time divvying up the property so that we can go out there, every day, with our watering cans and hoses-that-are-attached-to-pumps-that-are-dug-into-the-lake.

"Why do we have to water so much? The rain only

came once a week," Patricia asks as she types her work schedule into her cell phone calendar.

"You get more rain with a rainfall than a jerry-rigged hose," Dad says, touching the brim of his baseball hat.

"So no watering the regular rhubarb until Wednesday?" Patricia asks.

"You can water as much as you want by hand," he says. "That's what I'm going to be doing. I have to finish new tests next month for the Dunbar protocol and I can't risk my crop."

Basford's studying the chart like it's the subject of his next math test. But I can't think straight. The graph makes me dizzy, and while I totally understand why we have to irrigate, I can't shake the feeling that all of this is *wrong*. We're missing something.

"Maybe we should just sell," mutters Patricia.

I spin around. "What?"

Mom and Dad share a long look. Eventually, Mom shrugs. Dad actually allows a smile to cross his face. "Let me be clear about this." His voice is strong and proud. "She could offer me a hundred million dollars and I would say no. A hundred trillion dollars. Don't worry."

I let out a deep breath, relieved.

"Who's *she*?" asks Patricia. "And just out of curiosity, how much was she going to pay?"

"*She* is an old woman. Her name is Alessandra di Falciana. She's related to us, actually, and used to live here."

"Here? Why?" This is getting crazier and crazier.

"She's your great-grandmother Enid's sister."

"She must be a hundred," I mutter, thinking of Enid's portrait.

"Eighty-six."

"So how much?" Patricia insists.

Dad glances over at Mom. "Just a tad over fifty million."

I'm sure I didn't hear him correctly. "Fifty million?" I ask.

"Well, twenty-five for me, twenty-five for Edith."

Patricia's eyes brighten. "Maybe we should think about it." Mom instantly gives her one of her death stares. "Kidding, kidding," she says, recovering.

"Now listen." Dad's voice turns serious. "I don't want this blabbed around. No one needs to know that Edith was trying to sell our farm. It's no one's business."

"Who has that much money?" asks Patricia.

"Alessandra does. She married a duke. Or a lord. Something like that. She has enough money to think she can buy her way into anything."

"Why does she even want it?" Patricia asks. "It's not like she's going to be a farmer."

"She wants to move back. And she wants to uproot everything but the regular rhubarb. She would live here, and Girard would become the new manager. Edith had it all figured out."

"You can't sell it." Blood rushes to my head. "Dad, you can't sell it. You just can't."

"Don't worry, Polly. It would take an act of God for me to agree to this." He gives me a kind smile. "I've got it under control."

Which would be fine, except he's echoing Aunt Edith's words.

Instead, I think of Beatrice. *The bugs know what they're doing.*

When we finally leave Dad's meeting I run to my room. I pull out *Self Reliance* and the skeleton key. It's still laced through Enid's necklace.

WATER. NATURA NIHIL FIT IN FRUSTRA. +/−

Water. No rain on the farm. *Self-Reliance.* The two-headed spiders. I pick up the key, the gold necklace running through my fingers. It's all here, in front of me. What am I missing?

WEDNESDAY, SEPTEMBER, 10
Slugsand

It all clicked last night when I was staring out my window seat, *avoiding* the Dark House.

Natura nihil fit in frustra.

Nature does nothing in vain.

Spark wouldn't spell SILO unless it was important that I go there. I'm kicking myself for ignoring him before, but I guess I was just so scared of the idea that I pushed it far away in my thoughts. Not that I was thinking about anything better. In fact, yesterday was a complete loss. I overslept, wore mismatched socks, and forgot my homework. School was a nightmare. Jongy and Joe Josephs tag-teamed me with dumb jokes about the farm: *Hey, Polly, want to give up any of your umbrellas?* And also: *What do you call a farm that doesn't grow anything? The Peabody Money Well! Ha ha.* I managed to keep my head down for most of it, finishing up *Self-Reliance*. So far, my favorite line is *"A foolish consistency is the hobgoblin of little minds."* I've decided that's what Jongy's obsession with me is: a foolish consistency, which makes her (either) little-minded or a hobgoblin (whatever that is) or possibly both. The only time I laugh all day is when I imagine calling Jongy a "hobgoblin" to her face.

At least Freddy seems to be better. Dad said his blood tests were inconclusive, but they think he may have anemia. Apparently, that just means he has to eat more spinach. He's sleeping with his soccer ball these days because he's so upset about missing practice. Freddy's convinced he's 100 percent healthy. I'm not.

It's not even seven o'clock in the morning, yet the sun is already beating down on our fields. It physically hurts me to see how the lack of rain is affecting our farm. It's been seventeen days, and many of the plants seem to be swaying under the weight of their leaves. The rhubarb stalks are weak, unable to hold themselves up.

Mom mentioned the mist to me yesterday. Out of the blue, she asked me if I had seen the beautiful green fog that was spreading over our lake. I said yes and that it worried me. But Mom's not bothered by it at all; she just thinks it's pretty. Actually, I think the farm and Freddy take up all the worrying space in Mom's mind. By comparison, the mist is nothing.

I wonder what Aunt Edith is doing. Does she think of me at all? Does she know that at this very second, I'm heading to the Silo? Would she care?

No. I want to think that she would, but I think—at night, when I can't sleep, when I can't even read because I'm too upset—that Aunt Edith didn't care about me as much as I thought she did. Or maybe I'm just delusional, like Patricia thinks. Maybe the whole idea that I matter to Aunt Edith is wrongheaded. Maybe I'm just wrong about everything.

I cross the lower bridge, the one made of bronze, across the south end of the lake. There's a dirt path that leads to the door of the shed, but I think the slugsand crisscrosses it at a certain point. I have no idea where the slugsand actually is. I've worn my heaviest boots just in case.

The Dark House is about a football field's length away. To my left is the lake, sparkling and blue, as always. The mist hasn't reached all the way over here yet. I see Grandmom's bench, about fifty yards from where I stand. Teddy, Aunt Edith's Giant Rhubarb plant, remains upright, so far unaffected.

I take another step. I'm walking right on the edge of the dirt path, keeping my eyes trained straight ahead, determined to stay focused on my mission. I

find myself holding my breath as I stare at the Silo, but I don't move my head. I just march along, one step after another. I'm so focused that I almost completely miss *three black wasps* zooming straight at me like some sick air force squadron. They swoop by my head and I duck, but they switch directions fast and whoosh back, aiming for my chest. I jump out of their way as fast as I can, darting to one side of the dirt road.

My right foot doesn't land on the ground. It lands, instead, on a soft patch. A *really* soft patch. A pang of terror starts at my skull and crashes down through every bit of me as my other foot sinks, *sinks*, into the slush, the gunk, the *slugs*.

Cheese and crackers.

I'm in the slugsand.

The slugs are like snakes. Like pieces of fat wet spaghetti, black and deep purple and dark brown, flashes of yellow, moving, slithering, oily, disgusting.

A scream is stuck in my throat, tangled in the vision of the slugs. They're *everywhere*. Everywhere I move. I'm stepping in their muck, like the worst kind of pond scum—my boots squish as I force myself to move my legs, move over just a bit to the right, to the dirt road, where I can pull myself up.

184

Each time I move, my boot plunges deeper into the slush. The slugs are above my socks and on my legs, sliming my skin. They're on my legs. They're on my ankles. I'm going to vomit, I'm going to drown here, I'm going to die with slugs all over me.

But I can't do that. I can't die in the slugsand. Even though the slugs are winning. They are 110 percent, Victory-Dancing winning. They reach my knees. My left hand scrapes the top of them and the sickening gushy feeling wallops me.

No. I will not die of slugs. Who dies of slugs?

I close my eyes and raise my hands above my head, like I'm going to swan dive into the lake. One, two, three—*please please please*. And then I do it. I *dive* into the dirt road. My fingers touch the ground. I can't believe it. Using my elbows, I lift myself out of the slugsand, and end up staring straight at Beatrice—not six inches from my eyes.

"Sweet Lord, Polly!" she hollers. I don't know when she got here—I can't even think. There are still slugs, slugs everywhere. Crawling, sliming. I can't talk. It's like the slugs have paralyzed me, cutting off any sense of my feet and fingers and body. Beatrice yanks off my boots and lifts me up, as if I'm no heavier than a bag of sugar. I keep my eyes closed as she carries me all the way back to the castle, all the way up the stairs, all the way to the bathtub.

I hear my siblings and Basford, shocked, as Beatrice holds me, gripping me tight. I hear Mom saying thank you to Beatrice, and I hear the door close.

Mom has her arm around me. She whispers in my ear.

"You'll be fine, we'll just clean you off, that's it, my sweet Polly, you'll be as good as new."

Mom draws the bath and she slowly removes my clothes. She places me into the bathtub, gently pulling off slugs one after the other, putting them in a brown paper shopping bag.

"You'll be fine," she keeps saying, "you'll be fine."

I hear her, but I don't answer. Instead, I slide under the warm water and lean my head against the back of the tub.

"Keep them closed, baby. Keep your eyes closed."

I let Mom clean me, like I'm a little girl. When she's finished, I lift my arms out of the water, resting them on the ledge, and look down at my legs, still stained with slug slush. Mom squints, picking a tiny purple slug off of my foot. She dangles it in front of me before she puts it in the bag.

"What were you doing out there?"

I stare at my hands, on either side of the bathtub, instead of looking at Mom. Did Spark want this to happen? Is he on my side? "I decided today was the day I was going to see what all the fuss was about."

Mom pulls the washcloth over my face, smoothing it over my forehead, my cheeks, my chin. As she takes the washcloth away, my eyes meet hers. "You're growing up," she says quietly.

"I'm scared," I tell her. "I miss Aunt Edith." I look up at her quickly, feeling guilty. "I'm sorry. I know I should hate her."

Mom smiles. "No sweetheart, of course you shouldn't."

"You don't like her."

Mom laughs. "Not always. And not recently. No."

"I just think that if she were around, this wouldn't happen."

"What do you mean?"

"It's like as soon as she didn't get her way, she made it stop raining."

Mom lets out an easy laugh. "Oh sweetie, your aunt can do many things. Making it rain isn't one of them." But then Mom gives me a curious look. "She isn't around?"

"No," I tell her. "She took a private plane somewhere. Jongy thinks she's in Antarctica."

Mom soaks up more water in the washcloth. "Well, she never really fell in love with this place."

"How come?"

Mom starts scrubbing my other leg. "Think about it. She worked very, very hard to get to where she was. There is probably one percent of the population who can truly make a difference in this world. Your aunt was one of those people. She called the shots. She was important." Mom pauses. "If it's easier for a woman to achieve something in this world, it's because of people like your aunt Edith."

She continues. "Imagine having to come back here, to her childhood home, on a farm, making deals about trucking and rhubarb quantities after talking about ideas and philosophies and knowing people listened to you. If your dad wasn't such a goof, he could have run the farm after Grandmom, but he's always so focused on his research. Edith was kind of stuck, forced to return." Mom shakes her head. "When I'm being charitable, I feel sorry for her. I think it's very hard to come back to the place where you were a child, giving up everything you've done in some other, more exciting place. It must make her feel like she took a step backward." She chuckles sadly. "When I don't feel charitable, I think she's a power-hungry, charmless, selfish tyrant. How about that?"

I don't answer Mom because I'm picturing Aunt Edith growing up here. I didn't know until this second that I assumed her childhood was exactly like mine— that she loved the farm as I did, that she thought the exact same way as I do. But it wasn't. It was totally different.

She doesn't love the farm like I do. She doesn't think like I do. I've been wrong about so much.

Now I feel the tears.

"It's the slugs," I say, lying.

"It's okay sweetheart," Mom says. "You can cry."

FRIDAY, SEPTEMBER 12
Money

I didn't have to go to school yesterday. Mom said I was still recovering from the slugs. But she forced me out the door today. I don't know why I couldn't have just taken the whole weekend off. I don't feel like learning anything, anyway. I just want it to rain. And I want Harry to grow. And I want that stupid mist to disappear.

Someone grabs my arm. "I know something you don't know." It's Jongy.

"Let go," I grumble, trying to pull my arm away.

"No really. You'll want to know this."

"I really don't."

"Are you sure?" She smiles. "You don't care about Dunbar?"

For a second, I can't even remember who or what Dunbar is. Then I remember the name on Dad's folder during that dinner with Aunt Edith. I flick my eyes up at Jongy, who waits for me, grinning, one hand twirling her curly brown hair.

"What?"

"My father's on the board of directors there. He's not happy about the way things are going. They're going to drop your dad's funding." I feel my jaw sag. "I'm just telling you this for your own good. You've gotta start speaking up, Polly. You're way too passive."

"But . . ." I sputter, frustrated. "The irrigation system just started working . . ." This is true. Just last night, Dad and Chico rigged a pump by the lake that sprayed water over the Giant Rhubarb. We were all so happy we ran around the field as if we were playing under sprinklers.

She lets out a big, mean laugh. "Come on, Polly. Your farm's going to be completely dead any second now. Everyone knows that."

"I told you, we're irrigating."

"Great," she scoffs. "Then there's nothing to worry about." She dabs lip gloss along the lines of her big mouth. "I'm really just trying to be your friend."

Right. And I want more slugs to crawl up my legs.

"I have to go to class," I say, and turn away from her.

191

"Maybe St. X. will let you stay when you don't have any money."

"We have money," I mutter. "We have lots of money."

Her eyes tighten as she looks at me. "Your aunt has tons of money, you mean."

"You don't know anything," I tell her. "The farm's worth millions and my dad owns half of it."

"If you say so . . ."

"It is!"

"Good for you. My dad doesn't think so."

"Well, tell your dad that we could sell the farm for fifty million dollars if we want to!" The words fly out of my mouth so fast I can almost see them as they hang in the air.

Jongy's smile slashes through her face, her eyes bright and sharp.

Oh no.

"My father's going to love hearing that."

Oh no oh no oh no.

Dad explicitly said not to say anything and here I am, telling—no, announcing it to Jennifer Jong. What if she tells her dad? What if she tells her *mom*?

"Please, Jongy, don't say anything. Please. I wasn't supposed to tell anyone." I know I look pathetic, beg-

ging like this, but I don't care. She can't tell her parents.

"Oh sure," Jongy tells me. "I won't tell a soul. Cross my heart." She flashes both of her hands in front of my face. All her fingers are crossed.

What have I done?

There isn't a sports equipment closet at St. Xavier's. There's a sports equipment *room*. But I found a new spot to hide. The chapel. It's in the basement, far away from the schoolrooms, and I don't think people go there that often. It's cool. It's quiet. And no one can hear me cry.

SATURDAY, SEPTEMBER 13
Girard

I need to tell Mom and Dad what I told Jongy. What I *stupidly* told Jongy. She's going to tell her mother and then her mother's going to write about it and then everyone will know what Aunt Edith tried to do and even more bad things will happen.

It's a quiet afternoon. The churning noise of the lakeside pumps is soft, not any loud clunking. The plants alongside the edge of the dirt road are all slumping down toward the ground, which has changed from thick dark soil to light brown sand. The lake still shines under the sunlight, but I can see that the level of the water has shrunk. Before, water would slosh up against the ground, sometimes splashing up on the fields. Now I can actually see the muddy edge of the lake's shoreline.

The mist has continued to seep out from the truly

weeping cherry blossom tree and over the lake. It's covering about half of the northern part of the lake, up almost to the iron bridge. The farther it spreads, the thinner the mist gets. Now, when I pass my hand through it, it feels like my hand is passing through about a trillion soggy spiderwebs. Every time I ask Spark why he and his family are working so hard, he just bobs up and down and then zips back inside the mist, leaving his sparkling trail.

I'm trudging along the dirt road, on my way to Dad's cottage. Mom says he's been up late every night working on his research project, so that it doesn't suffer because of the extra work around the farm. I saw him for a second at breakfast; I could tell how worried he was, no matter how much he pretended he wasn't. He had given me two Vitamin Es and told me that "good things were coming! I promise." But I don't even think he believed what he said.

I'm about one hundred yards away from Dad's cottage when I hear someone calling my name.

"Polly?"

I turn. UGH. It's Girard, Aunt Edith's assistant. He stands directly in front of the sun, blocking it out like a dark, creepy planet.

"What are you doing here?" I hear how rude I sound,

195

but as soon as I see him, I can only think about Dad telling us that he wants to uproot all of our plants.

"I have a meeting with your father." Girard smiles one of his creepy smiles.

My eyes flash. *He* shouldn't be meeting with Dad. *He* shouldn't even be anywhere on our property. "Why?"

"To tell your father that the offer is still open." He smiles wider now, even creepier. It triggers something mean in me.

"You know, you're not even a farmer," I accuse. "You don't even like the farm. You want to ruin all the good parts!"

He steps closer to me. "What are you talking about?"

"The chocolate rhubarb, the Giant Rhubarb. Dad said you want to uproot all of that."

"I do," he says, looking genuinely puzzled. "It's the proper business decision." His eyes sweep across the fields. "I'm not the villain here, Polly. Neither is the buyer. I've been studying the business of rhubarb from a macro perspective." He walks away from me, lecturing. "Which means that the profit center of this farm is with the Juice Company contract. People around the world want juice. You can understand that, surely."

"People around the world want chocolate rhubarb too."

He shakes his head. "Not as much." He runs one of his hands through his thick, short hair. "There won't be any more so-called 'magic' crops." When he says "magic," he flicks the first two fingers of each hand in arcs, like he's showing me how to draw parentheses.

"You don't even like to walk in the dirt," I yell. "How can you run a farm!"

He laughs. "Do you think your aunt Edith has been getting her feet dirty all these years?"

"You're not like her," I say. "You're the exact opposite of her."

He doesn't even seem mildly annoyed with me, like he's just ignoring what I'm saying.

"Dad's not going to change his mind," I tell him.

"I'll let him tell me that." Girard looks over my head, his gaze pointed in the direction of the Giant Rhubarb fields. "Alessandra is prepared to sweeten, shall we say, our original offer."

"Why do you want it so much? What if it doesn't rain for you either?"

"It's all in the plans." Girard continues. "Luckily Alessandra is a woman of incredible means. It will require a massive reconceptualization of the infrastructure, of course. We'll be uprooting everything on the property that isn't regular rhubarb and installing a state-of-the-

 197

art irrigation system. The Juice Company is all for it."

"You'll get rid of the White House?" He nods. "And the Learning Garden?" He nods again.

"And your parents' house, the Giant Rhubarb, your father's lab, the Dark House. We may cordon off a section of the chocolate rhubarb field and see what thrives. Alessandra and I have discussed it—the Alessandra di Falciana Preserve, something like that."

"What about the castle?"

"The castle stays. Alessandra wants to live there."

My world—my whole life—is disappearing as he talks.

"You can't do this!" I plead. "This is our home!"

For once, Girard seems to really look at me. "I'm not a monster," he tells me quietly. "I realize how hard this will be for you and your siblings." He stops. "Believe it or not, I'm quite fond of all of you." He coughs, composing himself. "But children have to relocate all the time. In fact, I relocated sixteen times when I was a kid. You'll survive and it will make you stronger." He smiles. "And listen. You'll have so much money. Your father can take you guys anywhere you want."

"But we don't want to go anywhere. We don't care about the money."

In a flash, Girard's expression shifts to his typical

 198

smug face. "That's because you've always *had* money," he snaps. "People who have money have no idea what it's like for people who don't." He kicks the dirt. "They don't even know when they act like spoiled little brats because they don't know any other way."

I'm stunned.

Girard shakes his head. "Of course you don't see it. But you can't help it. You've always been rich. And now you're going to be richer. If your father stops trying to pretend he's some groundbreaking scientist."

I can't move my mouth to say anything.

"Think about it. The farm will die unless he accepts our offer." He straightens up. "Now if you'll excuse me, I need to stop by the Dark House before I see your father."

I try to imagine our farm without a White House or chocolate rhubarb or even the Dark House. I see a farm that doesn't have the name Peabody anywhere; I see a farm that's sunk back in the ground, with all the diamond sprigs and chocolate rhubarb and magic bugs.

"We all hate you," I say. "We all hate you: me, Freddy, Patricia. You're just a big, pompous loser."

Girard recoils, his shoulders drawing in, his eyes casting downward. But then he recovers, pulls himself back to his full height.

"You should tell your father to sell before it's too late. Before you all lose everything." He swallows. "And you should think about how calling people names is not only immature but unproductive." He smiles meanly. "Big pompous losers aren't likely to care if children have to leave their homes."

He whirls around and starts to stalk out of the field. I choke, as if I'm drowning in air.

"Stop!" I yell. But Girard doesn't stop walking. I run after him, breathless. "Please Girard! I'm sorry I called you a loser. Don't do this."

"Polly," he says tonelessly, "grow up. It's over."

SUNDAY, SEPTEMBER 14
The Organic Psychic

No one has to tell me that things are getting worse. I can see it every single day when I walk out to the chocolate rhubarb field. Harry, unsurprisingly, has not sprouted at all, but even all the rhubarb plants around him—the whole field, even—look pale and tired, ragged.

It's like our farm has become a walking tour of upside-down images.

So when the mist starts to take up the full northern section of the lake, I'm not surprised.

When my finger starts to throb as I walk around the PEACE maze with a watering can, I'm not surprised.

And then, when I hear Freddy couldn't even play a whole *game* on Saturday, I'm not surprised either. Don't get me wrong, I'm worried—*really* worried— just not *surprised*.

But this morning, I *am* surprised.

Ophelia Baird arrives at our house with a crystal ball, exactly like you see in movies and comic books. Nothing loony about it. Just a normal crystal ball.

"Hi Polly! The farm looks bad. I'm very concerned." Ophelia speaks in a high, strained voice, as if her nice, smooth voice was run through a cheese grater. She holds up a velvet bag. "I brought *everything*. Tarot cards, wheatberries, the crystal ball. Please get your mother! And everyone else! We should have all the spirits!"

I find Freddy in the playroom with a video game.

"Ophelia wants us upstairs." I pretend that I can't notice that his skin is basically white, like the bones of a skeleton.

"For what?"

"I don't know. A séance."

I'd never admit this to Freddy, but I'm counting on this séance thing to give us some answers.

Freddy grins as he stands up. "What are we waiting for? Maybe one of those spirits can tell my little sister here to relax so she stops looking at me like I'm some zombie."

A half hour later, my whole family plus Beatrice,

Basford, and Chico sit in a circle around Ophelia. (Actually, Dad and Chico sit in chairs behind the circle because Chico says his knees hurt and Dad is pretending to pay attention but is really sneaking looks in the papers he's hiding under his arm.) Dad has been on the phone with Dunbar all day, although I'm not supposed to know that. He didn't say anything about his meeting with Girard, and I didn't tell him that I spoke with him.

I also didn't tell him, or Mom, that I told Jongy about the sale. Every day I rehearse what I'm going to say to them. But I don't do it. Each day that it *isn't* in the papers, I think that maybe Jongy has found some streak of good in her evil mind and hasn't told her parents. Then I remember that I'm talking about Jongy, and that I should tell my parents before it's too late. And the whole cycle starts again.

Patricia keeps taking the wheatberries and eating them, right in front of Ophelia, but Ophelia doesn't care. She focuses on the crystal ball; her long, skinny, silver-tipped fingers flitting along the surface.

Patricia rolls her eyes. "I think we should be figuring out why there's an eerie green mist on our lake instead of sitting around a Ouija board," she says loudly.

203

"Don't be disrespectful," Mom whispers sharply. Mom's usually as calm as a rock, but it's obvious everything is getting to her. "It can't hurt."

Ophelia just keeps tapping the crystal ball . . . tap tap tap . . . and humming the song "We're Off to See the Wizard" from *The Wizard of Oz.*

"We're almost there," announces Ophelia. "Just one more thing." She takes out a football helmet and places it on her head. It doesn't have a faceguard, so we can see her expressions perfectly well, even though she looks 100 percent ridiculous. "It blocks the bad spirits," Ophelia explains, "like a defensive lineman."

I barely have enough time to ask Freddy what a defensive lineman is before Ophelia whirls around and fixes on Mom.

"Christina!" she commands.

Mom jerks her head up to look at Ophelia from her cross-legged stance in front of the crystal ball, her face taut.

Ophelia closes her eyes, splaying her hands on the ball. "The chocolate rhubarb in the western field asks that you discontinue *compsilura concinnata.*" Her face is stern. "I've told you that myself, I have to say. The ichneumon is much less harmful to the roots."

She's talking about parasitic bugs, another "natural"

204

form of pesticide. I think even Spark is considered a parasitic bug, since he *loves* eating mosquitoes.

Patricia groans. "Could you please stick a needle in my eye?"

"Sssh!"

But Mom smiles, somewhat relieved. "Thanks," she tells Ophelia. "But that's not—"

"Quiet!" Ophelia dances her fingers on the ball again. "Freddy! Freddy!"

"Ophelia! Ophelia!" Freddy grins.

She opens her eyes, splays her fingers again. She does not grin. "Follow the light," she says.

"What?"

She says solemnly, "The light! You'll know it when you see it."

"Uh, okay," he says.

Ophelia proceeds to give everyone something to think about. Dad has to consider the needs of his chemical solution for his etiolated rhubarb. Patricia needs to drink more water for her soul. Basford has to add more complex carbohydrates to his diet. Chico should be nicer to the sugar maple trees because they're not always happy with his pruning.

I wait for her to say something to me. But each time she closes her eyes, she reopens them and focuses on

someone else. Finally I'm the only one left. Patricia knows it too—she elbows me in my stomach.

But Ophelia just opens her eyes and smiles. "Well! That was wonderful, wasn't it?"

I can't believe it. I stick my head out farther, right in front of her face. But Ophelia ignores me.

"Guess organic spirits don't have your back," Patricia whispers.

I am so disappointed, I feel like crying. I wanted more than anything to hear something from Harry. Maybe Jongy's right. Maybe I am cursed.

Mom steps over to us and grins. "Okay, so maybe not the most productive session I've ever had, but it is good to know about the ichneumon."

"Right. And I have to go drink some water," says Patricia. "My soul is thirsty."

They laugh, and Mom leaves us to talk to Ophelia. I can feel my anger building. Ophelia is a fake. I'm a dope for even believing for a second that this could have helped.

I run to my room and pull the door shut. I'm about to flop on top of my bed, but I stop just in time to avoid sitting on the cricket. The Monster cricket.

"What do you want?" I whisper. He stares at me as if I'm the one who's supposed to tell him something.

I sense a fluttering above my shoulder. Spark hovers in the air by my side.

"I'm guessing you know about the slugs?" Spark writes "SORRY" in the air, finishing just as we hear a knock on my door.

"Polly," Ophelia says. "May I come in?"

I look back at the bed. The Monster cricket has left. Spark is nowhere to be seen.

Figures. You'd think magic bugs would be okay with an Organic Psychic, but clearly my magic bugs are cowards.

"Fine," I mutter. Ophelia doesn't look as strange now. She's removed her helmet, so she just looks like a typical mother, one who has wrinkles where she smiles and wears clothes that are just a little off.

Ophelia sits on my bed, smiling when she looks up at the inside of the turret ceiling.

"You've picked the lucky room," she says.

"Mom picked it," I say.

"No." She shakes her head. "You did."

She gives me that look that says that she knows more than I do.

"I know you're very anxious. You have so many currents swirling around in the mystical realm, it's probably hard to see straight. What to do, what to think, how to act."

207

"You saw all of this in your crystal ball?" I ask.

"No, I see all of this in you." She squeezes my arm. "I do have a message for you."

"You do?" I jump up from the bed.

She smiles widely. "You're such a believer, aren't you?"

"Believer?"

She smoothes the comforter cover as she talks. "Some people don't want to hear what I have to say. They think it's all nonsense." She drums her fingers on the bed. "They don't want to think that anything happens outside the realm of science." She turns, places her hands on her knees. "But people like you, Polly, know instinctively that our world is bigger than that."

Suddenly the Monster cricket is back, and resting on her shoulder like a black, huge parrot with bug legs.

"I presume you've met Lester?" Ophelia asks.

"I call him Monster. Monster cricket." I pause, just a little embarrassed. "Not to his face."

Monster cricket—er, Lester—rubs his feet together. Ophelia laughs.

"He doesn't care. He likes you."

"He does?"

She grins. Lester hops down and lands on her knee. "He's been trying to help. They all want to help."

Ophelia stops, curling her lips. "Spark can't come all the time. He needs to stay by the lake. But the condition of the farm breaks his heart." She closes her eyes. "Yes. There are legions of helpers, Polly. But one in particular." She pauses, directing a hard look toward me.

"Your best friend."

Ophelia says "best friend" in a way that makes me look up, wary. She stares back at me, waiting for my response.

A pounding *click click click* goes off in my brain, like the ratcheting of a roller coaster as it churns up a slope and you don't know if you're going to die or scream in delight.

"Basford?" I ask, too scared to say who I really want it to be.

"No." Ophelia smiles and puts her hand out, lightly touching my elbow. "He says his name is Harry."

I know it's stupid, but I burst into tears when I hear his name.

"Harry? Is he okay?" I leap toward Ophelia. "What did he say? What should I do? Can you tell him I'm sorry?" I look at Ophelia's dark blue eyes, remembering. "Can you please tell him I'm so sorry?"

"He knows," she says. "He has a special task for you."

"Will it bring him back?"

"I don't know."

"I'll do anything."

Ophelia looks down at her hands. "He says you have to find your ring. And then, afterward, your friends"—she gestures to Lester—"will help."

She pauses, shutting her eyes. When she opens them, she smiles. "But please avoid the slugs this time, dear. They understood you were in distress, but you did interrupt a birthday party."

I stare at my hands, my crooked finger. I lost that ring four years ago. I swam all over the lake looking for it, with no luck. It will be impossible to find it now, Spark or no Spark.

Ophelia stands. "I'm going to go help Beatrice with dinner. I need to make sure she doesn't chop off the wrong end of the carrots. It really hurts them, as you might imagine."

She smoothes down my hair. "I don't know what to do," I tell her quietly.

Ophelia nods, and gently leans down and kisses me on the forehead. "Trust yourself, sweet believer."

WEDNESDAY, SEPTEMBER 17
Fresh Air

Nature suffers nothing to remain in her kingdoms which cannot help itself.

I think Mr. Emerson is telling me that if I can't find the ring, I don't deserve to stay in my kingdom. (In my case, kingdom equals farm.) Right now, I'm undeserving.

I've looked *everywhere*. I've swum in the water under the cherry blossom tree, and I've looked in the fields, the castle, the cube, even Dad's messy lab. But I haven't found anything.

Looking in the lab ended up being a mistake. I was shuffling papers around on Dad's desk when I saw a new letter from Aunt Edith's lawyer. I found out that Alessandra di Falciana has added another *five million dollars* to her offer, which "was exceptionally generous considering the precarious condition of the property herein referred to as the Farm."

Everyone is trying to stay optimistic—even Freddy, who has had a fever ever since Sunday night. Dad wants him to go to the hospital for more tests, but Freddy flat out refused. "*I do not have to go to the hospital for a hundred and one fever!*" I think he's having soccer withdrawal. I know he's tired of people—specifically me—worrying about the fact that he's only gotten sick since it stopped raining. *I don't know how many times I have to tell you, Polly, but there is no connection between me and rain, none, nada, zilch. Stop being crazy!*

I probably don't have to say this, but it didn't rain on Monday.

And now we have a new problem. After twenty-four days with very little water and lots of sun, the regular rhubarb is dying by the acre. The Juice Company is not pleased. They keep calling and Dad keeps ignoring their phone calls. None of the other crops look very good either, despite our best effort. The only crop that looks kind of decent is the Giant Rhubarb. Maybe it's because they're bigger, or maybe it's because the plants know that they're going to be replanted soon to a place where they will get water. The shed of the Dark House has its own sprinkler system because of the Transplant-ing, although the water still comes from the lake. And the lake is not doing well either. Every day, the mist stretches out thinner and farther. Every day, the water level underneath the mist drops. Every day, we wonder whether the farm will survive.

Jongy stalked me yesterday just so she could tell me that she could not wait to come to our farm on Friday for our class trip. Mom absolutely refuses to cancel, no matter how ragged our farm looks, saying that this is a "teachable moment." Teachable for what? For Jongy to be able to make fun of me in my *own home*? Trying to explain this to Mom is useless, however, because she just says that I'm letting Jongy get the better of me when it's my farm and my house.

"But it's *dying*," I protest.

"Even if it is—which I personally refuse to believe— you're the one in control, Polly. You just have to stop letting her get under your skin."

Under my skin? She's blanketed my entire *being*. It isn't something to brag about, but at this point, I literally run away from her if I even sense her coming. I even know her schedule well enough to time my arrival to and from classes. Like today. I know she doesn't like Owen, so she won't come to science class one minute before she's due. I have a free period before science so this means that I can go to science class at least ten minutes before it starts, simply to hide from her. I know this is cowardly. But I've also been able to avoid her.

"Hey Pol." Owen strolls in the classroom, carrying an apple and a pile of papers.

"Hi," I say quietly.

"Whatcha doing?"

"Thinking."

"Excellente." He walks over to his desk and takes out what looks like a key with a white plastic blob on its head. "Want to help?"

"Sure. I guess. Help with what?"

He gestures to the closed roof over our heads, then waves the key in the air.

"What's that?"

"You haven't seen this yet? It's the key to the roof. Latest thing in all the roof-retracting buildings in the world. Or so I'm told. Want to try?"

He hands it to me. The shape on the top isn't a blob; it's a polygon with distinct sides. The key panel on the wall is actually an index-card-size plate that has a socket dug in the middle of it. The polygon fits inside, like a ball into a socket.

"Now twist it once to your right . . ."

There's a whirring noise, and then the rumbling of the roof. I tilt my head and watch it pull back, opening up to the sky.

Owen closes his eyes and does a yoga stretch. "Fresh air," he murmurs. "Can't beat it. Right, Pol?"

"Right," I say. I put the key back on his desk and walk over to the brick half wall, peering over the edge. Owen's planted a blueberry bush in a container. It's very small and there are no berries growing, just small little leaves that fall off as soon I touch them.

"Everything okay?"

"Yeah," I say. "Everything's great."

"Did you want to talk about something?"

"No. I just like coming early." I point to the sky. "You know. Fresh air."

"Exactamundo." He sits at his desk, puts on his reading glasses, and pages through a large textbook on his desk. "So, the farm's okay?" He still doesn't look at me.

"Oh yeah," I answer. "Fine."

"Good."

He turns some more pages.

"Well, not really fine," I say. "It's actually kind of bad."

He seems to study one particular page. For some reason my mouth keeps moving and more words keep falling out.

"The irrigation system Dad's trying isn't working. The plants are dying. It's a big mess. A really big mess. And I can't find this ring. And I killed my best friend."

Owen's eyes shoot up. He closes his book.

"He's a plant," I tell him, not even caring. "And there may be one root left. I keep watering him myself, but nothing's happening. He's not growing. There's also this weird mist, and Aunt Edith's gone and Freddy's sick . . ."

I blink, holding back tears. I tilt my head back and look up into the sky. *Stop crying this second, Polly!*

Owen gets up and walks over to the blueberry bush. He sits cross-legged on the floor in front of me.

"Can I help?"

Immediately, I shake my head. "No."

I wish he could. But he's a science teacher. He doesn't know about a farm.

Owen looks at me, his eyebrows knitted up in the middle of his head, like Mom does when she's worried.

"You think I'm a wacko now, don't you?" I close my

216

eyes. "I am. That's the truth. Look at where I live! We're a bunch of peculiar, pathetic wackos."

"I don't think you're a wacko. Someone like William Blake, maybe. You, nope. Not so much."

"Who's William Blake?"

"Poet. Writer. Genius. He died a long time ago."

"You're wrong."

"Nah. I'm hardly ever wrong. Well, that's not true. I'm a wrong a lot. *But* I admit it. Sometimes I even say I'm wrong when I'm right, how about that?"

"I really am a wacko." I look up at him. "Look." I show him crooked finger. "This is why Jongy hates me. And it isn't like I can do anything about it. Some women in my family have them. Aunt Edith. My grandmother."

"Polly, it's a finger. So it's crooked. So what?" He laughs. "It makes you different."

"Here's something else. I talk to bugs."

I expect him to be shocked. But he just smiles.

"Are they nice?"

"Yeah, a lot of them. The cricket's kind of annoying."

"So the problem is . . . ?"

"Well, one of them wants me to go to a place that terrifies me."

"Why?"

"Because—I don't know."

"Is it a real place?"

"Of course it's a real place," I say. "We don't live in Alice's Wonderland. It's on our farm and it looks just like the Tower of Doom. It's creepy and haunted and even though I never wanted to go there, I tried, I did—because Spark told me to go, but then I fell into the slugsand."

Owen just listens. I'm on some kind of rant—I can't stop. "You probably think this is all crazy. You're probably like my dad, right? All science, all the time."

"Actually, I'm stuck on the slugsand, frankly. Is it what it sounds like?"

"Even worse."

"Yuck." He checks his watch. "Listen, Polly. There's a big net out there, big enough for everything. Science and rain and talking bugs—"

"Spelling bugs."

"Spelling bugs, sorry, and religion and ultimate Frisbee and literature, the whole enchilada, as they say."

He stands up. "I like science. But I love *mysteries*. And that's what it sounds like you have on your hand. A mystery. Yes, the farm is in distress, Freddy's sick, the bugs and plants are talking, but who are they talking *to*? You, my friend."

I bite my lip. "I'm the only one who listens to them."

"No. You want to save your family, Little Miss Peabody. You just have to reframe how you're thinking about all this. Forget about whether you're wacko or not: You have a puzzle in front of you that you have to solve. Put your clues together. Use your mind." He grins. "In other words, let's go, Hercule Poirot."

"Who?"

"Never mind."

As I get up, the key on my necklace hits my stomach, which makes me think of its engravings.

"Wait. I do have one question." I remove the necklace and show him the key, pointing to the plus and minus signs. "What does this mean?"

"Could be anything." He hands it back to me. "I'm not sure. Math, naturally. But I don't get the relationship with water. Maybe polarization."

"What's that?"

"Polarization. Positive charges, negative charges. You've heard the saying that opposites attract? We're not really going to get into physics here, but essentially a positive charge here"—he holds out the index finger of his right hand—"and a negative charge here"—he raises the index finger of his left hand—"attract each

other. Like a magnet. It happens with all kinds of compounds, including water."

He shrugs. "But it could also be something called 'margin of error' or just addition and subtraction." He smiles brightly. "I know the Latin, if that's a help."

"I already figured that one out," I tell him. "Or rather, Basford did."

Just then, some classmates start streaming into the room.

"The ambassador, reading Latin. We are in very safe hands." He smiles again, very kindly. "Give yourself a break, Polly. You never know. The finger might be a good luck charm. Right?"

For the first time, I think he really may be out of his mind. "Sure, Owen," I tell him. "Whatever you say."

FRIDAY, SEPTEMBER 19
Class Trip

The dark thoughts came back again last night, just like they've been doing almost every night. At night, it feels like there's no way out; that we've—that *I've*—lost already. It's different when the day breaks. In the morning, I feel like there is hope—I just have to find it, whatever *it* is. Today, I decide that it would be plain wonderful to have Harry grow on the same day as the class trip. That would prove to me that the farm has a chance. I run down the stairs, headed to Harry's chocolate rhubarb field. But just as I'm about to rush out the door, I see Dad, sitting on a chair and staring out, as if he's been hypnotized. I skid to a stop and run back to him.

"Dad?"

A newspaper is on his lap.

"Dad?" I say again. He shifts in his seat, and is probably about to talk to me when I read the headline.

221

FOR SALE?
Rupert's Rhubarb Farm SOLD for One Hundred Million Dollars

Exclusive by Debbie Jong.

Today. Jongy had her Mom publish it *today*. The day of the class trip.

"Hi, pumpkin," Dad says mechanically.

This is worse than all of the night thoughts; this is reality, and it's awful. Dad's face droops; it's like he has disappointment etched right into his skin.

"I should have told you," I tell Dad as guilt floods through me. "I said something to Jongy even though you told me not to," I admit. "I'm so sorry."

"It was bound to happen." But Dad hasn't even flinched; I may as well be a robot.

Mom walks into the room carrying two cups of coffee. She gives me the saddest look I've ever seen, as if I were some kind of murderer. (I remind myself: *You are some kind of murderer. Or at least, a chocolate rhubarb plant almost-murderer.*)

Mom reaches over Dad's shoulder and takes the newspaper from his lap. She hands it to me.

Anonymous sources have confirmed that Rupert's Rhubarb Farm, home of the world-

famous chocolate rhubarb and Umbrella ride
has been sold to a private buyer for an exorbi-
tant amount of money in these tough economic
times. Attempts to reach a member of the Peabody family, including Edith Peabody Stillwater, were unsuccessful, but a close friend of the
youngest Peabody child alleged that a sale for
this outrageous amount of money was definitely
in the works . . .

Mom and Dad will never forgive me. They shouldn't.
I won't forgive me.

"I'm sorry," I say again, my voice cracking.

"Polly?" Mom's veins are popping out of her neck.
"I need you to go to your room and stay there."

"But—"

"I will come and get you. I just need some more
time to discuss this with your father."

I wish I had an excuse, but I don't. So I just turn and
go to my room.

Mom walks into my room two hours later. "You
should have told us you said something to Jennifer."
She stomps over to the window by my desk, grabbing
the drapes and yanking them open.

"Do you have any idea how many phone calls we've
received? E-mails, texts? Do you have any idea? That

223

story was carried by every major news outlet. We got a call from *Iceland* this morning, Polly. *Iceland.*" Mom slams her hand down on my desktop, shattering any attempt at seeming calm. "Your school is coming today. Today! I have to *pretend* that this article doesn't matter. It makes me feel dishonest."

She takes a deep breath and walks over to where I sit on my bed.

"I'm sorry," I say as genuinely as I can. "If I could take it back, I would. I really, really would."

After a long moment, Mom speaks. "Basford told me what she does to you."

"She wouldn't have known anything if I hadn't opened my big mouth." I look at my mom. "Mom, I'm really sorry."

She nods, short and fast. "I know. Now get dressed. Your class will be here in a half hour."

After she leaves, it's my turn to slam my hand down on the table. I've never done that before, and my hand stings. I take a deep breath, trying to control my anger at Jongy—my anger at myself. I pick up the first book I see. *Self-Reliance.* I open it up and read from a random page.

Your genuine action will explain itself, and will explain your other genuine actions.

Genuine action. Genuine action is me figuring out how to help the farm. Genuine action is *not* focusing on Jennifer Jong.

I hear the buses pulling into the castle's driveway and take a deep breath. I look in the mirror before I leave. *Pretend.* I can do that too.

I'm not out of the door, though, before Beatrice appears, swatting me on the arm with the newspaper. Her dark eyes leap out at me, angry, as she commences one of her full-blown tirades.

"What is the matter with you?"

"I know."

"I raised you better than that! Telling that girl!"

"I know."

"And this article. Don't they care if the facts are right? Any facts? One hundred million dollars? Who would print that? Does anyone care about the truth?" She swats me again, although I can tell she's reaching the end of her rant.

"I wish I could take it back."

Beatrice just looks at me sorrowfully, like I was a plant that deliberately didn't grow even after all her hard work.

"I promise you, as God is my witness, if that girl so much as looks at me in the wrong way, I'm—"

"Going to poison her with rhubarb?"

"What? No." Beatrice swats me again. "Foolish. You better be the most polite ambassador to this farm the world has ever seen. Do you understand me?"

"Yes," I say.

"Now go outside."

"Okay." I walk toward the steps.

"Wait a second!" Beatrice yells. She comes at me with a brush. "Could you just try to look a little less like a banshee?"

She pulls the brush through my hair, knots and all. It kills.

"There!" she snaps as she finishes. "At least you look like a human being. Now you can go."

Outside, my class climbs out of a yellow school bus. I see Christopher and Charlie to one side, looking up at the castle. Even if some of these kids have been to the farm before, they would have never been allowed to be so close to my home.

Margaret, the girl with the blond hair, spots me. "Hey! Polly!"

"Hey," I answer, a little tense. I wonder if my class-mates read the newspaper. But Margaret's face breaks into an honest, pretty smile. "This is really great."

Dawn, wearing pink terrycloth shorts and a match-

226

ing pink terrycloth hoodie, scurries over to me. "I've done some reports on ancient castles, like Neuschwanstein and the other castles of the German King Ludwig." She steps forward, examining the stone wall. "But I'd say that this is more like the Italian castle of King Maximilian. Am I right?"

"Maybe," I say. "The original owner was an Italian prince."

"No way."

"He was Polly's great-great-grandfather Leonardo," announces Billy Mills, who I didn't even know was listening.

"How do you know?" I ask.

"My mom has taken me here since I was little. I read it in the Archives."

Never in a million years would I think that a classmate of mine would be interested in Peabody history.

"We are so totally coming to the Transplanting," Charlie says. He's walked over with the other guys. "It's gonna rock. I can't believe I haven't been here before."

I quickly scan the farm and my classmates; the plants don't look especially horrible, at least from this distance, and the pretty blue sky does make it seem that the farm may not be on its last legs. My classmates seem genuinely nice. I feel myself start to relax.

Then someone behind Charlie announces, "There isn't going to be a Transplanting."

Jongy.

"True story," she says. "Sad but true."

"There will be a Transplanting," I say through gritted teeth.

Jongy's eyes flicker across the fields. "With dead plants? By the way, Polly. How did you like the article today?"

Everyone falls silent.

"Mom exaggerates a little, sorry about that." She smiles meanly at me.

"You should go home," says someone in a voice just a bit louder than a whisper.

I whirl around with the rest of my class. I'm shocked to see that it's Basford. His hair is wet and stuck to his forehead, and he carries a bag full of gardening gloves. He's at least a full ruler's length taller than Jongy. She glares at him and I can see how he's temporarily baffled her. Me too, for that matter. Up to now, Basford seems like someone who likes to watch from the sidelines.

"What do you know, beanpole?" she snaps.

Basford blinks again. "I know that you're a bully," he says in a low, quiet voice. Everyone stares, not just me.

None of us have ever seen anyone but Owen stand up to Jongy. He glances around quickly, as if casting a net around the castle. "Why do you even want to be here? You should go home."

"You can't make me," Jongy immediately sneers.

Then I do the weirdest thing ever. *I giggle.* I can't help it. I just keep remembering Jongy at the spelling bee, taunting the teacher with the same words. I stop pretty fast, but I've triggered something in all of my classmates: Everyone seems to be holding back laughter, even Basford.

"What are you laughing at?" she asks, embarrassed.

"You should carry a tape recorder around and hear what you say," Basford tells her. "You wouldn't believe how much you sound like a really mean person. You can't really want to be like that."

Jongy's mouth is open but no words are coming out. I realize that she's having her own private battle right now. She doesn't know what to do, or what to say.

I look over at Basford to say thanks, but he's already changed the subject. "So, Mrs. Peabody asked me to give each of you one of these . . ." He opens the bag of gloves.

Just then, Mom walks out of the castle and stands on a wooden box.

229

"Welcome!" She sounds so cheery that you would never guess how angry she is. "We're so glad you're here, helping with this important crop."

I catch eyes with Basford. He nods. I mouth the word "thanks." He gives me a small smile, then returns to handing out the gloves.

I'm ready to pick up my hand shovel when Beatrice sneaks up behind me. "Go get Freddy," she commands. "He should wake up. It's eleven thirty already."

As I walk toward the castle, Dawn Dobransky calls my name.

"What's all that?" She points to the mist. The funny thing is, it doesn't look like a mist right now. Some kind of reflective miracle has happened—the mist and the water underneath it have combined to make it seem like there's one flat, beautiful plate of blue-green glass lying on top of our lake, shot through with all different kinds of sparkling colors. At first glance, it takes my breath away. At second glance, I feel that familiar anxiety press up against my chest.

"I have no idea," I tell her, as honest as I've ever been.

I walk inside to find Freddy. He isn't in the playroom. I jog up the steps, calling his name. I check the kitchen in case he did wake up, and then I climb the circular stairs to his room. He actually has *two* rooms, one for where he sleeps, and another that leads to the rope bridge platform.

I knock on his bedroom door, but I still don't hear anything. Slowly, I push the door open.

"Hey—everyone's waiting for you." As usual, the room is a pigsty, though strangely, the windows are closed. It's stuffy. "Freddy?" I look around again. There's something pacing me, making my breath quicken with each step. "Stop it, Polly," I tell myself. "Don't be crazy."

I reach the other side of his room, the side with the platform, just as I hear someone yell from the crowd outside.

"FREDDY!" It sounds like Basford. Basford *yelling* at the top of his lungs.

I run over and yank open the door to the platform.

My brother, Freddy, is on the bridge, holding on to the rope railing. He looks ghostly, white. His knees are buckling.

From below, more people start to scream. We're *really* high in the air. It's hard not to be scared.

Somehow I stay calm. "Freddy," I say.

He tries to smile. "I wanted . . ."

I step toward Freddy as carefully as I can. I talk to him like he's a baby instead of my older brother.

231

"You should come inside," I tell him. Someone has quieted the crowd underneath us. I don't dare look at them. I just focus on Freddy. His eyes are glassy, his eyelids fluttering. I glance at his hands. They're still wrapped around the railing, holding tight. Good. That's good.

"I guess you wanted fresh air," I continue. "Makes sense. Fresh air is better than inside air. Your room reeks. You should really open a window."

"Poll." Freddy's voice is weak, but I can hear him better now that I'm closer. "You're babbling."

"I know." The bridge sways and Freddy's right hand clutches the top rope as his left clutches the left side. His left foot slips through the side. I suddenly think that even though nothing may drown in the lake, something—or *someone*—may get really, really hurt. What if there's a rock?

"Freddy, just hold on," I tell him. I make sure I keep my voice soft, quiet. I'm only two steps away. "Just hold on."

He looks over the railing, sees everyone. He tries to smile again, but he's too weak. "I heard them," he says, "but I've been having these headaches." His eyes flutter. "I didn't want to say anything, I thought they would go away."

232

I thrust out my hand. His eyes are shutting.

"FREDDY!"

He opens his eyes. He stares at me and very slowly takes one of his hands off of the rope railing and reaches for me. I take his hand, holding on as tightly as I can. I hear a sigh from the crowd below.

"Don't worry, Freddy. I've got you now."

Freddy manages a pale smile, but then his face changes and a confused, fearful look crosses his eyes. I stare back as I see his foot slip through the side of the rope railing, and while I hold his hand tighter, somehow I know we're going to fall, and we do, falling, falling, falling, forty feet down, in front of the shocked eyes of our classmates, our friends, our family, down down down into our own enchanted lake.

SAME DAY, FRIDAY, SEPTEMBER 19
Nobody's Okay

The water breaks our fall. I heard about it later, how when the two of us tumbled off the bridge people held their breath, waiting to hear the smack of us colliding with the water's surface. But that didn't happen. The water kind of opened up, hugging us as we plunged into it. I don't remember the fall at all. What I remember is waking up in the water, instantly wide-awake, like after a bad dream. Freddy was passed out next to me, so I immediately put my arm around his neck and swam upward as fast as I could, kicking with all the strength that my puny little body had. If I had been thinking more clearly, I would have remembered that he couldn't drown. But at that second, I just wanted us out of the water.

When we broke through the surface, the first person I saw was Owen. He had swum over to us holding a huge inflatable orange bubble attached to a long rope. Mom and Beatrice and about a thousand kids pulled us to shore.

I'm not sure what happened next. My teeth were chattering and I think Beatrice put a blanket around me and Mom hugged me and Basford pulled me aside. There was an ambulance that took Freddy and Mom and Chico to the hospital. Beatrice carried me up to my bed after a doctor said I was okay. Mr. Horvat put everyone into the school buses and went back to St. Xavier's.

When I wake up, it's Patricia and Basford who wait by the side of my bed.

"Is he okay?" I ask.

"Stable," Patricia answers. I blink.

"Wait," I say. "What happened to you?"

She's wearing a black eye patch across her left eye.

"I fell."

"When?"

"I was running to you guys, in the lake. I tripped and fell on top of a watering can. Fifteen stitches." She pulls the patch away. Her eye's a mess: yellow, swollen, black stitches sticking out.

"Eww."

"Thanks. You look fabulous yourself." She stands up. "I have to call Mom to tell her you're okay. I'll be right back."

After she leaves, I turn to Basford. He looks at me anxiously and then stands up, pushing his hair off his face.

"I didn't really say thanks before," I tell him. "When you stood up to Jongy."

For a second, Basford just stares at me.

"I don't like how this makes me feel," he finally says.

"What?"

"You. Freddy. The farm. You're all hurt and I can't do anything about it." He crosses his arms tightly over his chest.

"That's only because we don't know what's wrong. You'll help when we figure it out."

Basford shakes his head. "Why do you always do that?"

"Do what?"

"You can't always make things better. It doesn't work like that. Sometimes people can't help. Sometimes things can't be fixed."

I realize we're not talking about me, or Freddy, or the farm anymore. Basford's thinking about his mom.

"I'm not saying you can *always* make things better. But you have to try."

"Sometimes trying makes you feel worse." Basford stares at me for a second more, then he turns around and walks out of my room, leaving me alone. I don't call after him because I know that if my mother died, I'd be the biggest wreck in the world.

But I still think you have to try.

In a few seconds, Patricia comes back. "I told Mom you're awake and that you look okay." She stops. "Are you okay?"

"I think so."

"Wiggle your toes."

I wiggle them.

"Okay," she says. "You're fine. I saw that on a show

once. If you can wiggle your toes, you're not paralyzed. You don't have any brain swelling, do you?"

"I don't think so. How can you tell?"

She studies me. "I think you'd know."

She sits back in her chair and I stay with my head against the pillow. Neither of us talks for a long while.

"Did Mom say anything more about Freddy?"

"He's stable. Resting comfortably. Sounds like they have no idea what's going on."

"Where's Dad?"

"At the hospital." She stops. "I have something to tell you and I'm supposed to say that you shouldn't feel responsible."

I sit up higher in the bed.

"Dunbar pulled their funding," she says. "They would have done it no matter what. The article didn't help, but they had made their decision before then. Dad wanted to make sure I told you that."

We fall into silence, then she turns and looks at herself on a small wall mirror. "Sam's probably going to think I look like a dork," she says.

"You?"

She faces me with the eye patch. "I do look like a dork."

I shake my head. "Nope, you don't. You even look

good with that." I pause, thinking about something. "You always say you don't believe in magic. That's magic, though. You could go through a paper shredder, and you'd still look good." She stares at me with a weird expression. "I'm not complimenting you," I tell her. "I'm just stating a fact. I bet we could make a scientific theory out of it."

Patricia gives me the smallest hint of a smile. "Hypothesis," I continue. "Patricia always looks good. Testing: Have her trip on a watering can. Conclusion: She still looks good. Hypothesis proved."

She moves back to her chair. "I still can't believe you told Jennifer Jong about the sale," she says.

But she smiles, and I do too.

SATURDAY, SEPTEMBER 20
Grandmom

I fell asleep after Beatrice assured me that Freddy was okay. For once, I was asleep in a second. I think I have a dream—something with diamonds popping up, and psychedelic watering cans—but I'm not sure. What I do know is that I wake up completely alert at two in the morning. I know it's two in the morning, because I check my watch, which also tells me the date. It's September 20.

The day Grandmom died.

It's weird, I think, how understanding something flashes through your mind at the strangest times. Or maybe it isn't strange at all—maybe it's just some bigger force, Mother Nature, maybe, or God, waiting until the exact right moment for you to figure something out.

Spark spelled out Silo. But that's just because the

bench is right near the Silo. I'm suddenly sure that I'm supposed to go to the bench. Tonight. Right now.

If you ever have a question, Polly, just come sit on my bench.

I pull on a pair of jeans and a shirt and a pair of socks. I open my desk drawer and take out my book light.

Slowly, I open the door to my room, holding tight to the doorknob so it doesn't make any sound when it turns. I release it quietly, but when I push the door farther out into the hallway, there's a loud squeak from the hinges. I freeze, waiting for someone to come out in the hall. But Patricia and Basford fell asleep hours ago, and Mom and Dad are staying overnight at the hospital with Freddy. Beatrice and Chico are in their rooms on the other side of the castle. It should be okay.

As quietly as I can, I step down all the stairs to the living room. My work boots are lined up against the wall. I slide them on and push open the door.

It's very, very dark. The tiny beam of light from my book light barely illuminates anything and yet, here I am, taking steps in the middle of the night toward the one place on the farm I can't even bear to look at, even from the safety of my turret. But here I am, *step step step,* on top of brown dirt and a narrow, paved road, alongside unseen but dying plants.

240

There's some sense that this is directed by something—someone—I can't see. I'd like to think it's Grandmom, but I don't know. I just know *something* is pushing my feet farther and farther toward the Dark House, the slugs, the bench.

When I cross the bronze bridge, I stop. I can see the black outlines of the Dark House about one hundred yards ahead of me. My crooked finger starts to ache, but it's a dull pain next to the sudden image of Freddy on the rope bridge, dazed and gray and so unlike my brother.

This is for Freddy. This is for Freddy.

I step on something soft, making me jump. It isn't a slug. It's just a wayward patch of dirt. But the slugs are near here, I know it. I must be careful. *Step step step.*

The bench is about fifty feet away. I can barely make out its shape—its swirling framework, the tilted seat. The bench faces the lake, with Teddy, Aunt Edith's Giant Rhubarb plant, swaying next to it. It seems remarkably upright, relative to our other rhubarb plants.

The pain in my finger amps up: Now it feels like the electric shocks that shoot up my arm when I put my hand in the dragonfly mist. It hurts enough that I put the book light in my left hand and shove my right hand, clenched tightly, in my pocket. I'm not paying

attention to where I walk, and I step on another soft patch. This time, when I flash the light on the ground, I see that I have squashed a couple of slugs. *Sorry, Beatrice.*

I take a deep breath and lift my head, looking up to the moonless sky. Stars twinkle, but otherwise it's as black as the Dark House. I'm suddenly so scared, it's hard to breathe.

Something moves near the bench. I blink—it's still a black mass, but something is definitely moving. A moth? A bat?

A mutant vampire bat moth?

Coward Polly has returned. She's screaming for me to turn around, run back, pull up the covers, and shut my eyes until morning.

I take a step forward. Something moves *again*.

I'm close enough now to recognize the shape. It's a person. Someone sitting on the bench. I approach faster, shining the light to see who it is. The second I shine the light, a voice breaks through the stillness.

"Polly," says Aunt Edith from her seat on the bench. "I'm so glad you're here."

SAME DAY,
SATURDAY, SEPTEMBER 20
I Did It for You

"Aunt Edith?" My hand trembles and I stumble, my right foot almost smashing back into the muck of the slugsand. "Aunt Edith? What are you doing—how did you know I'd be here?"

"It's Friday," she says. "Well, now it's Saturday. I've been sitting here a long time."

I shine my book light at her. There she is, dazzling even under this dark, dark sky. "I had a feeling that if I sat here long enough, you might appear." She extends her hand. "Sit down."

My first impulse is to refuse. That's what Jongy would do. If Aunt Edith wanted to sell Jongy's home, Jongy would cut her off completely, no regrets, no second thoughts, no need to understand where she was coming from. In her mind, to do anything else would

243

be "passive." It's what I think Mr. Emerson was talking about: a hobgoblin with foolishly consistent thoughts, no matter what the situation.

But I'm not that kind of person. I know that about myself. I'm someone who has to hear and consider all sides. I love Aunt Edith. Or at least, I did. I think I still do. It's confusing and messed up and I don't know anything except that when I look at her, right this second, all I know for sure is that I missed her so much.

Jongy would *definitely* think I'm a pushover. Maybe she's right.

Teddy stands tall, shockingly tall, as if he's defying the lack of rain by pushing up his leaves like the most well-watered of plants. I realize that he must be reacting to the power of Aunt Edith's force field. That must be why he has energy. None of the other rhubarb plants can stand up at all.

I sit on the bench next to Aunt Edith, facing her, my back against the armrest. My crooked finger, still shoved in my pocket, feels like it's on fire.

"How is Freddy?" she asks.

"You know about Freddy?"

"Polly. Of course I know."

"He's getting tested," I tell her. "He's stable."

Aunt Edith laces her long fingers together. "I'm ter-

ribly sorry about that. You can't be out here very long. You have to get some sleep. That was a terrible fall today."

"But how—"

"Word travels fast. That bridge is a menace. I told your father not to build it." She pauses, her eyes flickering over the lake. "He didn't listen."

This doesn't sound like Aunt Edith. This sounds grouchy, like I sound when I'm mad at Patricia for not paying any attention to me.

"He liked the way the bridge looked," I tell her.

"So he said." Her voice is clipped, angry.

"I'm sorry," I tell her, "about the article in the paper."

"It was bound to happen. It doesn't matter." She turns, pressing her clasped hands against her knees. "What matters, Polly, is you." For a long second, she stares at me, serious. "Don't you want to know why?"

"Why what?"

"Why I want to sell the farm."

I don't answer her immediately. Instead, I bring my knees up to my chest, pulling my feet onto the bench. I circle my knees with my left hand, the one that's holding the book light.

"I've learned some things since you went away," I

 245

tell her. "About Alessandra di Falciana. Other things."

Aunt Edith turns to me with a beautiful, genuine smile. "Of course you did," she says. "You've always loved to learn. Even as a very little girl." Her whole face seems to brighten, even out here in the dark. "My own sons never showed any genuine appreciation for learning. Neither did Freddy or Patricia. Pleasant children. But no real interest, no seeking for anything."

Her emerald ring gleams. "But you. You're so interested in everything. You couldn't ask enough questions."

"I didn't ask everyone questions," I tell her. "Just you."

She nods. "So what did you learn about Alessandra?"

"A lot," I say. "She wants to uproot everything that matters here, she wants to keep a *preserve* here, whatever that is."

"You've been busy."

I can tell that I've pleased her, which makes me mad. Where has she been? Does she even know how bad the farm is doing? Does she know the plants are dying and that the lake is draining?

Does she know that Freddy and the rain are connected? I turn sharply and face her, shining my light directly on her face. She's startled, putting her hands up.

"Yes. I would like to know why you wanted to sell our farm," I say quietly.

Aunt Edith stares at me, her eyes trained on mine. "Good." She shifts on the bench, sitting more upright. "I have three reasons. The first is the most prosaic."

She shifts again, now facing the lake.

"I need money."

"But you're *rich*," I say immediately.

Aunt Edith smiles tightly. "I *was* rich. Now I'm not. Or at least, not as much."

"But—"

"You'll see when you grow up that there's a lot of talk about economic theory and arcane finance terms. But try to remember two rules: If you spend more than you earn, you'll get in trouble. And you can't expect other people to care about your money as much as you do."

"What does that mean?"

"I made some bad decisions and now I need an influx of money. The sale of the farm would fix everything." Her smile fades. "And your family would have enough money for the rest of their lives. Most people would be thrilled."

She sounds snippy, almost mad. It's hard to believe that Aunt Edith really needs money. But I think she's

telling the truth. She's not the type to make up stories, especially ones that show she's made a mistake.

"What's the second reason?" I ask.

A hopeful, young-looking smile spreads over her face. "I want to go back to work," she says softly. "I'm a writer. I'm not a farmer. I never wanted to be here. I did the best I could with it—made it what it is today, no matter what your parents tell you. But it was a sacrifice."

She takes a deep breath. "I spent years and years building my career, Polly, bulldozing over obstacles that other women couldn't begin to understand. It wasn't about my looks or my behavior. It wasn't about whom I married or whom I dated. It was about how hard I worked, my opinions, my *mind*." She pauses, grabbing my knees with her hands. "Polly, there was a time when I felt I was literally operating in the heavens, brushing the stars. People cared about what I had to say. People cared about what I did and, more importantly, what I thought."

She lifts her hands off of my knees, gently, replacing them on her own lap. "Then I came here. Thinking all the while that it was okay, that my family—your family—was worth it. More important than my achievements. More important than my work. No." She shakes her head impatiently. "It isn't.

"I'm going back to New York. I am going to return to the life that was meant for me to live—the life I've given up."

Aunt Edith sits back against the bench. When she turns, her eyes are glittering. "*A man is relieved and gay when he has put his heart into his work and done his best; but what he has said or done otherwise shall give him no peace.*"

"Mr. Emerson," I say, recognizing the quote.

She smiles. "This is important, Polly. Listen." I turn my face up to meet her gaze. "There's a feeling you get when you achieve something all by yourself that will bring you more peace and contentment than anything money or love can provide. Men or women, it's all the same. It is that moment when you can look around and say 'I did it'—and know no one can take it away from you. You don't need to brag about it, you don't need to try to get credit for it, because it is you, who you are, who you are meant to be."

She looks away then, toward the Dark House. "Unless you give it all up, throw it up in the air." I watch as her expression changes to all hard lines and strong eyebrows. "This farm is not who I am," she says simply.

I look at her. "You said three reasons. That was only two."

"Well, the last one, that's simple." She turns to me with a gentle smile. "I did it for you."

"Me?" I shake my head, not understanding. "But I love it here."

"I know you do. Of course you do. You're a child. But you're too smart, Polly. You have too much to offer the world to stay here." She grins. "I know you're going to tell me again what my mother told you." She imitates Grandmom's high-pitched voice. *"You can find all you need to find right here, in this rhubarb patch!"*

Aunt Edith shakes her head and speaks normally. "She was wrong, Polly. She was so wrong. For someone like you, who has me guiding your way—you can do anything, Polly! You really can!" She speaks so urgently that it propels her up, off the bench, to stand in front of me. "But you can't do it here."

"What if I want to stay here later, when I'm an adult?"

"The girl I know will grow up and understand she needs to get out into the world. That staying here is the same as surrendering to mediocrity. That keeping her gifts hidden is cowardice. That not fighting for oneself is unacceptable." She pauses, staring me right in the eye. "It isn't. It will never be."

I don't say what I'm thinking, which is that I don't

have any idea what I'm going to do, but I think it's entirely possible I can do all those things right here.

"What are you going to do if Dad won't sell it?"

"He'll sell it."

"I don't think so," I tell her. "I've never seen him so stubborn about anything."

"Dunbar just pulled their money. Now what is he going to do?"

"How do you know that? It just happened."

Aunt Edith doesn't answer. A horrible understanding cuts across my mind, silver scissors slicing open the curtain to a bright and awful room I didn't know was there.

No. It can't be.

"Did you do it?"

Aunt Edith turns her head away, toward the Dark House. This can't be true.

"Aunt Edith, did you tell Dunbar to take the funding away?"

She looks back at me. "Polly, the farm is dying. I didn't have to say much."

"But—"

She cuts me off. "Your father refused an astoundingly good offer. He would have been very well compensated to do his research wherever he wanted."

"But he's your brother—"

"He told me no." She pulls back her shoulders and suddenly, she seems as if she's sixteen feet tall. "I cannot accept that, not from someone who I've helped for so long and for whom I've given up so much. Do any of you realize that without me you would have none of this—no research, no private school, no *books*?" She's breathing hard. "I'll destroy this farm if I don't get what I want."

"What?" There is no way she said what I think she said.

"You heard me, Polly."

Doesn't she realize what she's saying?

"But what about Freddy?"

"Freddy?"

"Freddy's sick because the farm is dying, because there's no rain!"

"Oh, Polly." She gives me a sad look, like I'm the one who's ill. "Freddy isn't sick because it isn't raining."

"Yes he is," I say obstinately. "The only other time it didn't rain was when he was born. And now—now it hasn't rained in almost four weeks and he's gotten so sick . . ." My voice trails off, because I don't want to say out loud that Freddy might *die*.

"No, no, no. Polly, you're wrong about this. Freddy's sick because, well, Freddy's sick. Now look at me."

I do. I stare right at her bright, intense eyes.

"I will do anything I can to get Freddy the best medical help that exists. Do you understand that? I will get the best experts, the best everything." She reaches out and puts her hand on my shoulder. "But there is no connection between Freddy and the rain. I'm sure of it."

"If you destroy the farm, Freddy will keep getting worse."

I say this quickly, without thinking, but as I hear the words, I'm sure they're true.

Aunt Edith swallows and snaps her hand off my shoulder. When she turns to me, she's very serious.

"I love you and your siblings and your family as much as I am capable of loving." She looks pained, and I feel my heart rip again, another piece fluttering to the ground.

"You cannot solve this, Polly. I know you think you can. But you can't." She takes a deep breath, composing herself. "You should tell your father that everything will only get worse if he continues to refuse Alessandra's offer."

"I won't tell him that."

 253

Aunt Edith looks over to the lake, and I fall back against the bench. "I love you like my own child." Her voice breaks a little. "You will choose your parents. I suppose that is the right thing to do." She turns around. "I hope you never regret it."

Her face seems more resolved now and I suddenly have the feeling that a door is closing—no, a door is *slamming shut*.

I jump up from the bench. "Aunt Edith, don't do— whatever you're planning on doing. Please."

She bends down and hugs me as if it's the last time she'll ever see me.

"Good-bye Polly," she says.

"But—"

"Say good-bye Aunt Edith," she instructs.

"But—"Tears gather in the corners of my eyes.

Aunt Edith's smiles at me, a thin, lovely smile. "Say it." Tears fall down her cheek too.

"Good-bye, Aunt Edith," I hear myself say, softly, sadly. "Good-bye."

SAME DAY, SATURDAY, SEPTEMBER 20
A Green Slug

For a long time after Aunt Edith leaves, I sit on the bench. No book light, no moonlight, just me in the dark, staring at the lake.

Like the farm, I feel dry. Hollow, even, as if my blood has drained out of my body like the water is draining out of the lake.

I love Aunt Edith. But she shouldn't have tried to sell the farm. And she shouldn't get so mad just because someone told her she couldn't do what she wanted. And she definitely, definitely should not have told Dunbar about the farm so that Dad would lose his funding.

And there's something else. She's wrong.

I *am* going to solve this. I'm going to save Freddy and I'm going to make the farm live again. I am going to figure out how to make Freddy better.

I'm the biggest worrier in the world. Sometimes

incredibly horrible thoughts enter my mind and rip apart my heart. But even with all that, I can still hope that something good will happen. It's not even a choice for me: It's something that I actually *have* to do. I have to believe that something good can always happen.

In other words, I believe in magic.

I shift around and examine Grandmom's bench. It's wooden, not fancy. Slats held together by black iron side rails. I take my hand out of my pocket. Why does my crooked finger hurt so much? Honestly, Owen's out of his mind. How can he tell me this finger is a good luck charm? I flex my fingers back and forth, trying to fling off the pain. But I forget that I'm holding my book light, and it flies from my fingertips and lands in front of me.

In the slugsand in front of me.

There's no way I'm going to get it. I'd have to put my hand back in there. I'd have to touch more slugs.

But I can't see anything without it. For the first time tonight, with the Dark House at my back, I shudder. I have to get back to the castle and I can't do it in the dark.

I glance down at the muck. The book light is moving, courtesy of the disgusting spaghetti slugs,

writing and churning in the muck. Each time the slugs move, the book light flashes its narrow beam of light on more slimy creatures: big, small, yellow, gold, purple, and green.

Wait.

Green? I don't think I've ever seen a green slug.

I peer closer. The book light turns again, the slugs twisting it so that it shines directly on something solid, something shiny, something that *isn't* moving.

I jump off the bench. My crooked finger burns, so I plunge my left hand into the slugsand, closing it around the shiny thing and lifting it out of the mire.

I unclasp my hand. A disgusting black slug covers half my palm. I fling the slug away.

There it is. *My emerald ring.*

Another electric jolt goes through my right hand as I stare. The gold band, the green stone, the engraving.

For my dear wise Polly. Love, Grandmom.

I close my eyes, remembering. My ring fell off when she died four years ago. And now it's here. The book light turns again, shining light on more slugs. I take a deep breath and now reach into the muck with my opposite hand, the one that's in great, extreme pain. As my fingers circle around the black coiled neck of the light, my hand feels as if it's on fire. The slushy, watery

257

slugsand oozes over my wrist, my fingers, sickening me. I grasp the light and pull at it, hard, but it doesn't come. I tug some more, but it seems like the slugs are also gripping on to it, lacing my light to their bodies, pulling the light into the muck. It's an insane tug-of-war.

I crouch down, clutching the light as tightly as I can even though it means that now my hand is fully covered by the muck. Just as I am ready to yank the light away from the slugs, something stops me. Something I can't explain.

In the air above my hand, my *burning* hand, a thin column of white smoke rises from the muck.

My eyes open wider and I look down. The slugs are getting scorched and the watery mud around it is hot. *Hot*. With one massive tug, I yank the book light up, shining it over the muck. The vapor instantly dissolves. My finger burns.

What just happened? What *was* that?

"Polly Peabody!" A sharp voice slices through the air. "Polly Peabody, is that you?!"

SAME DAY,
SATURDAY, SEPTEMBER 20
Third Graders

It's Beatrice. She looks at me as if she doesn't know if she should scream or take me into her arms.

"What are you doing out here, with your hand in that muck?"

I don't know what to say, so instead, I pluck off two slugs that have attached themselves to my book light. When I fling them away, as far as I can toss, Beatrice flinches, grabbing on to the back of the bench, like she's in pain.

"Don't do that!" she mutters.

"Do what?" I move toward her, my arm around her shoulders. "Are you okay?"

She shakes her head like I'm some kind of nincompoop. "I asked you not to hurt them," she says.

"I didn't hurt them. I just—"

259

"Threw them so they landed smack on the ground, like a rock hitting a pavement. What's wrong with you?"

"It's a *slug*."

"It's a bug," she clarifies. "And you can't throw bugs around, because if you do, it feels like lightning strikes me clear from my head to my toes."

I stare at her dumbly. I don't understand.

"When a bug on this farm is killed, I get hurt. Okay? Even when a bug is hurt, I feel it."

"*What?*"

"You heard me, Polly. And don't go telling everyone my secret, okay? It's not something I talk about around town."

"I can't throw around bugs?" I sputter.

"No. You can't. Killing them is worse. That hurts so much that sometimes I have to cram a dishtowel in my mouth to keep from screaming." She lifts her hands off of the bench.

"You get hurt every time a bug dies? For real?"

"For real."

"Why?"

She shrugs. "I don't know. It used to affect my parents too. They lived on a sugarcane farm. Always said it was because we liked to be outside so much, it became a part of us."

She's solving a puzzle that I didn't even know existed. "That's why you came out that night—when I fell in the slugsand. Right?"

Beatrice nods. "Felt like a million needles puncturing me, all at the same time."

"Does anyone know?"

"No. Well, your grandmom did. But no one else. That's the point of a secret; it doesn't help anything to be let out to the world. No one should know."

There's one more slug on the book light. I pick it up and carefully place it on the ground, never letting my eyes leave Beatrice's. A small smile sneaks across her face.

"Perfect," she says softly. "Thanks." She puts her hands on her hips. "Now, what in the world possessed you to come out here at this hour?"

I think about the correct answer. "Grandmom," I finally say. "But someone else was here already."

Beatrice nods. "Edith?"

"How'd you know?"

"I remember the date of your grandmother's death as well as anyone. What did she want?"

For a second, I stare at Teddy, the Giant Rhubarb plant, who has now flopped over, like a dead green tree. I was right about Aunt Edith's force field. It was literally holding Teddy up.

Just like it usually holds me. I cross my arms tightly around my chest. "She said good-bye," I say very quietly. When the words hit the air, I think my heart is breaking.

I'm glad that it's so dark outside. This black night is perfect for the way I feel when I think about Aunt Edith: confused, alone, and sad.

"I'm sorry, Polly," Beatrice says simply.

"She told Dunbar the farm was dying. That's why they're not giving Dad any more money."

Beatrice nods, like she isn't surprised.

"And then she said she'd destroy the farm if Dad doesn't change his mind about the sale." I take a step toward Beatrice. "That's what people do in third grade."

Beatrice smiles at me. "Adults act like third graders all the time, Polly." She glances over at the lake, and then turns back.

"Let me tell you a story. One time at Christmas, Edith bought her mother this gold necklace from a fancy city jeweler. She was about your age, and had saved up a bunch of money to buy her something expensive. But your grandmother never liked presents like that. The only jewelry she ever wore was that emerald ring, and that's only because it came from her mother. She'd rather Edith make her something or work with her at the farm. So your grandmother told her that she would have been better off saving her money for a rainy day and learning more about the farm."

Beatrice shakes her head. "Edith was furious. But even more than that, she was hurt. Not that she'd ever admit it. She took the necklace back, got the money, and bought herself a fancy pen with gold trim and used it for all her assignments at school. I think it was the start of all her writing."

Beatrice leans back against the bench. "God knows, I loved your grandmom. But she made mistakes. She could have stopped trying to make Edith her little replica. She could have recognized all that was special about Edith. But she didn't. No one was surprised when Edith left.

"But parents are just people. Tall third graders. It's hard to find balance between your own stuff and your children—and the whole time you just watch as they grow up and you have to accept that they're a whole different person than you are. It's hard." She smiles. "You plant watermelons, out grows broccoli."

"I'll never forgive her," I say stubbornly.

"Never use the word *never*," Beatrice says. "It always bites you in the bottom when you least expect it."

Beatrice pushes herself up to the edge of the bench. "You have to get to bed."

"No," I say instantly. I suddenly remember the weird stream of vapor that appeared when I put my hand in the muck. "I need to stay here."

Beatrice gives me one of her nonnegotiable stares. "Not a chance."

"But—"

"Whatever you're looking for isn't going anywhere."

"I'm not looking for anything. I just *found* something."

She stands up. "What'd you find?"

"This." I flash my emerald ring.

"Where'd you find that?"

"Over there," I say. "In the muck."

Beatrice smiles. "You know, your grandmom lost her ring once too. When she was just a kid. She'd gone swimming and it fell off in the lake. Sound familiar?"

"Why didn't you tell me?"

Beatrice ignores me. "Then she found it right around here, about ten years later when she turned eighteen. Afterward, she told me the stone needed to roll around, soak up the dirt and the lake. Go back to its roots."

"What roots?"

"What are emeralds but stones, Polly? What are

stones but minerals squished together in the earth? Don't they teach you anything in that fancy school?"

My head is swimming. "But why?"

Beatrice puts her thick arm around my waist.

"You have the answers," she says. Beatrice pushes me down the path to the dirt road. As she walks, she points to my head. "The answers are all in here." Then she points to my heart. "And in here. You gotta think first, and then make sense out of it. Then you can figure out what to do."

"But I think I just figured out—" I stop. I'm not sure what to even tell Beatrice. That I saw a vapor rise from the muck?

"Not tonight, Polly," Beatrice says. "I promised your mom I'd take care of you while she's at the hospital. You can't fall off the bridge and see Edith and think it's all going to be solved in one second. Doesn't happen that way."

We walk the rest of the way without talking. I glance at my ring, noticing for the first time that it's not a perfect circle—that it's cut more like a stop sign, with eight gleaming green sides. Did it gain some power in the muck? Why didn't Grandmom tell me about this? Is Patricia's ring going to fall in the lake too?

The good news is that the farther I get from the

bench, the less my finger hurts. I glimpse Beatrice's face as we walk; her lips are pressed together tightly, but she's smiling.

"What is it?" I ask as we reach the castle.

"Just thinking about secrets," she says. "Know what I mean?"

"I won't say a word," I tell her.

"You're a lot like your grandmom."

I reach out then, touching Beatrice's soft arm above her elbow. "I *am* going to save our farm," I tell her, looking her in the eye. I don't say this like a crybaby or a showoff. I'm just telling her a fact, like George Washington was the first president. Still, I wait for Beatrice to tell me that I'm wrong, that I'm too young, or too scared.

But she doesn't do that. "I hope so," she tells me. "I really, really do."

SAME DAY, SATURDAY, SEPTEMBER 20

Genetics

I'm completely disoriented when Patricia throws off my covers and tells me that we're late.

"Late?"

"To visit Freddy at the hospital," she says. "Come on!"

It's only eight o'clock in the morning. I've been asleep for maybe three hours. Still, I jump out of bed and grab clothes. Later, when I climb into the car, Patricia notices my ring.

"Hey! Where'd you find that?"

"Near the lake," I say.

"I *knew* you'd find it," Mom exclaims from the front seat. "Maybe it's an omen. A good omen, for once."

When we get to the hospital, Mom has an appointment with one of Freddy's doctors. She tells us where to go, and Patricia and I walk slowly to his room, both of us eager to see Freddy but scared to see him too.

"Here it is," Patricia says when we reach the outside of Freddy's hospital room. "I'm going to call Sam first. Then I'll be right in."

"Did he think you looked like a dork?" Patricia's eye patch doesn't make her look odd. It makes her look even *more* beautiful.

"He said I reminded him of a pirate." She reddens. "A *sexy* pirate."

This may be the first time I've ever seen Patricia blush.

She sees me smiling at her and scowls, which makes

me smile even more. "Take this," she says, grabbing a brush from her bag.

I'm still grinning as I yank the brush through my hair. She's already dialing the number when I give it back to her, and she puts it back into her bag without looking.

When I face the hospital room again, my smile fades. I haven't seen Freddy since they put him in the ambulance yesterday. I push open the door.

Freddy is asleep in a hospital bed with steel railings. The sheets are white, and there's a blanket pulled up to his neck. It is pretty warm outside, but Freddy is shivering. Although, if I'm to be honest, this is the least of his problems. One side of his head has been shaved, and he has an oxygen mask on his face.

"Hi," I say. His eyes are closed. *How did all of this happen so fast?*

Dad reads from a notebook, checking something with a thick manual he holds in his other hand. His hair stands at an odd angle from the rest of his head, like he pulled it to the right and left it there. A man stands next to him.

"Hi, Dad," I say.

Dad looks up and tries to smile. "Hi, Pol. This is Emory Jackson, Freddy's doctor."

Dr. Jackson is really handsome. I don't usually notice

this kind of stuff, but he's tall and has thick, dark, wavy hair and a really nice smile.

"Hello," he says.

"Hi. How's he doing?"

"I think he's . . ."

"Hey Pol," Freddy whispers.

I turn to my brother and for a brief instant, I see him as he was just two weeks ago, assuring me it was going to rain.

I hadn't realized he was awake. His eyes are barely cracked open. I can only look at him for a moment before I shift my glance to the big windows on the side of his bed. There are huge sycamore trees outside of his room.

"Hi," I say to Freddy, still looking at the window.

"Scared?" he whispers.

"No," I answer immediately.

I hear Freddy laugh, a weaker laugh from how he usually sounds, and I turn. "I look like a shaved-head weakling, right?"

I try to look at him scientifically. "Yes," I say. "And you're gray."

He laughs again, that weak, watered-down laugh. "Like Dad?"

"No, your face. Your face is gray."

"They're not giving me any mirrors."

"Well, I'll tell you the truth," I say.

He smiles weakly and flutters his eyes closed. I gasp, but in a second he opens them again. "Slow down, Polly. It's not that bad. I'm just tired."

"Right. Tired people always have all these tubes and oxygen." I look back at Dad, who's completely focused on his books. "Why did they shave your head?"

"Something about my brain." He says this pretty matter-of-factly, but his eyes look serious. "They're going to do some more tests."

"They don't have any idea? Why has it happened so fast? It's been crazy fast, right?"

"No answers," Freddy says. "Dad keeps giving me Vitamin E pills, like that's gonna do anything."

"Maybe he should squeeze some on your brain," I say.

"He would if he could," Freddy said.

His eyes are the same, still bright blue and shiny, and I force myself not to concentrate on his gray skin, his white lips, the eerie way you can see blue veins crawl across the sides of his forehead.

Dr. Jackson leaves the room as Dad walks up to the bedside.

"Are you okay, Polly?" He's looking at me strangely.

"I'm fine," I tell him.

He holds me out at arm's length, looking at my eyes, my appearance. "Are you sure?"

"Yes, why? Don't I look okay?" I'm getting nervous.

"It's the hair," Freddy whispers.

"That's it!" Dad grins. "You brushed your hair."

"Not funny," I tell them.

Just then my mom walks into the room. She goes straight to Freddy and kisses him, as if he's not gray and lying there like a long, thick slab of stone, but like he's the little boy from the baby pictures, all fat and happy.

"Still cold?" she asks him.

"I'm okay," says Freddy. "Tired."

"Polly's been chattering away?" Mom turns to me.

"No," Freddy says. "She's been telling me how good I look."

Mom reaches over and grabs Freddy's hand from under the sheet.

"You look fine," she says. Mom grips his hand as if there isn't any tube at all, that he's just another seventeen-year-old boy who is holding hands with his mother.

We watch Freddy as he falls asleep.

Despite Aunt Edith's assurances last night, I still have

to ask my parents the question I can't get out of my head. I lean over to make sure that Freddy's asleep so that he doesn't hear my question.

"Do you think that the reason Freddy's sick is because it isn't raining?"

A sad smile creeps over Dad's face. "Oh, honey, I understand why you think that. But no. It's just a terrible coincidence. Whatever Freddy has, my guess is that he's had it for a long time."

"A long time?"

"It's what I was afraid of before, when it seemed like it was just anemia." Dad pauses. "I think it's genetic."

"Genetic."

"My dad had a genetic mutation that can cause the nervous system to start to fail. A common symptom is anemia."

"Granddad fell off a horse," I say.

"Yes, but he fell because his nervous system was giving out."

"This is good news!" Granddad didn't die until he was an old man.

"No," Dad says gravely. "No, it isn't good news, Polly. If Freddy does have my father's disease, he's going to be sick until some kind of remedy is found. Also, the fact that he's contracting it at an earlier age is . . . troubling."

272

"What I meant is that if all Freddy has is a genetic disease, if it doesn't have anything to do with the rain, it would be a good thing. He could live for a long time."

I smile at Mom and Dad, but they look sadder than before.

"What? Wait a minute. Are you saying he *isn't* going to live for a long time?" A horrible thought blazes up in my mind, a sudden fire I can't stop. "Is he going to die?"

My dad holds his finger up to his lips, warning me to be quiet.

"We're doing one day at a time here," Mom admonishes. "Nothing more, nothing—"

She's interrupted.

"I'm not going to die." Freddy's awake.

He's speaking so softly, I can barely hear him.

"But—"

"Seventeen-year-olds don't die," he whispers. Mom reaches over and holds Dad's hand, and I realize that we're all thinking the same thing.

Seventeen-year-olds do die. Rain or no rain, they die all the time.

SAME DAY, SATURDAY, SEPTEMBER 20
Heat

My tree weeps. My beautiful, lacy weeping cherry blossom tree sobs in front of me, tears falling from its pink petals as I stand underneath its branches.

There is no mist under here anymore, although I don't think it's why the tree is crying.

The tree cries because the farm is dying. We can't pretend that it isn't happening. The mist now stretches over the lake, exactly as it did four years ago. If it is protecting the water underneath it, it's not doing a terrific job. The lake is still shining, still crystal blue, but it looks about half full. If we're lucky.

The dragonflies have left my tree too, going with the mist over to the lake. Thousands and thousands of sparkling dragonflies still spin their green mist, an army gone to war against the relentless sun. I now believe the mist has good intentions. But it isn't paying off.

I'm wearing my emerald ring on my left hand because my right hand started to ache as soon as I walked over here. When we left the hospital tonight, Mom tried to hide the fact that she was crying. Patricia and I didn't say anything either. Now Mom's back at the hospital, this time taking Basford and Beatrice with her. I came straight over here. I have a theory I need to test. I've been thinking about it ever since we got into the car at the hospital.

The whole way home, as Mom pretended to smile and Patricia pretended not to notice, I stared at my crooked finger. Mom was talking about how fun it would be when Freddy returned home from the hospital and how she hoped it would still be warm enough for him to go swimming in the lake. It made me remember that last time I went swimming, with Basford and Patricia, when Patricia accused me of peeing because the water around me was so warm.

Which made me think about the bottle I held during science class, when the water boiled inside the plastic and I showed Owen my crooked finger.

Which made me think about last night, when I pulled out the book light from the slugsand, and the stream of vapor lifted up from the watery muck.

Which is why I'm here, right now, at twilight. With my own scientific inquiry.

THEORY

Hypothesis: My crooked finger can create water vapor.

Testing: Put finger in water and observe if heating causes water vapor to rise.

Result: ?

Before I walk to the water's edge to test my theory, I turn to the weeping cherry blossom tree's narrow trunk.

"You're very pretty," I say, which I know sounds dumb, but I don't want to lie and say everything's going to be okay, because I don't know if it is, and I don't want to tell it to stop crying, because there's a part of me that wants to cry right now too. So I do what I think makes sense: I tell my pretty tree that it's pretty. Which is not a lie, and which is something a lot of things—people, anyway—like to hear.

Then I walk to the water's edge. Without any hesitation, I kneel down and thrust my right hand, the one with the crooked finger, into the water.

My chest gets tight and my eyes go wide as I feel a bolt

276

of sharp pain strike through my finger, lighting up my arm to my shoulder. I force myself to focus on the water, which has begun to swirl around my hand in small circles, a scant foaming crest appearing on the water's surface. Another pang shoots through my arm, but I keep my hand swallowed up by the lake, as I feel the water grow warmer, as the water grows intensely hot.

And then, just like last night, I watch something incomprehensible happen, as another electrical *ping* runs up and down my arm.

Very, very slowly, up past my eyes, up to the lowest hanging petal of the cherry blossoms, a trail of vapor starts to rise from the swirling water. I can see it, thin droplets of water smearing into the air, forming a blotted column of water vapor. Just like we learned in science class, the vapor rises, up, up, up, past my eyes—past my head—moving so high that I have to crane my head back to look at it rising up and through the tree branches.

I've never seen a ghost, but I think the vapor might look like one: It's white-ish and thin, and if you look at it a certain way, it could look like a very skinny phantom without a face. I forget about the pain in my finger; I just stare at the vapor continuing to rise up into the air.

Then it hits me.

Water heats to form vapor. Vapor condenses into ice crystals as it rises. And ice crystals form . . . *could it be?*

Ice crystals form a cloud. That's a fact. Ice crystals form a *cloud*. And from a cloud can come . . .

Rain.

At first, I feel a warm sense of triumph seeping through my bones. But just as I'm about to scream from the thrill, from the magic swirling around me—from *my* very own magic—those bright scissors in my mind return, cutting sharply through another curtain, revealing another truth that is terrible and ugly, and true.

Aunt Edith has a crooked finger. Aunt Edith could do this. Aunt Edith *was* doing this. Aunt Edith is deliberately not doing this now because Dad told her no.

Aunt Edith knew I could do this and *didn't tell me.*

Aunt Edith *wants* the farm to die.

I yank my hand out of the water, falling back on the shore, trembling.

Aunt Edith. *My* aunt Edith.

I can't help it, I start to cry, and the lacy pink petals of the cherry blossoms start to cry again too. I sob, and my tree sobs, and it feels as if it's all I will ever do.

But my finger throbs, and it jolts me out of my

heartache. My finger. I look back over to the water, watching the tail end of the skinny vapor keep winding its way upward. It is far too skinny to make a cloud. I'm still missing something.

I press my eyelids closed, thinking about Aunt Edith, willing her to tell me this one last thing. Willing her to tell me how to make it rain on our farm again. Willing her to be my savior one more time.

But then I feel myself harden, as if that force from before—the one that propelled me to the bench on the anniversary of Grandmom's death—has yanked the controls away from Aunt Edith and switched the focus from her to me.

Is it Grandmom? Mr. Emerson? Mother Nature? God?

I don't know. I just know the message.

Trust thyself: every heart vibrates to that iron string.

I go back to my scientific process, now feeling like a professional scientist.

THEORY 1

Hypothesis: My crooked finger can create clouds.

Testing: Put finger in water and observe if heating causes water vapor to rise and condense.

279

Result: Vapor rises. Kind of.

NEW PROBLEMS:

Vapor too skinny to do much of anything. How can I make the evaporation more powerful?

THEORY 2

Hypothesis: Need to get one.

MONDAY, SEPTEMBER 22
Mutations

Last night, after I got back from the cherry blossom tree, I almost told Basford about making the vapor. He was in the playroom, staring at the wall, although as soon as I entered, he snapped open one of his history textbooks and pretended that he was working. I think he was surprised that I was energetic; he was the complete opposite, his long frame sunk into the cushions of the sofa, his eyes downcast and sad. I opened my mouth, ready to tell him why I was so energized, when he cut me off.

"Did Beatrice ever tell you about the devil's needle?"

"Devil's needle? No. What's that?"

"That's what they call dragonflies in Bermuda. That's why I stared at it that first day on the porch. Some people think dragonflies find evil spirits and stick to them, trying to ruin their lives."

"That's crazy," I told him. "Grandmom loved dragonflies, which means they have to be good."

"They bring bad luck," he said stubbornly.

"What's the matter with you?"

Then he gave me this sorrowful look like I was the only person in the world who couldn't see what he was seeing.

"Have you noticed everything that's happened? All the bad things?"

"It's not because of the dragonflies," I said, thinking of Aunt Edith. "It's because of a person."

"Exactly," Basford said, but he looked at me strangely. "That's what I think too. The dragonflies are just one of the bad omens."

"No," I argued. "It's the person who is the bad omen." I wondered if he knew about Aunt Edith too but before I could ask him, he said he was tired and wanted to go to sleep.

Since then, Basford hasn't talked to me. On the way to school this morning, he kept his lips closed tight, staring out the window. When we got out of the car, everyone rushed to me to ask about Freddy, and Basford instantly disappeared. I think I'm going to have a chance to ask him what's wrong in science, but just as I sit down, Owen enters the classroom.

"Hello, hello, hello," Owen says. "Please tell me you did the homework, Eve."

"I'm Pia."

"Of course you are."

My thoughts wander back to the vapor. If I could only figure out how to make more of it; generate more heat, perhaps, or maybe make it wider, thicker through some other method I haven't figured out. I sit back in my chair, my eyes inadvertently locking with Owen's for a second. I pretend I've been paying attention.

" . . . each of our cells have twenty-three pairs of chromosomes," Owen is saying. "Half contributed by your mom, the other half from your dad. No choice involved, thank you very much. You there wanted your mom's big brown eyes? Not so fast! Someone in your family had those green suckers and that's what you got. But today, everything's changing. Genetics, the new frontier! You can alter some individual traits. Right? Think about it."

Wait a second. This is what Dad was talking about yesterday. About Freddy.

I don't even raise my hand. "Can you change them? Your genes, I mean?"

"Change? Like change, change, make blue eyes brown, without contact lenses? Not exactly. Some scientists are

learning how to manipulate genes. And sometimes genes get all willful and manipulate themselves."

"How?"

Owen notices the worried tone of my voice, but he pretends as if this is all still a normal class discussion. He turns back to the rest of the class.

"It's called, ladies and gentlemen, *mutation*."

"What does that mean?" asks Margaret. "Mutating?"

"Come on, Marcia! Have you not seen all those movies with mutants?"

"Mutants have something messed up," says Charlie. "Something in their chromosomal line. Right?"

"Well, they have something that isn't typical," Owen says. "I wouldn't say it's necessarily messed up. Sometimes supremely superb things happen."

"Like what?" asks Charlie.

"Like superheroes," Owen answers. "I *love* superheroes."

"They're not real," scoffs Jongy.

"But they illustrate the example," Owen answers. "All mutations aren't a bad thing. Or rather, all mutations don't result in something bad, or diseased. Some actually have pretty amazing consequences. Think about it: What is evolution but a series of mutations?"

I sit up straight in my chair. "Is that what a genetic disease is? A mutation?"

284

"They're all different. But let's take the big one. Cancer. Cancer isn't inherited. An inclination to having a specific kind of cancer can be dictated by the kinds of genes you have, but it isn't a straight-up inheritance. It's like having a great relationship with your grandfather, who *may or may not* leave you with a lot of money. Possible, not definite."

"But what about other diseases?" I say.

Owen knows why I'm asking. "Diabetes? Genetic component. Bad heart? Genetic component." Owen chews on the end of a pencil. "We can work on those because we've figured how to manipulate the mutation."

There's a sad look in his eyes as he continues. "But there are some genetic diseases that we haven't figured out at all. All we know is that the mutation exists. Without a remedy, no matter what we do, we cannot change it. No matter how well we eat, or how much we exercise, the mutation will not change. Hardwired."

"Can someone figure out the bad genes, the ones screwing it all up?" I hear the change in my voice; it's shaky and scared. Everyone's staring at me, including Basford.

Owen sits back in his chair, placing the pencil slowly on the desktop. "I'm sorry, Pol. I wish I could tell you

something different. But there is no exact date. Scientists are working on this kind of stuff—people like your dad try to figure out the gene sequences, or else find some kind of remedy that relieves the symptoms, but there's no exact date."

He looks up to the class. "Here's something to think about, all you future politicians and scientists. It becomes a question of priorities, and funding, and general interest. Science, as a rule, is never as interesting as, say, gossip. People think that there's no room for humor, for accessibility, for magic. We're to blame for it—scientists, I mean. We like to be the king of the mountain, taking credit, assigning blame, not sharing." He pauses, cracking a small smile. "Not me, of course. I'm here with you. But the good news is that there are a lot of people working really hard, every day, to solve these genetic puzzles. They've made a lot of progress, and there's no reason to think they won't continue to do so."

"Soon?" I can't help it, even though I know the answer.

"No one knows," Owen says. "Like anything, you've gotta go one day at a time."

That's not good enough. I don't think Freddy has much time.

TUESDAY, SEPTEMBER 23
Ask for Help

When we get home from school, Beatrice tells us that we can't go to the hospital.

"Why not?" Patricia asks.

"Your brother needs to sleep," Beatrice says. "He's been in tests all morning. You can go tomorrow."

"Why don't they give him something? What about Dad's medicine? Maybe that would work?" I ask Beatrice.

"I have no idea, and don't you go mentioning it to them," she warns me. "They're already going out of their minds." She stretches her arms wide and herds us over to the castle. "Once you've done your homework, go and visit your Mom, Polly." Beatrice puts her hand on my shoulder. "She's a wreck."

Then Beatrice turns to Basford, who's leaning against the wall. "I made some strawberry rhubarb soup," she says. "Come have some."

Basford's eyes flicker around the room, briefly stopping at both Beatrice and me. He shakes his head so that his hair flops over his eyes, and leaves the room without even answering her.

"He's in a bad mood," I tell Beatrice.

"I got that," she says. "Everybody needs to sort this out themselves, I guess."

I walk down the hallway to Freddy's room, the one with the platform leading to the rope bridge. But I shudder as I push open the door; it's the first time I've even come near here since I fell last Friday. I try to remind myself that it wasn't the rope bridge's fault we fell. Freddy's foot slipped.

Outside, the rope bridge seems as sturdy as it's ever been. There is no wind at all. But as I take my first step, the hair on my arm rises so high I feel like I'm going to transmit sound waves.

I turn back and walk to Basford's room. I want him to help me across.

He's in Freddy's other room, at Freddy's computer.

"What're you doing?" I ask.

Basford turns around, hair flopping over his eyes. On the screen, behind him, is an image of Freddy's team in the middle of a soccer practice.

288

"I'm livestreaming his practices and editing them together. Then I'm going to burn it all on a disc." He's speaking so low I can barely hear him.

"What for?"

"So he doesn't miss anything."

He turns around and focuses again on the monitor. His hand is on the computer mouse, but it doesn't seem as if he has anything to do.

"Basford," I say.

He ignores me, pressing on the mouse a few times.

"Basford."

I watch his hand freeze. Slowly he wheels the chair around to face me. I can't see him behind his bangs.

I reach out then and push his hair away from his face. His eyes are red-rimmed. He's crying.

Basford's *crying*.

I let go of his hair and let it fall back in front of his eyes. He turns the chair around.

"That's a good idea," I say softly. "Freddy will like that."

Basford's hand is on the mouse again, as if he's about to go back to work. But I see his shoulders shake, and I know he's still upset.

"Thanks." Basford's voice is muffled.

"Sure," I say. I'm ready to walk out of the room

when I glimpse a duffel bag leaning against the wall. It's filled up and zippered, and there's a nametag hanging over the dark green canvas.

VON TRAMMEL.

"What's that?"

Basford doesn't turn around. "What?"

"That duffel bag."

It's one of those moments when your sense of sound goes into overdrive. This is why when I hear Basford tell me he's going back to Bermuda, I have to cover my ears, close them to the echo chamber of words I don't want to hear.

"I'm the bad omen," Basford says, pushing out his chair from the desk, spinning it around. "Just like you said. I'm the reason all the bad things happened." He speaks like what he's saying is the most obvious thing in the world. "Ever since I came here, your farm started to die. If I go home, it will live."

I grab on to the foot of Freddy's bed, swinging myself around so that I can sit down.

"I never said you were a bad omen."

"Yes, you did. You said it to me. '*The person is the bad omen.*'"

He's getting everything so wrong. "No! I was talking about—"

Do I want to tell him about Aunt Edith? I can't. Family secrets.

I try to straighten out the crooked words in my head. "I wasn't talking about you. I was talking about someone else, someone who *isn't* an omen. Just someone who's—someone who is deliberately trying to mess everything up around here. Not you."

"Who?"

"I can't tell you."

"You can't or you won't?"

"It isn't you, Basford."

He turns away from me, walking over to the window. "I still think I should go. You asked me if I noticed all the bad things that happened. Well, I have. Starting with that dragonfly who flew around me on the porch."

"That dragonfly is my friend!"

Basford lifts his eyes to mine for a second, curious.

"His name is Spark, and he's a *good* omen, not a bad one. Not one of those devil's needles, or whatever you said."

"Fine. So it isn't the dragonfly. It's just me."

"That makes no sense!"

"Why is that you're the only one who makes sense? The one who knows what to do?"

291

"Me? I never know what to do. I'm a big coward."

He turns to me, his cheeks bright red, his eyes blazing. "YOU ARE NOT A COWARD. Stop saying that."

"But—"

"No." He cuts me off. He's all worked up—his face is red and he's sputtering words. "No, you just pretend you're a coward. You stuck your hand in a motor, Polly. You're not a coward. You just say that when you want to give up."

"I don't give up!"

"Yes, you do! You always give up when you have to deal with people who make you confused or upset. Think about Jongy. She's a jerk. Anyone with a brain can see it a mile away. You act like she's a queen or something. Like you're her slave. You just do it so you don't have to deal with her. Plus you act like all the other kids are mean, just like her, which they're not, if you'd give them a chance, which you don't."

He's breathing very hard, his face flushed.

"I do give them a chance."

"No, you don't. You act like you have no friends, but you do."

"I know I do," I say softly.

"Yes. Margaret and Billy and Christopher—"

292

"No. You. You're my friend." I turn to look out the window, at the dying fields. "You're my friend. That's why you can't leave. I won't let you leave."

He sits down on the bed, wiping his eyes with his hand. Neither of us speaks for a long time. Finally, he says something, while staring at the wall.

"Are you sure you were talking about someone else?"

"Yes." I sit down next to him. "Do you really think that I say I'm a coward so I don't have to deal with things?"

"Yes."

We both just sit there for a while, hanging our heads. Eventually, I stand up and walk to the door.

"You can't leave," I say. "Promise me you won't leave."

Basford flicks his eyes up at me. "Okay."

"Promise."

"I promise."

"Good," I tell him. "Freddy would have been so mad."

Then I take a deep breath and climb back up the stairs to the rope bridge. Now I feel braver.

I open the platform door and boldly—or as boldly as I can—stride across. The sun has almost set, and the air is a bright navy blue. I hold on to the rope railing and place my feet steadily, soundly on the planks. I don't look down the entire way.

When I reach the cube, I pull open the sleek black door and run inside, down the white-walled hallway, and over to Mom and Dad's room. I don't knock. I just run inside.

Mom is awake, sitting in front of the window seat, staring at the lake.

"Polly?" Her voice is low and sad. "I've been sitting here thinking of you."

"You have?"

"I miss you, sweetheart. And Patricia. I haven't seen much of any of you these past days." She's curled up by the window, her arms around her knees, her chin tucked down.

"How's Freddy?" I ask.

"The same," she says. "They don't know." She turns to me. "They think his body is failing."

All the words I want to say dissolve as they get near my mouth. I sit down next to her.

"I need you to do something for me, okay? I need you to contact your aunt Edith and tell her to do anything she can to help Freddy," Mom whispers. "You have her number, don't you?"

I nod.

"Tell her we will do anything she says. Anything." Mom blinks, her eyes dry.

"But—"

"Listen to me, Polly. I know that your aunt loves you three so much, and I know she'll do anything for you." She pauses, and I can hear her breathing. "I need her help. We need her help."

She looks down then, to her knees, and as she does, I stretch out my skinny arms around her and hold my mother as tightly as I can, just like she did for me four years ago. I haven't even been thinking about how this affects Mom, how real this all is to her. She doesn't have a crooked finger, after all. All she has is a son who is very, very sick.

"I'll call her tonight, Mom. I promise."

FRIDAY, SEPTEMBER 26
A Kiss for Lester

I cannot form a cloud. I try, and I try, and I try, but each time, the stream of vapor is thin and scrawny, disappearing within minutes. I feel pressure every time I step out from the castle onto the farm: Every second that passes without rain means that the sun is destroying our farm, killing my genie.

There is no part of the farm that is unaffected. The PEACE maze now barely reads PACE. The *E* is completely dead, flattened on the ground. All the plants around Harry are basically dead, their wide, flat leaves sluggish and limp, like a rag doll. I still pour the lake water on Harry's spot and I still make the sign of the cross. But nothing has changed. My cherry blossom tree cries every day. Sometimes I think she hangs over the lake, weeping, just to replenish the lake herself. It doesn't work, but it is a nice idea.

There is no good news from the hospital either. In fact, at the hospital there is only bad, terrible, awful news. No one has a clue what to do, so they all watch, every day, as Freddy gets worse and worse and worse.

Tonight I'm trying something different. I'm in the playroom, in front of the fireplace, spreading out all of my clues on the coffee table. The necklace. The emerald ring. Just as I place the skeleton key on the coffee table, Lester, the Monster cricket, springs up out of nowhere, landing right near my crooked finger.

I want to be mad at him. Lester and Spark have disappeared this week, even after I called their names, searching for them, asking them for help. But I'm too desperate. Instead, I look at Lester and talk to him as if I just saw him yesterday.

"Hi," I say. "Just trying to figure this out."

Lester jumps up on the mantel. I pick up the emerald ring and put it back on my left hand.

"See what I found? It was in the slugs," I tell him. "But you probably knew that."

I tilt my head back against the cushion, closing my eyes. *What am I missing?*

When I open my eyes, I find I'm staring at the portrait of my great-grandmother Enid. She has an emerald ring on her finger too.

My eyes flicker over to Lester. There's something about the way he's watching me that makes my heart start to race.

I look back at the portrait. Enid's emerald ring.

Lester picks up his front leg and points to the portrait. Then he points back to me. He does it again and again, back and forth, back and forth.

In the portrait, Enid isn't smiling. She's composed, hands folded on her lap. Her emerald ring is on her right hand, the same hand as her crooked finger.

My eyes widen. I look at Lester. He nods, then points to the portrait. To Enid's hand. To Enid's right hand.

It's so obvious.

I switch the emerald ring from my left hand to my right.

Instantly, a sensation that my lungs are expanding, taking in more and more air, overwhelms me. My heart pounds. My brain seems to be exploding.

As quickly as I put it on, I take it off.

Then I put it on again. The same *whooshing* feeling, as if I'm propelled by a greater force than myself. I take it off. Everything slows down again, returning to normal.

I remember something else, from Dad. *All gems are minerals at heart.* Patricia called Grandmom's diamond sprigs "naturally occurring." Beatrice yelled at me because I didn't consider that emeralds are "minerals squished together in the earth."

I stare at the ring. *Nature does nothing in vain.*

Suddenly Lester leaps from the mantel down to the coffee table. He rubs his two feet together.

"I don't understand leg rubbing. Is that supposed to be a word?"

Lester just looks at me. I check my watch. It's late, after ten. He leaps on my chin.

"Yuck!" I swat at him, but he's too fast. He jumps back to the coffee table.

"I need to go outside, right?"

Lester moves his head up and down.

I've become an expert at sneaking out of the house. I'm outside in a matter of minutes with my book light in the pocket of my jeans. I wait for Lester, shining my light on him because he's as dark as the ground. As we walk to my spot under the cherry blossom tree, I spot Spark's brothers and sisters and friends, still at work on the mist. In the black night, each of their movements leaves a sparkling trail, so that teeny, tiny pinpricks of color glitter on top of the lake.

I spread apart the branches and walk over to the water's edge. Lester jumps up on the same rock where Spark ate his mosquito.

"Okay," I say. "My turn."

I'm about to put the ring on my finger when a dragonfly swoops by my shoulder.

Spark.

"Perfect timing!" I say. "But where have you been?"

Spark bobs up and down before he zooms back into the sky to spell his answer.

H . . . O . . . M . . . E.

"Home?"

I watch as Spark zooms up to the top of the branches of the weeping cherry tree, then back down again, hovering above the water. When he's sure I'm watching, he dives in the water, now about three feet lower than it was when the mist first appeared.

It's my night for sudden realizations. I understand.

Ever since I've begun to communicate with the bugs, I've understood that bugs, like people, have different ways of communicating. Not just the language itself. The meaning. As I watch Spark dive over and over again into his water, I remember that Grandmom said dragonflies are made up mostly of water and that water is their home.

That's it. It's so simple. The lake is the dragonflies' home. Just like the farm is mine.

The dragonflies aren't building a shield. Not even

300

years ago, when Grandmom died. They were building their own water-drenched net—not to take water
from the lake, but to give water *to* the lake when it was
needed. They started early because they knew Aunt
Edith's plans. They built the mist under my tree, and it
was all packed together tightly, like wet cotton. Then
they pulled the strands apart, spreading it out over the
lake. They wanted to protect the water underneath.

But there's been too much heat, and the mist can't
release enough moisture to replenish the lake. No matter how much they spin. It's not enough.

"I understand," I whisper to Spark. "You're just like
me. You want to save your home."

Spark flies over to me, bobbing up and down. *Yes.*

"Okay, then." I hold up the emerald ring so he can
see it. "Here goes."

I ceremoniously put on the ring. Again that *whooshing* feeling, power surging from head to toe to finger.
Specifically my *crooked* finger. Then I dip my hand in
the water.

Instantly, there's a difference. My finger throbs. New
energy flushes through me—I feel as if I'm vibrating.

*Grandmom, is this right? Is this what it's supposed to feel
like?*

I turn to Lester. "You really have to start talking," I

tell him. "This could have saved a lot of time."

Lester leaps down from his perch to my shoulder. We watch the water surrounding my finger swirl into a bigger and bigger whirlpool. Pain shoots through my arm and out my fingertips—the emerald the motor for this new response.

It's a massive change. Tonight, when I shine the light onto the column of rising vapor, it seems wide, a bold white stripe intensifying as it goes up and up and up. I take my hand out of the water and sit back along the shore, balling my hand into a fist and covering it with the palm of my left hand. I tilt my head far back to look up to the sky. The vapor is climbing through the air and then fading. The stars are out, pinpricks of light, but the vapor has disappeared.

"Do you think it's going to be a cloud?" I ask Lester.

I watch as he lifts his leg straight up, extending it like an arrow above his head. I look back to the sky.

And I see it. Far above me, a soft trail of white gathering in the dark night sky, the beginnings of a cloud.

I can't help it. I kiss Lester. At least, I think I kiss Lester. Slimy and kind of strange for kissing. Anyway, he hops away. I think he's offended.

"Sorry," I call after him. "I'm just really excited."

 302

I look up at Spark. "I'd kiss you too, but you're too little."

My finger still aches, but I don't even mind. At this very second, above our own very farm, a cloud, a small cloud, has been formed by Polly Peabody.

I am very proud.

SATURDAY, SEPTEMBER 27
A Cloud Moves

Before I even look outside my window, before I even brush my teeth, I run down the hall and bang on Patricia's door.

"Go away!" she yells. But I push the door open and run to the side of her bed. "I promise, this is not a waste of your time." I must look serious, because she swings her legs around the bed and puts on her sandals.

"What is it?" Her scar is healing, although I think she may always have this thin red line at the very top edge of her cheekbone.

"You'll see."

"Eww!" she grumbles. "You didn't brush your teeth."

"I will. Come on!"

Patricia trails me down the stairs. The house is very quiet; it's early, before six o'clock. I'm so excited, I feel

like I can float up to the sky. Everything will change today. I know it.

Patricia looks over and sees me grinning. She glares. "This better be good," she says. "I haven't been sleeping well."

"Trust me." I probably should have woken up Basford too. He would love to see the cloud. There are still questions, of course. I don't know when clouds decide to make it rain—when the cloud gets too heavy, I think, but even if it doesn't rain, the presence of a cloud should change *everything*.

Dunbar.

The Juice Company.

Freddy.

I push open the side door. Patricia's got a slight little smile on her face too. My giddiness is making her excited. I swing open the door and run to the center of the driveway.

"Look!" I yell. "Look!"

I lean back and look up to the morning sky. Patricia looks up too.

But it's just blue. There are no clouds. Nothing. I've never been so disappointed in my life.

"What am I looking for?" Patricia asks, her eyes still trained on the sky.

"A cloud," I whisper.

Patricia tilts her head back down and scans the sky with her eyes. "Did you see one?"

I blink. Do I tell her the truth? That I made one? Suddenly, I hear Aunt Edith's words in my head.

You don't need to brag about it, you don't need to try to get credit for it, because it is you, who you are, who you are meant to be

Patricia is staring at me. "Polly? I don't see any clouds."

"There was one," I insist. "I saw it."

"When?"

I'm stuck again. "This morning," I say. But where did it go? It's been only four hours.

"Do clouds move?" I ask Patricia.

She shrugs. "Sure, with the wind, air pressure, whatever."

I'm miserable. "My cloud must have moved."

I ready myself for Patricia's insults, for her to yell at me for waking her up for nothing, but she surprises me. She reaches out and touches my shoulder. "It's okay," she says. "I wish I could imagine clouds."

"I didn't—"

She keeps talking. "I can't imagine anything. Scratch

that. I can imagine the farm going into bankruptcy, and I can imagine that Freddy dies." She looks back up to the sky. "You're lucky."

"Lucky?"

"You keep thinking the sky will open up and gold or diamonds will rain down. You're sure that if we find the right magic potion, Freddy will drink it and get better. You think that if you pay enough attention to the plants that they'll talk to you."

"They do talk to me," I say. I look over to the dragging, dying plants. "Well, they *did* talk to me."

She steps toward the door to the castle. "You live in the clouds, Polly," Patricia says. "That's why you think you saw one." She sighs. "As if a cloud could solve all our problems."

"A cloud *can* solve all our problems," I insist.

"I'm going back to sleep. Wake me if it rains." She pauses. "And brush your teeth."

After she leaves, I scan the sky for my cloud. I think I see it finally, far off, away from our property. I need to know how to keep the clouds together, how to keep them over our farm.

I look around for someone or something to help me—a plant, a bug, anything. But the entire farm is

asleep or dead. I scowl at the ground and tramp back inside.

Things get worse at breakfast. I'm the last one there, and they're all eating silently, turning over scrambled eggs and grapefruit slices with their forks and spoons, not really eating.

"I checked it over," Dad is telling Patricia. "It's okay."

She pretends to brighten up. "More clothes for me."

Basford just stares at Dad with the sorriest expression I've ever seen. Mom's back is turned.

I sit next to Chico. He grunts. I look over at Dad, who has one hand on his baseball cap and one hand on the handle of his coffee mug.

"What are you talking about?" I ask.

"Promise me you won't overreact," Dad warns me. He looks over, leaning down across the table.

I glance over to Patricia, who avoids my look by chomping on her carrot. "Overreact about what?"

"Well." Dad gives me one of his weak smiles. "We're going to be rich." He pauses, reaching over and grabbing one of my hands. "I'm going to accept the offer from Aunt Edith."

I whip my hand back. Dad's face falls, his eyes clouding over.

"No. NO!"

"Polly, we don't have a choice—"

I stand up, ramming my chair back so hard it falls over. I feel Mom's hand on my shoulder.

"No. You have to give me more time."

"You?"

"I mean us," I say. "You can't give up yet. The Giant Rhubarb will be okay. We'll make money from that, right? And what about your medicine? Somebody else may want it, won't they?"

No one answers. They all stare at me with hooded, sad eyes.

"Why are we giving up?"

"Because," Mom says, spinning me around to look at her. "Because Freddy's getting worse." She puts both of her hands on my shoulder and looks me in the eye.

"How much worse?" I ask.

She shakes her head. "We're all going there after breakfast. Go comb your hair."

"But—"

"Not another word."

Dad must have worked some special arrangement at the hospital, because they let all of us in at one time. I head down the hallway to the general patients' rooms, but Beatrice steers me down a different corridor.

"He's in Critical Care," Patricia whispers.

Everything inside me is loose, rattling around, frozen icicles broken off from the eaves, clattering together on the black pavement. We reach two wide doors, opening in the center. Dad presses a card against a black panel. The doors swing open, and we follow Dad into the unit. I don't dare look to my left or right, not to the nurses or the patients. There are too many beeps and drips and whispers.

We swarm around Freddy's bed. He has more tubes than before, and there's a little monitor hooked up with red and blue lines and numbers. He's asleep.

Dad glances at the numbers. I let everyone else crowd around the railings. "He's resting comfortably," says Dr. Jackson, who stands in the corner of the room, a gray metal medical chart in his hand.

I will do anything I can to get Freddy the best medical help that exists. Do you understand that? I will get the best experts, the best everything.

Aunt Edith still has not called back.

"He's stable?" Mom asks, her voice quaking.

"For now," Dr. Jackson says.

Mom and Dad are going to stay all day, but the rest of us can only stay in his room for about fifteen minutes. So when Basford and Patricia have stepped away from Freddy's bedside, I move closer. His hands are white now, almost clear. His freckles look like someone flicked orange paint dots on a piece of white paper.

"The farm looks pretty bad," I say very softly. When I stop talking all I hear are the blips and beeps of all the machines. I bite my bottom lip to stop it from quivering. "I wish you'd get out of this thing, Freddy. It's time. I'm not a chicken anymore."

I lean over to make sure I can hear him breathe. "You said you were fine." I blink. "So be fine. Get *fine!!!*"

Nothing.

"Please."

I kiss Freddy's forehead and make the sign of the cross, as I do with Harry's root. Then I walk out of the room, down the hallway, and outside, by the pickup truck.

This is how desperation must feel. If I saw Aunt Edith right now, I'd stomp her like a bug. I'd scream and holler and force her to show me how to make clouds so that they stick, so that they don't move away, so that they arrive on time and rain and make our farm healthy, *make Freddy healthy.*

What am I missing?

How could she do this to us?

How could she do this to me?

SAME DAY, SATURDAY, SEPTEMBER 27
Despair

It's late when we get home from the hospital. Mom and Dad stayed by Freddy's side, but Beatrice decided we had to go on a bunch of silly errands before we drove home. It was obvious she was trying to keep our minds off of Freddy, but we didn't complain. We went shopping for socks, stopped at a park, and ate dinner at a hot dog stand. Then she brought us to church. There wasn't a service. She said she thought it seemed like a good idea, and we agreed. The whole time I was there I prayed for some sign, some answer to our problems. I was praying so hard that I didn't even notice when Beatrice tapped on my shoulder to leave.

When we finally get home, Beatrice asks us if we want anything to eat—a fresh strawberry rhubarb pie, a chocolate rhubarb cookie—but I think it is obvious that we are all so filled with sadness that we couldn't fit anything else inside. Everyone goes into their rooms and shuts the door. But I'm only in my room for a moment, long enough to grab my book light. I figured out where I needed to go in that last second in the church.

Enid's turret.

I race up the stairs as fast as I can. As soon as I cross the threshold of Enid's room, I wait for something to move. But it's completely silent, completely still. The ivy is coiled up all around me and I don't see one cricket. Not even Lester.

They're here. I know it. They're watching me to see if I get this right. I stand in front of the window, the one where Aunt Edith yanked down the curtain rod. I look down at my feet, placed around strands of ivy. It's completely still—not even the slightest twitch of a leaf.

I wait for help—for one of the bugs to emerge, to write the answer that will save *everything* in the air.

Outside, the sun is setting and it's getting hard to see. I walk around the room, stepping carefully to try to avoid touching the ivy, or trampling on a book. I go round and round, searching for something, waiting for someone.

313

"Please? Someone? Something? Help!" I know my voice sounds desperate. But the lack of rain must have sucked out the life of this turret too. I'm failing. I've failed.

I want to cry but I don't—I'm so far beyond crying. I've lost. I never once thought that it would really end, not even in the slugsand. But here, right now, it feels like it's completely over, that all hope has been drained from me, from Freddy, from our farm.

Aunt Edith is going to win. The farm is going to die. Freddy is going to die.

I look out the window. The sky is that perfect blue and purple color of twilight, lit up by a sparkling white crescent moon. The moon casts a crooked slant of light across the farm, slashing over the Giant Rhubarb, the mist-covered lake, even the Dark House. The moonlight bounces on the top of the shed; it shines directly on the Silo.

We will lose it all. I won't have my home. My family won't have its farm, which it's had for all these years. I try to imagine what it would be like. As usual, my mind searches out a place for hope: Maybe it won't be so bad? Maybe it's okay to lose a family business? Everyone dies anyway, just like Charlotte the spider said in *Charlotte's Web*. There will be some point when none of this exists.

The Silo seems to glare at me, underneath the silver ray of the moon, as if it knows my thoughts are wandering in this direction. I realize I'm being a coward—these are the wanderings of someone who isn't trying. Someone who is giving up.

I can see Grandmom's bench from the window. And Aunt Edith's Giant Rhubarb plant, Teddy, standing straight up next to the bench, just like the night Aunt Edith was there.

My breath catches. Teddy's standing straight up? I squint, leaning out over the windowsill. Teddy's completely upright, his leaves facing the Silo.

The Silo.

I never did make it to the Silo. I made it to the slugs. The slugsand. I made it to Grandmom's bench.

But I never did make it to the Silo.

I glance directly down, at the field of regular rhubarb nearest to the castle. Something catches my eye. The regular rhubarb is sluggish, of course, but the plants look odd, misplaced. Their leaves seem pushed to one side. Like they're bowing or pointing at something.

From my perch on the window seat, I scan the fields. The plants are all like this. All of them. My whole body seems to freeze up.

The Silo. The plants are pointing to the Silo.

At the very moment it all begins to tie together, bugs swarm the room. Lester bounds into view, along with some of his cricket friends. The ivy lifts up, forming a tangled arch over my head. The stinkbugs show up. Some fireflies and mosquitoes and bumblebees too. Even one or two black wasps fly around the room, whizzing by my head.

Polly Peabody, the girl who hates bugs, here amidst her friends.

I develop a new scientific theory.

> **Hypothesis:** The secret to keeping the clouds on the farm will be found in the Silo.
> **Testing:** Go to the Silo.
> **Conclusion:** Rain. I hope.

"The final secret," I murmur as the ivy begins to move. I walk underneath it as it winds me to the doorway, the bugs following me in a procession to the door. Right before I walk out the door, I turn back around.

"I can do this, right?" I ask, my voice shaky.

Spark bobs up and down. Lester nods his big black head. The rest of the bugs flutter and buzz and hover, which I think means that they're all saying the same thing.

"Thanks," I tell them, and I leave.

SAME DAY,
SATURDAY, SEPTEMBER 27
Trust Thyself

Trust thyself: every heart vibrates to that iron string.

Very quietly, I push open the door of the turret. I clench my fist closed and walk silently down the stairs. When I get closer to the first floor, I hear something, a soft murmur. I tiptoe to the bottom steps and then peek around the wall.

Beatrice is standing in the living room. She's got her head covered by her hands. Chico sits on the sofa, looking straight ahead, like an old dog with flappy skin around his neck.

"Come on out, Polly," Beatrice says. "I know you're there."

I walk down the last two steps. She waits for me across the room, her hands on her hips. She doesn't look angry. She looks like she's been expecting me.

"You think you can go outside every night and I wouldn't know about it?"

I stare at her. The truth is I haven't been thinking much about Beatrice. "Sorry."

She smiles, but then she turns her face quickly around, avoiding my gaze. Chico doesn't move.

"Beatrice?" I say. "Are you okay?"

She lifts her head up slowly. I step closer to her and see that her cheek is stained with tears.

"What is it?"

"You should be asleep," she says. "Most eleven-year-olds sleep at night."

"What is it?" I ask again.

"Sit," Beatrice orders. I do as she says and she follows, sitting down next to me. She closes her eyes tightly, her fingers laced together as if she can't unlatch them or else risk some kind of collapse.

"I don't know how to tell you this," Beatrice says.

"Tell me what?"

"Freddy," she says. Her voice breaks. I look over at Chico again, who has now tilted his head down, holding it in his large hands.

"What about him?" I ignore the shooting pains in my hand, the trembling in my knees.

Beatrice turns to face me. "Your mother just called."

She closes her eyes. "He's in a coma." Her eyes flash. "They don't know why. We just have to pray."

She puts her arm around me and pulls me to her side. I feel myself swallowing, as if I'm gulping down these horrible words, taking them out of our shared space.

Beatrice pats my shoulder, but I barely can feel it. Am I too late? Freddy has to hold on. He *must.*

"Is he—" I'm not even sure what my question is. Is he dead? Is he going to die right this second?

"I don't know anything else, sweetie," Beatrice says. "Maybe you should try to get some sleep?" She's treating me like a child, which I understand.

But I don't feel like a child right now.

I pull back from Beatrice, who gives me a surprised look. Then I propel myself off of the couch and stand in front of her.

"What are you—"

"I have to go and do something," I tell her. "Something important."

"Polly, not tonight . . ."

"I'll be back before you know it." I give her the most reassuring smile I can muster. "And honestly. You want me to do this." I pause. "I promise you that."

Chico moves to stand up. "*Voy contigo,*" he says.

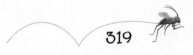

"No," I tell him. "You can't come."

Chico looks over to Beatrice for her decision. She looks from him to me and back again. Finally she motions for Chico to sit down.

"I just got a feeling," she says, looking at me.

"Thanks, Beatrice," I say as I kiss her on the forehead. "I've got one too."

SAME DAY, SATURDAY, SEPTEMBER 27
The Silo

Outside, I take a deep breath and look up to the sky. The moon is crescent shaped, so it's both starlit and moonlit. Still, it isn't bright enough for me to completely find my way around the farm. I turn on my book light and shine it over to my left, by the dying chocolate rhubarb field.

Here is what I see: The plants, all of them dying, all of them depleted, have lifted their leaves up off the ground. I was right: The plants are all pointing toward the Dark House.

I lift my light higher.

It's the same everywhere I look. The plants have lifted up their northern leaves and somehow swung them over the crown to lie on top of the southern leaves. I don't know how they can do this, as weak and thirsty as they are. But I know as clearly as I know anything that they are talking to me, pleading with me to go to the Dark House. Go NOW.

I look quickly at the lake. The mist is faint, sparkly, but as thin as tissue paper. The lake is shrinking, despite the dragonflies' best efforts. The genie—the one I imagine is the face of the farm—can't stay alive without rain.

Suddenly, I hear a new noise. "Daaak! Daaaak!" I flash my light over the ground. The talking two-headed spiders are awake too. They stream from the chocolate rhubarb field in straight rows, hundreds of striped, black, eight-legged, two-headed creatures crawling behind me like a private army. Everyone's outside tonight.

I point my book light in front of me. I smile. Lester's arrived without me knowing. Spark has too. I can feel his comforting flutter behind my ear.

"Ready?" I ask.

"Daaak!" answer the spiders.

I take my first step to the Dark House. As I move, I flash the light over the fields, observing more and more

dead and dying plants guiding me to the Silo. From here, I can see that the level of water in the lake, under the mist, is dangerously low, probably half of what it was just a week ago, when Freddy and I fell.

The image of Freddy asleep in the hospital spurs me on and I pick up the pace. As the Dark House comes more and more into view, I start to jog. The bugs match me, step for step, scrambling over the ground like a creeping black shadow.

Finally, the wooden door of the Dark House looms in front of me. In front of us.

I race up the incline and put my right hand on the doorknob. Then I yank my hand back because I receive the sharpest stab of pain I've felt yet.

I fall back, but then I think of Freddy and reach for it again, turning the doorknob and opening the door.

A mutant moth, the kind I always expected would live in the Dark House, swoops by my head. I duck. This entryway seems like it is blanketed in all our farm's bugs, none of them dying and browning like our plants. I look over to the Giant Rhubarb plants, now standing like soldiers in tight, packed rows of barrels. Then I look behind me, at the spiders.

"Gooooood! Luuuuuck!" they say, waiting outside

the door. Lester stands near them, a giant to their little selves. Spark zips in, hovering by my shoulder. I take my first step inside.

I shine my book light to my right. It's the entrance to the Silo, built within the gray wall shared by the Silo and the shed. It's painted white, and seems to shine. On the door, there's a small sign hanging from a tiny nail.

NO ADMITTANCE.

I turn the doorknob of the Silo, but it's locked. And then, every hair on my neck raised, I pull out the necklace and use the skeleton key, inserting it into the lock.

It fits perfectly.

Just as I start to turn the key, I hear a rustling noise. I turn around, shining my light over to the shed part of the building.

The leaves are clapping for me. Rather, the Giant Rhubarb plants are clapping for me. With their leaves.

Rustle. *Thwap!* Rustle. *Thwap!*

A smile sneaks across my face, even though I know it's strange timing. I have the wishful thought that Harry claps along with them, wherever he is. But then I spin around, facing the door. Slowly, I finish turning the key. The door is heavy, and I have to lean my shoulder into it to move it at all. I put my head down

and press as hard as I can, my feet accidentally smashing some wayward slugs.

I'm sorry, Beatrice.

The door sweeps open, dragging a bit on the floor. I take a deep breath, trying to push aside my image of a silo haunted by ghosts and terrors and instead remember the plants guiding me, dragonflies and crickets, all helping out.

And much more importantly.

Freddy is in a coma.

It's time.

SAME NIGHT, SATURDAY, SEPTEMBER 27
Diamonds in the Sky

Grandmom is here with me. Not that I see her, or that she's shimmering in front of me, like a ghost from a Halloween story. She isn't visible—I don't smell her or feel her hand—I just *sense* that she's here. If I could see her, I'd be jumping, grinning, crying. I'd be happy just to stay in her arms, thinking that nothing had changed.

But that would be a different Polly. *That* Polly would not understand or accept that everything, and everyone, dies. *That* Polly would think that Aunt Edith is perfect. *That* Polly would believe "change" was some kind of animal, one that would stare her in the face, snarling.

That's not who I feel like anymore. *This* Polly is plain old desperate. And exhausted. And, as luck would have it, fearless.

I step over the threshold, into the chamber of the Silo. The pain in my finger intensifies, blazing from the tip of my nail through my hand. It hurts so much, I squeeze shut my eyes and push my fingers into my palm as hard as I can and chant: *for Freddy, for Freddy, for Freddy*.

My eyes blink open and I absorb the interior of the Silo. It's cavernous and tall, so tall that the domed roof above my head seems like it's in outer space. I flash my tiny book light on the wall until I see a rectangular panel of light switches. I flick them on, wiping my whole hand across the panel, and suddenly enormous beams of white light flood down on me from wide, round lamps attached halfway up the soaring wall.

I'm a speck in here, a tiny, almost indistinguishable speck. Anyone would be—even Basford, even Dad,

even the tallest person in the world. I crane my head back and look up at the roof. It's the strangest thing: I can see the sky. The partitions holding the clear plate are visible, but it must be made of glass or clear plastic or something like that, because I can see stars, bright slivers of white stars, hanging above me. The walls are painted white, and the floor is wooden, swept clean. Someone comes in here; someone comes in here and sweeps the floors, keeps the space clean. Beatrice? Aunt Edith? Who?

Understanding spreads through my mind: secrets. My family has secrets. My farm, my genie, has secrets. Secrets that are kept hidden, secrets that may creep out from the corners like streams of tiny ants. Secrets I'm learning, right this second.

Again I feel that rush of Grandmom's energy, as if she's behind my eyes, in my brain, forcing me to see the Silo as *she* would see the Silo. If I were Grandmom, I'd be practical, forthright. I'd know that I was just following in tradition's footsteps. That before Grandmom, there was Enid. After Grandmom, there was Aunt Edith. And now, courtesy of my crooked finger, there's me. And whatever has to happen, has to happen in here. So where is it? Where do I go?

I tilt my head back again, gazing at the stars. This

room isn't scary. That's the truth of it. It's weird, but it isn't scary. The inside wall is bright white, and there aren't any bugs. Or if there are, they're flying far above me, under the dome. I bring my head back down and start to pace around the edge of the room. It isn't that wide: maybe just a little bigger than one of those parachutes you play with when you're a little kid, when everyone grabs the edges and you float it up and down and then duck underneath. I make a complete circle of the room, running my hand against the wall as I move. The wall is made of that crumbly concrete, which makes me think that pieces could break off, that I could rub parts of the wall in between my fingers and it would dissolve into little particles of sand. I walk around and around the empty room. It's in here. It has to be. I'm not looking hard enough. I can't fail, I CAN'T FAIL.

I'm not trusting myself.

Grandmom? I stop, my hand still on the wall, now near the light switches. My finger hasn't stopped pounding since I walked in here. What am I missing? My eyes sweep over the room again. The only "artificial" part of this space is the lights and the light switches. Otherwise, it's just walls and a roof and a floor. Walls and a roof and a floor. Walls and . . .

My eyes narrow as I notice something. On the light

panel, the same panel of switches found in an ordinary kitchen, is something different. There are three normal light switches and one other thing. A tiny circular socket.

I walk over to it, breathing hard and fast, my eyes riveted to this one small difference. An odd-shaped hole, formed like an octagon, only about a quarter of an inch deep, as if a tiny stop sign was pushed into the panel.

An octagon. Eight sides. Like my emerald ring. A ring that could be a key in a socket, like the polygon from Owen's class.

I move so fast, I don't have time to think.

Freddy. Freddy. Freddy.

I push my ring, my eight-sided emerald stone, into the circular opening. Immediately, there is a faint but strong whirring noise, followed by a crackling, whooshing sound. It's coming from high above, from the roof. Just like in science class, the roof of the Silo is pulling back. Amidst loud rumbling noise—the sounds, no doubt, that have haunted me—the entire curved roof of the Silo folds over to one side, opening it to the night sky. The stars seem to burn against the dark night and my heart and lungs and mind feel as if they're in overdrive because then, just then, there is a rumbling under my feet and I jump, pressing my back against the wall, removing my ring from the socket, staring as the floor begins to *move*.

That is, the central plate of the floor *retracts*. A long, cut-out rectangular piece pulls back, revealing water—free-flowing, bluish water—streaming underneath the open roof, the night sky.

Water under the Dark House. Water that gives the slugs a home, that breeds dragonflies, that feeds into our magical lake. It is always, always about the water—the water that saved me and Freddy and that took my ring and that feeds our plants, our rhubarb, our family. Until it stops raining. Until the clouds don't form. Until the water cycle *is stopped*.

As I kneel down on the floor, next to the open water, I keep my hand in a tight fist, casting a quick glance up to the sky, breathing hard, taking it all in. I'm joining my family in a different way right now, a subset of my family: all women, all crooked fingers, all programmed—genetically hardwired—to keep their farm alive. It isn't like First Communion or graduation from middle school: it's more specific and natural and *certain*—like that instinctive certainty you have when you plant one seed, give it water and sun, and know something will grow.

I'm growing.

I look down at the water. I feel it: all of them—Harry, the farm, Grandmom—are waiting for me to take my place as the newest rainmaker in my family.

I plunge my hand in. The swooshing sound, the opening of my lungs, the volt of electricity shooting through my fingers—everything happens at once. I shut my eyes tightly.

Freddy is in a coma.

I keep my eyes closed until I can't bear it. Then I open them, eyelids fluttering, realization pushing me back off of my knees and onto my bottom, so that when I see the thick ribbon of white vapor rising from the water, I'm sitting down, ignoring the water churning around my hand and the relentless jolt of energy surging up my arm, only staring as the vapor rises, spotlighted by the floodlights, heading up to the waiting sky.

I, Polly Peabody, am making a cloud.

A smile fights its way across my face, battling all my worry and fear, as I watch a very scant trace of a white cloud appear up against the black sky, blocking out some of the twinkling stars.

I stand up slowly and shake out my hand as I continue to stare. That's when something else happens, something I don't expect. The tip of my crooked finger pulses—

 330

it's a strong and almost metallic feeling. I fling off more water droplets from my hand, but as I do, it becomes harder to keep my hand level, to keep it at, say, waist height. My eyes widen as I feel my arm pulled up, my finger drawn up above to the sky. It is as if there's a magnet in the sky and a magnet in my finger—

Plus or minus. PLUS OR MINUS.

Polarization. Positive charges, negative charges. You've heard the saying that opposites attract . . .

I stretch out my fingers wide, far above my head, and then I bring them in close, making a fist, except my one small, bony, crooked index finger, which I extend, as straight as possible, pointing at the vapor. I don't know that I'm holding my breath; I don't know what's compelling me to start twirling this finger in the air. But that's what I do, and the truth is, I'm not surprised when I watch the cloud move with my finger, spinning itself into a more perfect circle.

Like Spark, I start to draw in the sky. I'm not forming words. I'm *making a cloud*.

I grab at little bits of the trails of vapor, pointing and swirling, mixing the vapor together until a cloud forms in front of my eyes. A large, white, puffy cloud, almost the size of the dome itself. I picture it attaching itself to the stars, little twinkling clips holding my cloud

331

in place. Maybe this is how it works. The stars hold the cloud in place—they're *starclips*—until tomorrow at one o'clock. Then the starclips open wide and the cloud is released, free to break apart into tiny, scattered, life-giving raindrops.

It could be. Maybe not. But I do know this: Tomorrow, it will rain on our farm.

I stand there, under the sky, under my cloud, for a long, long time.

I wonder if this is what being an adult is like. I don't really feel like jumping around or doing a victory dance. I'm glad that there's a cloud above my head and I'm awed, but I'm sad too. Aunt Edith stopped making it rain. That's a fact. She didn't want to be here anymore, no matter what she says about the other reasons. And what she wanted was more important than anything else: more important than our farm, our family, or me.

I wonder what Mr. Emerson would think about Aunt Edith. There's a part in his essay when he says *"I shun father and mother and wife and brother when my genius calls me."* Maybe Aunt Edith's genius will cause her to write something wonderful—something that does a lot of good for a lot more people than my family and the people who love our rhubarb. Wouldn't that be better than staying here?

I slowly bring my hand down. The throbbing has mostly stopped. I stare at my crooked finger and suddenly, despite all these hard thoughts, find myself giggling. Jongy has shown up in my mind: an image of her, waggling her red-painted fingernails at me, telling me I need to be more assertive, as if she knows everything there is to know in life. If she only knew what my finger could do! Not that I'd tell her. I suddenly realize that this is *my* secret. The secret that I will hold on to my whole life, until I tell it to the next girl in our family born with a crooked finger.

Before I leave the Silo, I look up one more time. Peeking behind my cloud are more stars. They look like diamonds to me, like the same ones that poked out of the ground when Grandmom died. She's here. She'll be with me always. It's a good thing to know.

I check my watch. It's almost morning. I've been up the whole night.

Later, as I walk up the stairs to my room, I peer out the window and see my cloud. It looks small from here—meager, almost—but that doesn't matter. It's still hanging from the stars, filled with water, full of life.

Even after I pull up my covers, I can still see my cloud, this time sprinkled with tiny diamonds. I can see it even with my eyes closed, even as I begin to dream.

SUNDAY, SEPTEMBER 28
Rain

When I climbed into bed, I never thought in a million years I could sleep. But I crashed, sleeping well past morning and waking up sometime around one o'clock.

What woke me up was the sound of raindrops.

SAME DAY,
SUNDAY, SEPTEMBER 28
Freddy

If I have to be honest, it wasn't a full rainstorm. More like a full drizzle. It only rained over the medicinal rhubarb field and a little bit of the chocolate rhubarb. The regular rhubarb is still as dry as dirt.

Mom and Dad had come back to the castle to get clothes so they could stay in the hospital. I think they also wanted to check in with Patricia, Basford, and me

one more time while our family was intact, in case the worst happened.

But the best happened instead. They walked out of the castle, disbelieving, even as the raindrops bounced off of their arms. If I could have taken one picture of this day, it would be this: Dad's arm around Mom, his baseball cap off of his head, and Mom crying, simply sobbing, as her tears add to the pool of rain water gathering at her feet.

Basford was out there too, kneeling to the ground, running his fingers through the softening dirt. Patricia just kept looking from the sky to the ground and smiling. (Then, of course, she pulled out her cell phone and started to text.)

When Dad and Mom saw me, they stretched out their arms and I ran into them.

"Isn't this wonderful?" Dad said, hugging me.

"I can't believe it," Mom kept saying, over and over. "I just can't believe it. God answered our prayers, He did. He must have."

I guess I didn't look like I was surprised enough, because Dad pulled me a little closer and whispered, "Don't tell me you expected this?"

I looked him in the eye. "Course not," I said. "I just believe in magic, that's all."

"I think I do too," Dad said.

He pulled me tighter and hugged me so hard, I felt his heart beating. Or maybe it was mine. Over his shoulder, Beatrice grinned at me and put her hand on Chico's tall shoulder. She winked. I winked back.

Then, right before Dad released me, I saw Spark zipping about all of us, threading some invisible net of joy around. I glanced at the lake.

The mist was gone. *Gone.*

"You know," Patricia said from where she was texting. "It could all stop again in a second. We shouldn't get our hopes up."

"It's not going to stop," I assured her.

"How do you know?"

"Because," said Basford. "She's Polly Peabody." He smiled at me and I started to grin.

"Whatever," Patricia said. "I hope you're all right."

"Let's go see Freddy!" I yelled.

At first, when I said his name, everyone froze. I thought I had really ruined this moment. But then Mom smiled and said that yes, we should all go to the hospital immediately.

It was a good thing we left when we did. As we drove out of the farm, news vans were just beginning to arrive. I spied Mrs. Jong stepping out of a white one, a plastic bag over her hair. She tried to run in front of Mom's car, but Mom just beeped the horn and drove through.

When we get to the hospital, we are in for another surprise. Dr. Jackson meets us at the doors to the Critical Care Unit.

"I have some news," he says. We all stop in our tracks, waiting. Dr. Jackson is not a smiley guy, so seeing him, very serious, made us all forget for a second how happy we were about the rain.

"Is something wrong?" Mom's voice trips up, and we all look at one another, scared.

"No," he says. "Not at all." He smiles then, a thin-lipped but hopeful smile. "It seems I have some reinforcements."

"Reinforcements?" Patricia asks.

"Two medical specialists were flown here today by private plane. They are the leading researchers in your son's specific genetic condition."

I feel a smile growing, pulling up the corners of my mouth.

"Dr. Alexander Noble and Dr. Ella Roman are in there right now, examining Freddy. They have a number of ideas for his treatment." Dr. Jackson stops, looks over at Dad.

"One of them is to consider the use of your own research," he says. "Apparently Dunbar has been quite open with them about the results of your testing protocol and they feel that the possibility of retarding the growth of the mutated gene is greater than any associated risk of detrimental side effects."

Dad picks his baseball cap up off his head, looks at it, and then puts it back on. He's trying to hide that he's pleased. "Well, obviously, if that's what they think could help . . ."

Basford's the only one who still looks confused. "What's going on?"

I lean up and whisper to him, "Aunt Edith."

He turns to me, surprised.

"No need to be quiet about it," Mom says to everyone. "I knew Edith would come through." She stops, wiping her reddening eyes. "For you kids, she'd move the world."

Dr. Jackson leads us into the unit and we all race to Freddy's side. I think I'm not the only one who fully expected him to be revived too—saved by the drizzle, out of his coma. But he isn't. He's still there, sleeping soundly, beeps and drips going nonstop. The two new doctors stand in the back of the room, introducing themselves to Dad and Mom.

I push past Basford and Patricia and lean in over Freddy. "It's time to wake up," I tell him.

And honestly, I can't tell you if it was magic, or the doctors, or something inside his brain that told that stupid mutating gene to stop it already, but I saw Freddy's eyes flutter. They didn't open and he didn't totally wake up, but I knew when I saw his eyes flutter, that it was all a matter of time.

SAME DAY, SUNDAY, SEPTEMBER 28
The Book of Secrets

I went to sleep certain that my Dark Thoughts were gone for good, like the mist. And they were. But the bugs weren't. Particularly Lester. I'm having a wonderful dream when I'm forced to wake up because there's a Monster cricket on my nose.

"You are an official pain in the neck." I swat him away from my face.

Lester hops off. I swear, I think that cricket *likes* to freak me out. I pull my head slowly off the pillow, and Lester lifts up his front legs and points to the door.

I swing my legs over the bed. "The turret?"

Lester jumps high in the air and lands right back where he started.

"Silly me. Where else?"

I grab the skeleton key and my book light and put on my slippers and follow Lester out the door. We move through the hallway quietly. He starts to hop up the circular staircase toward Enid's turret, and I trail him, climbing up the cold stone steps. We reach the door and I unlock it.

When I push it open I'm met with twinkling Christmas lights. Only, as I look around, they're not lights at all—they're fireflies. About a million fireflies align the top of the turret, blinking flashes of light that lets me see the many things happening at once: more Monster crickets, jumping up and down in the corner, the ivy reaching up and twirling around as if it's dancing, black two-headed spiders crawling over the bookshelves, and—best of all—Spark with hundreds of his best dragonfly friends.

I smile as soon as I step inside the room, closing the door behind me.

"Is this a party?" I ask.

"Yeeeeessss." I look over the bookshelves and see the spiders stopped, mid-scramble, as each of them nods their two heads. The stinkbugs have returned, and are now dancing round and round in what seems to be the hokeypokey. Even some wasps have flown into the room, taunting me by aiming right for my head before swerving away at the last possible second.

"You guys are so weird."

The ivy untangles itself and starts to float in my direction. I stand there as the vine encircles me, stretching behind my back. It starts to tug the two floating pieces on either side of me, pulling me over toward the window. Lester waits on top of the mosaic table. Spark buzzes around my shoulder.

"What are they doing?" I whisper.

He skywrites. R . . . E . . . . A . . . D.

I look at him, confused, but then the ivy drags me closer to the table. I glance down to see the book underneath Lester. It is brown and square and has dust all over it.

Lester looks up at me, nodding slowly with his big black head.

"Reeeaaaadd it." I hear the spiders from the bookshelves. More of Spark's friends have flown over here too, so I'm surrounded by crickets and dragonflies and spiders and fireflies and ivy, yards and yards of ivy.

Lester jumps off the book. I reach over and grab it;

it's heavy in my hand. The title is etched into the cover in gold letters.

THE BOOK OF SECRETS

Underneath the title, another phrase is etched in Latin.

Sapere Aude!

Someone's taped a scrap of paper next to the phrase. A child has written very neatly on top of it.

> I translated this from Horace (65-8 B.C.) It means "Dare to be wise." Lucretia di Falciana, age 10

Two dragonflies zoom down and pick up the pages. They flip over the first one, revealing a broad, yellowed sheet with handwriting on it.

> I write this after the rain has stopped. I have found that it helps to soak my right finger in warm salted water after the clouds are formed, as it returns the polarized charges to their original state . . .

"Polarized charges?" I mutter as one of the dragonflies turns the page. This heading says "Weekly Rain Timing: 1:00 p.m."

My sister, Lucretia di Falciana, died on Monday from tuberculosis. She was twelve. The time of her death was one o'clock in the afternoon. From now on, all cloud formations will occur at this time, hidden in the silo, in tribute to our beloved sister.
Enid Peabody, October

I skim the pages. Piles of ancestors—female relatives with crooked fingers—heap on top of one another in my crowded, messy brain. Besides Enid's sister, Lucretia, there's someone named Charlotte, and Katherine, and Olivia. My history, my heritage—all on these pages.

The bugs flip up another page. This one has a sheet of paper stapled to it. It looks like a science worksheet, with a grid.

POLARIZATION PROCESS

1. Cloud formation occurs during evening hours. Preferably before ten o'clock p.m.

2. Return to Silo at approximately 12:45 p.m. the following day.

3. Confirm that cloud is in precise raining position.

4. Activate polarization in finger with cloud, inciting rainfall.

"Precise raining position?" My mind is whirling; I look at the bugs, who are all watching me. "I have a lot to learn."

Spark flutters over to me, hovering.

"You could have given me this earlier," I say, glaring at them. But I'm not a very good actor—I start to smile almost immediately. I guess it's better I learned it all myself. The crickets jump and Spark flies and the ivy dances and the bugs turn more and more pages as I learn more and more secrets.

I must sit in one of the black iron chairs for hours, as puzzle pieces fall into place. The reason it didn't rain on the day Freddy was born? Grandmom went to the hospital with Mom on Sunday, and stayed there until Freddy was born on Monday afternoon. Who keeps the Silo clean? The Peabody woman in charge of the rain. When does the Peabody woman discover this genetic trait? When she turns eighteen. (This one, obviously, didn't apply to me.) Why doesn't it rain anywhere else but on our farm? No one knows. The pain in my finger? It will go away. Or rather, I'll get used to it as I get older. Why did it only drizzle today? Full rainstorms don't come until the female is fully matured. That's why my rainstorm was kind of feeble.

It turns out that if I want the rain to occur exactly at a certain time, I'll need to trigger it with my finger. Today, I just got lucky. I made the cloud late enough that I think the polarization lasted long enough to make it rain.

Or something like that. Actually, I don't really believe that. I still believe in something much more basic.

Magic.

The dragonflies turn to more pages, filled with photos and rhubarb research. Everyone who has the crooked finger seems to write in this, keeping their history and keeping their secrets in one place.

Before I go back downstairs, Spark flies over one more time. He picks up the final page of the book. I swallow when I recognize the handwriting. It's from Aunt Edith.

I'm tired of being here. I'm restricted. It was all easier in New York, without any of this, this hardship, this banal reality. The only bright spot is the children, those glorious nieces and nephew. They remind me that the life of the mind, the child's imagination, is not just important, it is absolutely essential in order to live life fully. I worry though—I see Polly's finger and I wonder about her future. What if she wants to leave? What if she wants to truly be all that she can be? Can she do it on a farm? Is this fair, this tie to her heritage, this worthy but perhaps-individual-destroying tether to the past?

Honestly, I don't know.

Edith Peabody Stillwater

I close the book and look up at my friends. Carefully, I place it back on the table; I have the key. I'll read more in the days ahead.

"Now what?"

I stand in the middle of the room as the ivy moves over to me, picking up my right hand, the one with the emerald ring, and holds it. Like we're friends. The Monster cricket jumps in my left hand. More and more stinkbugs fly in, plopping down and joining their brothers and sisters in a circle. Bumblebees fly over my head, and the dragonflies, led by Spark, fill the air before me.

It's a little silly. A lot silly. And very, very weird.

But we dance. We all dance—silly dances, wild dances, disco dances—everything. It's the best party I've been to in a long, long time.

Finally, though, I have to stop. I'm really tired.

"Keep up the party," I tell them. "I'm going to sleep."

Right before I walk out the door, Lester jumps in front of me, startling me yet again.

"What is it?" I ask him.

He puts his leg straight up to his mouth, the same as when a teacher tells you to be quiet.

"I know," I say. "It's a secret."

FRIDAY, OCTOBER 31
The Transplanting

Harry's *growing.*

His spindly root has thickened and a crown is developing. I think, I really, really think, that a leaf has begun to sprout.

I do such a crazy dance that I'm sure Basford thinks that the whole farm thing has made me permanently affected. He's right.

Since the rain—the drizzle—started a month ago, we've been able to rejuvenate a bunch of our crops. For about two straight weeks, I made it rain every day. Well, "rain" is too strong a word. But it did drizzle at one o'clock daily until I could get the farm back into shape. The truth is, I've messed up the timing so much that the news reporters are going insane; it gets harder and harder to sneak out of the castle at night because there are so many of them trying to hide all over our property. All of them are trying to be the person to figure it all out. But they won't. I've learned something else during this process. No one, absolutely no one, suspects that an eleven-year-old girl is capable of anything. Especially not reporters. I think I could tell them the truth and none of them would do more than tap me on the head and ask me to find my father.

For the last two weeks, I've resumed the weekly rain, only I have to do it on Saturday night and Sunday because of school. Of course, the media would never figure this one out. There are all kinds of theories, some of them just silly, and many of them outright mean. Mrs. Jong wrote that she thinks our farm has undergone some kind of violent transfer of power from one evil spirit to another. It's okay. Especially since I now know for sure that there aren't any evil spirits, even in the Dark House.

The regular rhubarb crop is still pretty dismal, but the Juice Company "is open" to resuming our business. Patricia and I told Dad he should tell them no way, and change all the regular rhubarb to chocolate rhubarb.

But really, Dad is too focused on his medicinal rhubarb project for Freddy to think about anything else. Dr. Noble and Dr. Roman have become our friends, along with Dr. Jackson. They're over our farm all the time, working with Dad in his cottage and then coming over for dinner. Freddy came out of his coma about a week after they started injecting him with some of Dad's medicine. The only person in the room then was Basford, and the nurses say that he screamed so loud he woke up another person who had been in a coma for twenty years. (I'm pretty sure they were joking.) Freddy's still really weak, but he's much better. He told me that when he was in his coma, he had a dream that he was walking down a long hall toward a light seeping out from under a door. He did what Ophelia said—he followed the light and swung open the door.

"And Pol? There were like five thousand televisions with all the sporting events *in the universe* going on. Plus all the chicken wings I could eat. It was *heaven*."

I check my watch. It's 4:00 and my class should be arriving soon to help with the preparation for the Transplanting party. This was my idea since (a) the last trip was a little bit of a disaster and (b) we need help. Mom's been pulled between the hospital and the farm, so Patricia and I have had to step in to arrange everything. We're not having the big blow-out party we usually have. No news cameras. Not one. A couple of reporters from major newspapers and websites, but

Mrs. Jong is not on the invitation list, obviously. Neither is her husband.

We decided to take it back to Grandmom's original idea—a Halloween party where people had fun and got to do some work too. We were all allowed to invite as many friends as we wanted. Ophelia is planning a mass séance to talk to the Ghosts of Rhubarb Past. Mom made us invite Girard, but luckily he's moved to Maryland to irritate other people.

The day is bright and sunny. I squint when I see my classmates step out of the yellow bus.

"I want to wrestle a Giant Rhubarb!" yells Joe Joseph.

"You are such a loser," Charlie Lafayette tells him.

Jennifer Jong holds her pink cell phone to her ear as she walks off the bus. I think we are in a kind of cold war. (That's what it is called when two people don't like each other but don't do anything to hurt each other either.) On my first day back to school after it rained, Jennifer strolled over to me and sneered.

"Finally got lucky?" she said.

"No," I told her, smiling. "Actually, the witch doctors came and did their rain dance. You should come next time. You can burn some sacrifices and howl at the moon too."

"You're not funny, Polly. I'm still going to find out how it rains."

I smirked. "You don't have to look far. It's kind of what we've been studying all semester."

She glared at me and stomped off. I've spent the rest of my class days actually meeting some of my other classmates. It turns out that Margaret Hess and Billy Mills and Will Skalley and Christopher Taylor and Charlie Lafayette are all pretty cool. Chirpy Dawn is still annoying, but that's okay. I'm nice to her anyway.

Patricia comes out of the shed and starts to bark orders. She's made for that kind of thing.

"Okay, the boys start with the candles. If there's a raging inferno tonight, I'll know who to blame." She points to two big boxes behind her.

"The girls are going to help organizing all the shovels and light stands. We need them for later, when we actually get the barrels outside and replant the Giant Rhubarb in the ground.

"You, over there, with the pink cell phone. Take this." Patricia holds up a brown broom.

Jennifer puts her phone down. "What's that for?"

"You have to clean up the slugs," Patricia says with a big smile on her face. I look back at her. She winks.

Basford comes over with the wheelbarrow. He's

begun to talk a lot more, especially once Freddy came out of the coma.

"I checked on Harry," he tells me.

"So did I," I say. "He's looking good, isn't he?"

In fact, I go out there every morning, telling him everything, just like I used to. Today, I was explaining how my friends Margaret and Charlie were coming, and how the Giant Rhubarb looked healthier than ever. Then I told him that Freddy's coming home in a week.

I'm pretty sure Harry's almost-leaf almost smiled.

Mom and Beatrice and Chico are all the same. They like to act like nothing happened—that the farm wasn't in jeopardy, that Freddy didn't almost die. Instead, they're working and cooking and harvesting as much as they can, squeezing out every second of the day in the pursuit of healthy, delicious, ozone-protecting rhubarb.

I've read the Book of Secrets about one hundred times, in between *The Railway Children* and my third time through *Self-Reliance*. I'm excited to write something there myself, when I'm older. But as much as I like that it explains many of my questions, I still have the sense that the answers are really bigger than all of it, the book—the farm—everything. It's some combination of nature and God and science and, of course, magic. Maybe this is what I'll write about, when I get old enough.

I wish I could talk about this to Aunt Edith. But she's gone. It's weird to think that she knows that I figured it out. I think of her all the time, every single day. I make lists and lists of all the things I am going to talk to her about when I see her again. I want her to be proud of me—more proud than she's ever been of anyone. How can I grow up without being able to tell her what I'm doing, what I'm learning, what my life is like? Sometimes, in the dark of the night, I have an awful feeling that I really won't see her again—that, like Basford said, sometimes things can't be fixed.

But I can't accept that. It makes no sense. So every day I just wait for her to contact me. I know she will. I just have to wait.

She was right, of course. When she told me about how good it feels to do something all by yourself.

There's a feeling you get when you achieve something all by yourself that will bring you more peace and contentment than anything money or love can provide. It is that moment when you can look around and say "I did it"—and know no one can take it away from you.

That's exactly how I felt that first day it rained. I

felt as if all the rips and holes in me had been sewn up, like some invisible hand was busy sewing all the time I was distraught over Aunt Edith or crying over Freddy. But when I was there, in the Silo, pulling the clouds together, it all made sense. Even with all the other things going on, I kept just saying one thing over and over to myself. I still say it, almost every night before I go to sleep. They are the most hopeful words I know.

I am Polly Peabody and I can make it drizzle.

Acknowledgments

If I were to write my superstar editor's name—Kate Harrison—seven trillion times, it wouldn't be enough acknowledging. Essentially, she whacked and shaped and honed my mountains and mountains of pages until this novel emerged. What's more, she divined the spirit of my story even before I did. Anything good in this novel is because of Kate; all of its faults are mine.

Laura Dail is not only the agent of a writer's dreams (although she is that), but she's also my friend, and for that I am so grateful. Liz Van Doren is an inspiration, and a treasure, and not just because she was the first person to encourage me to write for children.

I studied Matt Ridley's fascinating *Genome* and Richard Dawkins's equally compelling *The Selfish Gene* in preparation for writing this novel. Middle school science teacher Dan Meiselman also thoughtfully gave of his time and expertise, as did molecular biologist Kristin Baldwin. Physics student and brilliant guy David Crisanti deserves special praise. He made me promise not to use his theory of polarized charges in fingers until I checked with an "expert." I didn't listen to him because I consider him an expert in most things, including but not limited to gardening, finance, Ibiza, and yes, polarized charges in fingers. Also, thanks are due to the wonderful Charlie Van Doren ("Big Charlie"), for telling me about Ralph Waldo Emerson's essay *Self Reliance*. Finally, I would know little about rhubarb without the incredibly comprehensive website The Rhubarb Compendium (www.rhubarbinfo.com).

I am so grateful to my adult readers: Danielle Ganek, Gerry Van Doren, Julie Cohen, Jamie Levitt, Malek Lewis, Diana Weymar, Dan

Wigutow, and especially Alison Flaggert, who (thankfully) didn't mince words with her first (wholly accurate) criticism.

My middle-grade readers are the kind of great kids who make one hopeful for the future. They are Eve LaBalme, Kate Horvat, Ella Van Cleve, Will Van Cleve, Charlotte Berl, Declan Smith, Amelia Smith, Mac McHugh, and Olivia Case.

Special Mention to my nephews: Christopher Reiche, Billy Van Cleve, and Charlie Van Doren, all of whom spent hours with me improving, scheming and developing Polly's story. Sarah Weldon and Polly Weldon contributed the all-important element of spelling bugs, which propelled the book in a new and better direction. My sisters-in-law, Andi Van Cleve and Anne Van Cleve, read the book so many times, I'm sure they regretted that I married into their family. My sister-in-law Jennifer DeMarco, who read the book in one sitting, gave me insightful and important suggestions. My own sister and brother, Barbara and Mark DeMarco, had no choice but to read it over and over again. I couldn't be more thankful for all of their help.

Jessica Carroll, Natalie Jordan, Peter Walters, Melinda DeCesare, and the great people at Germantown Friends Nursery Program not only took care of my children, but took care of me too.

My brother Anthony DeMarco, truth be told, didn't read any drafts, but he's a great brother and wants an acknowledgment, so here it is.

I continue to be awed by my mother Lucy DeMarco's limitless love and support. My father, Mark DeMarco, was thrilled with the idea of *Drizzle*, and I know he's up in heaven, hawking the story to St. Peter (and telling him that he might have written it just a little better).

Finally, I acknowledge, with delight and love, my sons, Jackson and Emerson, and my husband, Emory Basford Van Cleve. I cherish them more than all the raindrops in the world.